Save Me Twice

Terry Toler

Save Me Twice
Published by: BeHoldings Publishing, LLC

Copyright ©2021, **BeHoldings Publishing, LLC**
Terry Toler
All Rights Reserved

Book Cover: BeHoldings Publishing
Book Editor: Jeanne Leach
For information email: terry@terrytoler.com.

Our books can be purchased in bulk for promotional, educational and business use. Please contact your bookseller or the BeHoldings Publishing Sales department at: sales@terrytoler.com

For booking information email: booking@terrytoler.com.
First U.S. Edition: November, 2021
Printed in the United States of America
ISBN: 978-1-954710-07-8

OTHER BOOKS BY TERRY TOLER

Fiction

The Longest Day
The Reformation of Mars
The Great Wall of Ven-Us
Saturn: The Eden Experiment
The Late, Great Planet Jupiter
The Mercury Protocols
Save The Girls
The Ingenue
Saving Sara
Save The Queen
No Girl Left Behind
The Launch
The Blue Rose
Body Count
Save Me Twice
The Cliffhangers: Anna

Non-Fiction

How to Make More Than a Million Dollars
The Heart Attacked
Seven Years of Promise
Mission Possible
Marriage Made in Heaven
21 Days to Physical Healing
21 Days to Spiritual Fitness
21 Days to Divine Health
21 Days to a Great Marriage
21 Days to Financial Freedom
21 Days to Sharing Your Faith

21 Days to Mission Possible
7 Days to Emotional Freedom
Uncommon Finances
Uncommon Health
Uncommon Marriage
The Jesus Diet
Suddenly Free
Feeling Free

For more information on these books and other resources go to terrytoler.com.

Thank you for purchasing this novel from best-selling author, Terry Toler. As an additional thank you, Terry wants to give you a free gift.

Sign up for:

Updates
New Releases
Announcements

At terrytoler.com

We'll send you the first three chapters of *The Launch*, a Jamie Austen novella, free of charge. The one that started the Spy Stories and Eden Stories Franchises.

FROM THE AUTHOR

The story line in Save Me Twice, overlaps another book I wrote called, The Cliff Hangers: Anna. Anna is written from Cliff Ford, Rita, and Anna's perspective. Save Me Twice is the same story, but written from Jamie Austen and Bae Hwa's perspective. Each book can be read as stand alones and the story is brought to a conclusion in each. For the best reading experience, I'd recommend reading Anna first and then Save Me Twice, although it's not necessary.

Enjoy. Thanks for reading my books.

Terry Toler

The National Center for Missing and Exploited Children estimates that 1 in 6 runaways become victims of child sex trafficking.

1

Where does a seventeen-year-old girl go to find danger?

Hitchhiking. Alone. At night.

There are few things more dangerous than getting in a car with a stranger. Or at least I hoped that was the case.

Perhaps I should explain why I'm looking to put myself in harm's way. The idea came to me the day I read a Reeder Rich novel. Actually, when I finished book nine in the series, and I ran away from home.

Not home. College actually. My parents would freak out if they knew I'd dropped out of school.

The reason. I'm bored.

My name's Bae Hwa, and I'm not your typical seventeen-year-old. They say I'm gifted. I graduated high school when I was fifteen. Started college one month later and will graduate at the end of next semester. Or I'm supposed to, anyway. But I have other plans. My mom wants me to be a doctor. I want to be a CIA spy like Jamie.

Jamie Austen.

She works for the CIA and kills people for a living. I want to be just like her when I grow up. Actually, I am grown up. That's why I ran away from college. To get out on my own. Prove to Jamie that I could do what she does.

Jamie and her husband, Alex, rescued me when I was thirteen-years old from Iranian terrorists. Two men who killed my parents and were after me in North Korea. Alex and Jamie saved my life and brought me to America. Some friends of theirs adopted me.

Not that I wasn't thankful for the new family. I was. I love my new parents. They took me in when I needed a home.

But I'm seventeen and have to make my own way in life.

I know.

The last time I was bored is how I got into trouble with the Iranian terrorists. I stole their backpack full of nuclear codes. How was I supposed to know what was in the satchel? If not for Alex, no telling what would've happened to me.

But... I'm older now. More mature. I learned my lesson.

And I have skills.

Jamie taught me martial arts. Self-defense. How to fire a gun. How to kill a person with my bare hands in a hundred different ways. Alex got me into a two-week training session on The Farm. That's the CIA training facility for new recruits. A man named Curly put me through the best and worst two weeks of my life.

I heard he died. Makes me sad, but I digress.

The time with Curly was the worst two weeks of my life, because I thought I was going to die. By the end, I had bruises up and down my body. Every muscle ached. The best of times because I'd never been happier. It made me who I am today. A trained killer. Like Jamie and Alex. Like Reeder Rich.

Reeder Rich was a former navy seal who went off the grid. He had no family or friends and hitchhiked around the U.S. wherever the road took him. With nothing but the shirt on his back. He tried to find bad guys and take them out. He's a small guy, so people underestimate him. Like they do me. I'm small. People overlook me. They think I'm weak. Big mistake.

Reeder Rich can beat up five guys at one time. Without a weapon. With only his hands.

I want to be just like him.

So, I left college. Yeah! It's stupid. I know Reeder Rich is a fictional character.

But... I'm going to graduate college someday. I'll eventually finish my degree. A degree is required to join the CIA. Just not right now. There's so much good I could do in the world. For a semester. Then I'll go back and finish.

I want to try out what I've learned. I'm determined to find some bad guys and 'Jamie' them. My term for beating the living daylights out of the human debris, as Alex likes to call them.

So, I was on a mission.

To find some bad guys.

Hitchhiking. At night. Alone.

Hopefully, a low-life scumbag will pick me up.

That's where I was now. On a road leading out of Richmond, Virginia. I may have forgotten to mention that I go to Virginia Commonwealth University. It's supposed to be one of the best schools around for pre-med. When I do graduate, it'll be with honors.

It's a little after nine. The sun has set. It's still hot out and I'm drenched in sweat.

I adjusted my backpack. I wasn't like Reeder Rich. Traveling with just the shirt on my back. I needed several changes of clothes. Two pairs of shoes. One pair of sneakers and one pair of flats. Reeder Rich traveled without toothpaste or deodorant. I couldn't do that. Ew. That's the only thing I didn't like about him. I bet his breath and body smelled like a pigsty.

So, I carried some basic necessities. I didn't need makeup, *but a girl needs a brush!*

I was so excited. Earlier that evening, I walked out of my dorm and went north to Broad Street. My plan was to stay off the interstates. It's illegal to hitchhike on the main roads anyway. A cop might stop me. My entire plan would be out the window if I got arrested within thirty minutes of leaving my dorm.

If I had to, I could take down a cop. But I couldn't resist arrest. Jamie always said we only use our skills against bad guys. Not against cops who were just doing their jobs or innocent civilians.

I had to admit that I was a little nervous. Reeder Rich probably was too the first time he got in a car with a stranger.

Not Jamie. She's not afraid of anything.

The problem was that no one stopped. No one even noticed me. Even when I was walking through some bad areas. I thought someone might try to steal my backpack or my cell phone which I left conspicuously sticking out of my back pocket. Enough to where someone could easily snatch it.

No takers.

I needed to be patient. These things take time.

I was looking for the worst of the worst anyway. I should be able to find them on Highway 6 leading out of town. I had just stepped onto that road. Headed west.

I took a deep breath.

Surely, I'd find a bad guy on that well-traveled thoroughfare.

I saw a car coming. The headlights almost blinded me. I stuck out my thumb.

Let's get this party started!

2

Hitchhiking was harder than I thought it would be.

After nearly two hours, I still hadn't found a ride. People stopped. A family with kids. Some girls who went to my college. That's not who I wanted a ride from.

My feet hurt. I was hungry. I had money on me and a credit card, so I stopped at a dive just outside of town. A truck stop. I'd heard that a lot of bad guys hung out at places like that one.

I'd find one there. If I was lucky.

I ate a stack of pancakes lathered in syrup. Along with two slices of bacon and a side of eggs over medium. Even though I barely weighed a hundred pounds, I had a big appetite. The food hit the spot but made me sleepy. Midnight was fast approaching, and I hadn't encountered a single bad guy.

This wasn't going well.

I needed a pick-me-up. So, I bought an energy drink. It felt like I'd been given a B-12 shot. Curly said to always be alert when on a mission. Know your surroundings. Plan your escape route. At dinner, I sat with my back to the wall just like Curly taught me, so no one could sneak up on me.

Eventually, I paid the check and got back on the road and started walking. Every time I saw a car, I stuck out my thumb. For twenty minutes, I struck out. No one stopped. I was about to give up. Maybe this wasn't such a good idea after all.

The thought occurred to me that I could go back to my dorm and regroup. Come up with a different plan. Richmond had a lot of bad areas. Where I could find bad guys to confront. I'd been downtown before. Never alone though. Perhaps if I went there after midnight, I could draw attention to myself.

No! If I turned around, then I will have failed. I didn't want to go back to school. Not yet anyway.

I decided to give it a few more minutes.

A car approached me from behind. I stuck out my thumb. Not as enthusiastically as I had before because my arm was getting tired.

An old pickup truck passed me. I saw the red brake lights come on. The truck slowed, then pulled off on the shoulder. About thirty yards in front of me.

I ran to it, as I felt a jolt of energy like I'd been struck by lightning.

Maybe this was a bad guy.

The window on the passenger side door was down. The truck had seen better days. Faded blue. A couple of dents in the front fender and one on the back rear fender. A confederate flag decal was on the back rear window.

Seems perfect.

"Where ya goin'?" the man asked, in a southern, redneck drawl.

I eyed him carefully. I didn't want to waste my time if he wasn't a threat. It was hard to tell.

"Anywhere west," I answered.

"How old are you?" he asked.

"Old enough to make my own decisions," I said smartly.

He turned his head to the side. Skeptically.

"I'm eighteen, if that's what you're wondering." I lied.

Truthfully, I still looked thirteen. I'm taller, stronger, and fitter than I was at that age, and I worked out with Jamie at the gym as often as I could. But I had a baby face. Something that worked to my disadvantage at the moment. Although, if he truly was a bad guy, he wouldn't care if I was underage.

"Hop in," he said.

That's a good sign.

The man opened a rear sliding window and picked up several items off the front seat and flung them into the bed of the truck. Including a couple empty beer cans. Another promising sign. I got into the passenger seat.

He held out his hand.

Was it a trap?

I prepared to twist his wrist and jerk him into an armlock if he tried anything.

He didn't. Much to my disappointment. He simply shook my hand and released it.

His hand was calloused. Rough. Thick with wide knuckles. He looked larger once I was inside the truck.

No problem. I could handle him. Curly always said if I couldn't beat up two men at the same time, he hadn't done a good job training me.

I wondered how Curly died. I thought he was as strong as an ox.

Redneck's hair was greasy and slicked back. The inside of the truck was warm. It must not've had air conditioning. Or if it did, it didn't work.

"I'm Ben," the man said. "But my friends call me Rascal."

"I'm Bae," I answered.

A bolt of fear shot through me. My heart jumped into my throat. I tamped it down. This was the plan. This was what I wanted. No turning back now.

Hopefully, Rascal was a bad guy.

It wouldn't take long to find out.

3

Rascal was sending me mixed messages.

Most of the time, he acted like a perfect gentleman. Even called me ma'am several times which irritated me to no end. I was seventeen years old! You don't call kids, ma'am. That's a term reserved for someone over forty! I reminded myself that I wasn't a kid.

I'm no ma'am either!

He also sounded like my father half the time.

"You shouldn't be accepting rides from a stranger."

"You should be more careful. There are a lot of bad dudes out there."

"A girl like you should be in school."

Blah. Blah. Blah.

Rascal was making me madder by the minute. I'd use that aggression when he made his move.

Which I hoped was soon.

There were times when I thought he might. When Rascal wasn't being Mister Nice Guy, he acted like a scoundrel. He cussed like a drunken sailor. Not that I'd ever met a drunken sailor before. Jamie used the term occasionally to describe someone with a potty mouth. She always said cursing showed a person's ignorance. Their lack of vocabulary.

Rascal didn't have much of a vocabulary because he couldn't go ten minutes without spewing out a word of the four-letter variety. He did admit that he never finished high school. I could tell. Not that I was a snob. I just didn't care for all the bad language. Curly was that way. During training, I saw him chew some people up one side and down the other. He never cursed at me. Probably because of my age. I was only fifteen at the time.

Rascal's swearing was annoying. He didn't use the entire word. He'd say shi... Or fu... Son of a bi...

Jamie said damn and hell were okay to say because they were in the Bible. Those were the only two bad words Rascal didn't say. He'd say *gol darn, dang,* and *dagnabbit* instead of damn. And for hell he'd say *hades*. Or *h-e-double hockey sticks*. It took me awhile to figure out what that meant.

Honestly, I didn't know if Rascal was a good ol' southern boy or a serial killer. I was hoping for the latter.

Truthfully, I was getting bored. I'd been in the car with him for nearly two hours, and he hadn't tried anything. The only thing he did that might be suspicious was get on a back road. Said he liked to stay off the main ones. He didn't offer a reason why.

I thought that was a good sign. If I was going to try to kill a girl and dispose of her body in the woods, I'd find someplace secluded. A swamp. Or deep forest. A river or stream. Rascal seemed to know the area. I think he mentioned he was from a small town on the other side of the border in Kentucky.

When I found a baseball bat under the passenger side seat, things looked even more promising. I found it by accident. Kicked it when I moved my feet around, trying to get comfortable. The seat on the old truck had seen better days, and the lumps were causing my back to hurt.

I pulled it out and asked Rascal, "What's this?"

"That's my girlfriend, Bertha. I take her everywhere I go. She's been with me almost as long as the underwear I'm wearing."

Rascal cracked himself up with that joke. The closest thing to off-color he'd come. I was beginning to lose faith in my fellow man.

Rascal might be stupid, but he also came across as harmless as a garden snake. Still a snake. But his bite wouldn't kill you.

The bat was made from blond wood and had several indentations and chips in it. It had some noticeable brown stains.

"Chewin' tobacca," Rascal said, when I asked what those were. Not blood stains.

"What's she for?" I asked, hoping I knew the answer.

"She's for protection. In case I run into trouble."

I wasn't bored anymore.

"Have you ever hit anyone with it?"

"Dang shootin' I have. That bat right thar's cracked many a skull. Ain't nobody gonna mess with me when I got that baby in my hands."

"Who tryin' to mess with ya?" I asked, as I suddenly found myself talking like Rascal with the same southern accent.

My curiosity was through the roof. The conversation had just turned interesting.

"Oh, you know. Mostly guys in bars. Think they're tough. They ain't tough when Bertha's around. Most of em take off runnin'."

"Can we go to a bar?" I asked.

"It's two in the mornin'. And if you ain't noticed, we're in the middle of nowhere."

I had noticed that. The road was dark, and the moon was behind the clouds. If Rascal was going to make a move, I figured it'd be any time. We hadn't seen another car for miles.

My blood was pumping now that my heart started racing.

I gripped the bat. The thought of hitting a man over the head with a baseball bat was energizing. Forgetting that Rascal might intend to use that bat on me. One strike with that club and my head would split open.

Which reminded me.

"I hit a man once," I said, in a bragging way.

"No, you didn't!"

That comment made me mad. I wanted to smack Rascal on the head right then and there.

"I most certainly did."

He chuckled dismissively, like he didn't believe me.

"I did! A man grabbed me from behind. I smacked him over the head with my laptop. Knocked him out."

"The devil you say."

I immediately regretted telling Rascal that story. I'd gone to great lengths to make him think I was a vulnerable female. That I didn't know how to defend myself. I hoped he wasn't thinking twice about attacking me.

"I got lucky, I guess," I added to try to undo the damage.

I remembered it like yesterday. Alex and I were in North Korea. Running from the terrorists. An armed soldier grabbed me from behind. Alex had been teaching me some self-defense moves. I used one of them. I stomped on the soldier's foot or kicked him in the shin. I don't remember which. He released his grip. I had the laptop in my hands. I reared back and hit him in the head with it.

Alex said I killed him. All I know was that it felt good. Hitting a bad guy. That's the first and last person I've ever hit. That's what's so frustrating. Jamie and I work out all the time. But all I hit were punching bags. Shadow boxing. Ad nauseum. Jamie said it honed my skills.

"When can I hit a real person?" I had asked her.

"Hope you never have to."

Jamie did let me get in a ring with another kid once. It wasn't the same. We wore boxing gloves. Headgear. Shin and knee pads. A stomach protector. I could barely move, much less hit the other boy who was actually younger than me.

Not being able to hit a bad guy was driving me crazy. It sounded weird in my head which was why I never told anyone. Not even Jamie. She wouldn't understand. Maybe she would. Jamie got to kill bad guys all the time.

She was so lucky!

It's what she did for a living with the CIA. That's what I was going to do someday.

It seemed like it might be an eternity from now.

Best case scenario, I'd graduate from college next semester. Then go through the application process. Alex and Jamie would be able to get me approved, but it'd take time. If accepted, I'd be sent to the Farm. I'd go through six months of intense training. I'd get to hit people there, but it'd be controlled.

I'd spend a year or two in the field as an analyst to learn the ropes. Then, if I was lucky, I'd be given an assignment. I'd probably go to Asia, given my background. Maybe South Korea. There wasn't any action there. It's possible I wouldn't see real danger for four or five years. If at all. Jamie said some officers went their entire careers without firing a gun.

I'd rather die!

I put the bat back under the seat and started messing with the glove box with a latch that was hanging on by a thread.

Rascal didn't like that. When the glovebox popped open, I realized why. A handgun was in it. I recognized it as a Glock. He tried to drive with one hand and shut the glovebox with the other, but it kept popping open. When he went around a curve, I took out the gun and held it. Pretended I didn't know what to do with it.

Actually, I could take it apart and put it back together in a matter of seconds. Curly taught me that. Along with how to fire it. I got pretty proficient after the two weeks of training. Better than most my age, Curly had said.

"Put that gun back," Rascal said roughly. "You'll hurt yourself. Or me."

I put it back and managed to get the latch to work and closed it up.

Rascal made a sudden movement.

It startled me.

He jerked the truck off the road at the last minute onto a dirt side road.

The road came to a stop at a dead end.

Rascal turned off the engine and the lights.

The cab was almost pitch black.

Finally!

He was going to make his move.

What would it be? The bat. The gun. His fists.

Didn't matter. I was ready for anything.

4

Jamie was having a hard time getting over the death of Curly. Her mentor and father figure. Curly was her trainer at The Farm. He was the one who made her into the CIA's most skilled officer and the most lethal female assassin in the world.

She probably felt an affinity to Curly because Jamie never really had a relationship with her own father. Her mother, who died when she was seventeen, told her from an early age that her father was dead. Turned out, he was very much alive. And he'd been looking for her.

Adam Lang was an astronaut. On a one-way mission to the ends of the universe. Jamie was at NASA headquarters to send him a message.

Jamie's husband, Alex, had suggested it.

"Why don't you go to Florida and send your dad a message? It's been a while. The break might do you good."

It had been over a year since she had done so, even though she had an open invitation to come anytime she wanted. Her dad was a hero in NASA circles.

"I don't even know if he's getting them," she said.

General consensus was that he was traveling away from earth too fast to receive the messages. The first few years, she sent them anyway.

"Whether he is or not, talking to him will be cathartic," Alex said.

"It'll be what?" she asked.

"Cathartic. It means psychologically cleansing."

"I know what it means. I just didn't know you knew such a big word."

Alex got a huge grin on his face. "Don't let the pretty face fool you," he said, pointing at it.

So, she took his advice and flew down to Cape Canaveral. They led her into a room with a desk, one chair, a microphone, and a video camera facing the desk. Same room she'd used in the past to send her dad messages. Jamie sat down behind the desk and fidgeted nervously. She never knew quite what to say.

It seemed weird having a one-sided conversation. Especially not knowing if he would ever hear it.

"When you're ready," a voice from another room said to her over a speaker.

"I'm ready."

"Three. Two. One. Go."

"Hi Dad. It's Jamie. Hope you're doing well."

She immediately began to tear up. Jamie didn't show emotion much. Seemed like the only time she did was when she recorded these messages. It made her sad. Reminded her of the fact that she'd grown up without a father. When they finally found each other, he was gone out of her life forever. It seemed unfair.

Jamie only talked to him once. By the same kind of video camera. He'd already lifted off into space and was about to go into the space stream. They talked for less than twenty minutes. The sum total of the entire interaction with her dad.

Twenty minutes. Hardly seemed like much, yet enough time to make an indescribable bond. He was always in her heart.

"Sorry it's been a while," Jamie said. "I've been busy."

She chuckled.

"Listen to me. Telling you I've been busy. You're in outer space. Only God knows where. I've been praying for you. Every day. Well. . . Almost every day. When I remember anyway. Which is as often as I can."

Jamie shifted positions in the chair. This always made her uncomfortable.

"I've been killing lots of bad guys lately. And rescuing girls. I just got back from Hong Kong. We helped more than two thousand girls get out of sex trafficking. You know I work for the CIA. I told you that. In case you don't remember. They say I'm really good at it. Senator Robinson got me in. I love it."

She shifted again in the chair as the tears welled up for a second time. The whole situation suddenly felt overwhelming with a force she couldn't control.

"I got bad news while I was in Hong Kong. A good friend of mine, Curly. . . he passed away. Died of a heart attack. The sad part was that I didn't get a chance to say goodbye."

Curly was running a mission in Costa Rica. Alex was there with him when he died, but Jamie was in Hong Kong. It'd been a while since she talked to Curly as well. She would've called more often but Curly never stayed on the phone longer than a minute. She'd barely say hello and he'd say, "Thanks for calling. Talk to you next time."

She once asked him why, and he said he didn't want to run up her phone bill. Jamie tried to explain to Curly that she had unlimited minutes on her cellphone, but the argument fell on deaf ears. If she wanted to spend significant time with him, she had to make a point of going to The Farm where he trained recruits. In person, Curly would sit and talk to you for hours. Now that he was gone, she realized how much she missed those times.

Jamie tried to choke back the tears, but they escaped from her eyes and ran down her cheeks. She brushed them aside with her hand. Roughly.

"Curly was kind of like a father to me. Is that bad? I mean...
I hope you don't mind. I don't mean to hurt you, but I never really
knew you. Curly took me under his wing. Taught me everything
I know about being a CIA officer. I feel like I lost another father.
You know. I'm sorry the words aren't coming out right."

She took a deep breath. This time, she did successfully stop the
flow of the tears.

"Alex is great though. I told you about him. He's my husband.
We don't have any kids yet. Someday. I hope."

Jamie had a picture of Alex in her pocket, and she took it out
and showed it to the camera.

"Alex is a CIA officer as well. Actually, we aren't CIA officers
anymore. I don't think I told you this. We started a corporation
together. AJAX. We buy and sell art. Did you know I minored in art
in college? I don't know if I told you that. We still work with the
CIA. Just not *for* them. Off the books. AJAX is a cover for our covert
operations."

Jamie let out another chuckle.

"Don't tell anyone though. It's top secret. Who are you going
to tell? Have you run into any aliens yet? Met any pretty green
women?"

That caused Jamie to burst out laughing. The conversation was
cathartic. She was already feeling better.

"Courtney says hi, by the way. She misses you too. We keep in
touch. She never married. I think she's still in love with you."

Jamie met Courtney on the same day she talked to her dad for
the first time. She knew instantly the two of them were in love.
According to Courtney, they never acted on it. What was the point
really? He was leaving forever. It's not like they could carry on a
long-distance relationship.

"What else? I'm sure I'll think of something after I'm done.
I won't wait as long next time."

Then the sadness returned with a vengeance. It always did
when she had to say goodbye.

17

"Take care. I love you. I really miss you. Thanks for listening. I'm praying for you. Stay safe. Bye."

The last bye was barely above a whisper.

"We got it," the voice said soberly but matter-of-factly.

"Thank you," Jamie said, as she stood and walked out of the room.

She looked at her watch. *4:03 p.m.*

Courtney said to come by her office at four. They were going to dinner. Then Jamie would stay with her that night before heading back home tomorrow.

Jamie's phone vibrated in her back pocket.

She took it out and looked at the caller ID.

Page McBride.

Bae's mom.

Bae Hwa was a girl they rescued in North Korea. She was living in America now with a woman Jamie went to college with and her husband.

"Hello Page."

"Hi Jamie. How are you?"

"I'm doing well."

As well as could be expected, considering the emotional upheaval she'd been through over the last few days and weeks.

"How about you guys?" Jamie asked, trying to muster up some enthusiasm. "How's Bae?"

"That's why I'm calling. I wondered if you'd heard from her?"

"Not in a couple of weeks. Why?"

It'd actually been more than a couple of weeks. Maybe even before Jamie went to Hong Kong.

"I've tried to call her a few times, and she doesn't answer," Page said.

Jamie could hear the concern in her mother's voice.

"She's in college now. You remember what that was like. We didn't have much time for parents."

"Don't I know it. I remember. But Bae's usually pretty good at calling me back. I'm starting to worry."

A slight stab of fear hit Jamie's emotions. She slapped it back down.

"I wouldn't worry," she said. "I'm sure Bae's fine. She's probably studying for a big test or something. Maybe she met a boy."

Page laughed nervously.

"Let's hope that's not the case. I'm not ready for Bae to start dating college boys. She just turned seventeen. Anyway, if you hear from Bae, please tell her to call her mom."

"Will do. Good talking to you."

Jamie hung up and then called Bae's cell phone. It went directly to voicemail.

"Hey girl! Jamie here. Call me. Bye."

Jamie refused to be worried. Bae didn't have time for adults. She was having fun. She used to call Jamie every day before she went to college. The calls were getting fewer and further between.

Jamie had expected as much.

Bae's probably with a boy.

5

Somewhere in Virginia

A loud noise awakened me from a deep sleep. A familiar sound. An engine cranking. Then a roar. A muffler sound, then a vibration as the truck roared to life.

It took several seconds to get my bearings. The sun beat through the windshield and into my eyes, temporarily blinding me. I had to put my hand on my forehead and squint to see anything.

What I did see caused the events of the previous night to come flooding back to me.

Rascal. The blue truck. The side road. Hitchhiking.

"Mornin'," Rascal said, flashing me a grin. I wanted to slap him and knock the smug smile off his face.

In the light I could see he was missing several teeth. His nose was slightly off-center. Probably from being broken several times in fights. He was rougher looking than I'd realized. I'd only seen him in the dark of night.

Then I felt the anger and suddenly remembered why I was so mad at him.

The mission.

He'd shown so much promise. Now in the light, even more so. He was a carbon copy of what I thought a bad guy would look like. Dirty. Mussed hair. Rough features. Ill mannered.

Disgusting.

So, what happened? Rascal pulled off the side of the road in the early morning hours, around two a.m. I asked why.

"I need some sleep," he said. "We're still a couple huner'd miles from the border. A few hours of shuteye will do us both some good."

Rascal leaned his head against the driver's side door, crossed his arms, and closed his eyes. I was convinced it was all a ruse. His attempt to lure me into complacency. Get me to fall asleep then he'd make his move. When I was most vulnerable and unable to defend myself.

I'd been determined to stay awake. Even pretended to be asleep for Rascal's benefit until I realized the futility of it. He snored like a mule. It wasn't hard to know that he was dead to the world.

At some point, I must've fallen asleep.

Rookie mistake.

Curly would've chewed me out if he knew. Jamie would be disappointed in me. I was disappointed in myself. I should've stayed awake. Slept with one eye open. Curly always said you can sleep when you're dead.

Which is what you'll be if you fall asleep while in a dangerous situation.

Curly's words still resonated in my ears.

That's not why I was mad though. Rascal hadn't tried anything. Even while I was asleep. Much to my chagrin. He had every opportunity. The question was why not? I was determined to find out.

He must have sensed my animosity. I met his smile and good morning with a glare that would've broken a plate glass window if such a thing were possible.

"What's eatin' you?" Rascal asked.

I had no idea what he meant. *Eating me?* That's not a term I was familiar with. Did he mean, like, an animal? What a stupid thing to say. No animal was eating me. As if I couldn't be angrier at him. Now he was mocking me with stupid southern phrases.

I didn't answer.

He gave me a dismissive shrug. That only made me madder. Jamie's pet peeve was people dismissing her. I think I got that same trait from her.

Rascal backed the truck out of the dead end, turned around, and drove back to the main highway. Neither of us said anything for a good five minutes. Until I couldn't hold it in any longer. The anger was building inside of me like a volcano filled with boiling lava about to erupt.

"Why didn't you make a pass at me?" I said angrily.

"Is that what's got them crawdads in your britches?" Rascal asked.

Again, I had no clue what he meant. I didn't have any crawdads in my pants. I didn't even know what a crawdad was. I also wasn't sure about britches, but I believed those were pants.

"What the hell are you talking about?" I demanded, deciding to curse for effect. I could count on one hand how many curse words had actually ever come out of my mouth. I liked the sound of it. It made me sound tough.

Rascal kept his eyes on the road.

"I was asleep," I said. "You could've had your way with me. Why didn't you?"

Rascal shrugged his shoulders a second time and refused to look in my direction. Like the conversation was making him uncomfortable.

"I guess you're not my type," he finally said, somewhat sheepishly.

Wrong answer.

Now I was offended.

Rascal didn't try to kill me because I wasn't pretty enough!

Of all the nerve!

"What's wrong with me?" I asked roughly.

He shrugged again.

If he didn't stop shrugging, I was going to break one of his arms so he couldn't lift his shoulders anymore.

He explained. "I guess... You know. You don't have enough goin' on upstairs."

I exploded in fury.

"I'll have you know that I go to Virginia Commonwealth University! I'm a premed student! I'm going to graduate from college in one semester! At seventeen years old! I can't believe you think I'm not smart enough for you."

"I thought you said you were eighteen?" he said, in more of a question than a comment. Another rookie mistake. Jamie always said to remember your cover. Memorize the details. One slip up could get you killed. I'd forgotten I told him I was eighteen.

"Whatever!" I said, not having a better comeback than that.

I folded my arms in front of me again and purposefully put a scowl on my face.

"Anyway. That's not what I's meant," he said defensively. "You're plenty smart."

"What's wrong with me then? You don't find me attractive? There are plenty of guys at my school who think I'm pretty."

"Yars pretty nough. By upstairs, I mean... in the chest area."

I looked down at my chest, then at Rascal. He wasn't making sense.

Rascal took both hands off the wheel and cupped them in front of his chest. "You don't have enough boobage. I'm a breast man. You're as flat as a pancake."

The pancake comment distracted me. A stomach growl at the exact same moment notified my mind that I was hungry. Pancakes sounded good.

I tamped down the feeling and refocused. Now I understood what he meant by my upstairs. I did have the chest of an eight-year-old. Not long ago, Jamie took me clothes shopping. In the fitting room, I lamented about how small my breasts were. Jamie said tiny breasts were good for a CIA officer. Large breasts were vulnerable to strikes to the chest. They also weren't good for undercover work. A spy wanted to be inconspicuous. Unremarkable. People remembered pretty, voluptuous women. A spy didn't want to be remembered.

Regardless, I didn't take what Rascal said as a compliment. He didn't try to kill me because I wasn't his type. What a pig. I didn't even know serial killers had a type. I thought they went for the easy prey. Like me. A small girl. Young. Alone. Hitchhiking. At night.

It didn't get any easier than that. What did I have to do? Put his hands around my neck for him?

Rascal might be a serial killer, but he wasn't very good at it. That, or he was picky. Apparently, he only attacked big-busted girls.

I was beyond offended and let him know it.

"I thought for sure you'd try and attack me while I was sleeping."

"Attack you? What in hades are you talking about?"

Another mistake.

Never give away your mission. I'd already told him my name which was a serious lapse of judgment. Jamie drilled in me that, when on a mission, you never tell anyone your name or any details of the operation. Technically, I wasn't on an official CIA job, but this was practice for one.

I was failing miserably.

Then I blurted out, "I'm a female Reeder Rich."

"Who's he?"

"A character in a novel I'm reading. He's my hero. I'm not surprised you've never heard of him. You don't seem like the reading type."

"I read. I may not have all that college learnin' like you do, but I can read."

That seemed to have offended him, judging by the tone. Good. He deserved it. He'd wasted more than twelve hours of my time.

"Reeder Rich is a bad dude," I said.

"If he's a bad guy, why's he your hero?"

"What?" I didn't understand.

"You said this Rich character was a bad dude. What is he, a murderer? Kidnapper? Bank robber?"

"No. He's a good guy."

"Make up your mind."

"A bad dude means he's a good guy."

"You ain't makin' sense. Reeder Rich sounds like a loser."

"Reeder Rich is dope."

"He does drugs?"

"No! He kills it."

"Kills what."

"Will you shut up and let me finish?"

Rascal threw a free hand in the air. The other was on the wheel and his eyes were focused on the road. Although, they'd yet to see a car for the several miles they'd been driving.

I explained. "Reeder Rich is a *good* guy who hitchhikes across the country looking for bad guys. Then he kills them. Or beats them up. I'm a female Reeder Rich."

"You?"

I nodded my head up and down for emphasis and recrossed my arms.

"Little ol' you? You don't weigh ninety pounds soppin' wet. I think a mosquito'd have a better chance of beatin' up a bad guy than you. No offense."

I hit him on the arm. Hard.

"Ow! What'd you go and do that fer?"

"You deserved it. I'm tougher than I look. My job is to find bad guys and take them out. I thought you were one of them."

Rascal started laughing at the top of his lungs.

That only made me madder.

"And you thought I was a bad guy," Rascal said, laughing even harder. "You wanted me to attack you."

"Yeah. Well. You didn't. I guess my boobs weren't big enough," I said, sarcastically.

"Are you sure you didn't just escape from a mental institution?"

"Pull over and let me out."

The truck was flying down the road at seventy miles per hour.

"You are one crazy bee... atch!" Rascal said, mockingly.

"I said pull over or I'll make you regret it."

I opened the door even though he hadn't slowed down. Fortunately, I had my seatbelt on and only opened the door slightly for effect. Gripping the handle tightly. I hoped it didn't break off in my hand.

"Okay. Okay. I'm pulling over," Rascal said, nervously.

He slowed down and pulled off onto the shoulder.

I grabbed all of my stuff and got out of the truck. Put my backpack over my shoulder and stormed off in the direction we were headed.

Rascal followed along behind me. I kept my stare in the direction I was walking and refused to look at him. Wouldn't give him the satisfaction.

After a quarter of a mile, Rascal pulled the truck alongside me. He was still in the road, but nothing was coming. The passenger-side window was down.

"Get in the truck," he said. "I'll take you to a town just past the border."

I kept walking. The truck matched my pace.

"Come on, Bae. I know a great breakfast joint," he said. "I'll buy you breakfast. Let me make it up to ya."

I stopped walking. Then looked in both directions. Didn't see anything coming for miles. Breakfast did sound good.

I got back in the truck.

The taste of pancakes was causing my mouth to water.

"I'm sorry I didn't try to kill ya while yous was sleepin'," Rascal said, with a wide grin.

"It's okay. I forgive you."

6

Jamie boarded her private jet and took off from Melbourne International Airport headed back to Washington D.C. Feeling better. Taping a message to her dad and spending the evening with Courtney had done her a world of good. As Alex said, cathartic. She called him to let him know she was on her way home.

"Was your time away abreactive?" Alex asked.

It sounded like he was eating lunch and his mouth was full and he struggled to get the word out. Jamie knew what was going on and was prepared.

"It was extremely depurative," Jamie quipped.

Jamie had googled thesaurus words for cathartic. Alex had probably done the same thing. Abreactive was on her list.

"I knew it'd be lustral," Alex said, not even acknowledging her word. They'd see who laughed first.

Lustral was also on the list of about twenty-five long words.

"More purgative than anything," Jamie replied.

"I find those things very laxative," Alex answered.

Jamie laughed first. "That's the noun version of cathartic. Cathartic, abreactive, depurative, and lustral are all the adjective versions of cathartic. Totally different meaning. You lose."

"Shoot! I was doing so good."

"So well."

He ignored the correction. She wasn't even sure she was right.

"How did you know I was going to be prepared with more big words?" Alex asked.

"You are predictable, honey. I've known you long enough to know."

"Hard to put one over on you. You are very perspicacious."

Jamie quickly typed that word into the search engine of her computer for the definition. It meant mentally discerning.

"You're quite the sesquipedalian," Jamie retorted.

"What does that mean?" he asked.

"Someone who uses long words."

"You're prepared to do this all day, aren't you?"

"Until you give up and admit that I'm the winner."

"I give up. You're making my head hurt."

"When I get home, I'll rub it for you."

"I can't wait. You are the best osculator I know."

The line went dead.

"Alex?"

He wasn't there. He'd gotten the last word. Jamie looked it up. Then smiled broadly. Osculator meant one who kisses. She was already looking forward to giving him an abundance of kisses as soon as she saw him. She'd only been gone for two days but missed him intensely.

Perhaps the nature of their work kept the passion alive between them. Being near death several times a month, carried over to their relationship. They lived on the edge. Going from one adrenaline rush after another. They'd sometimes go weeks without seeing each other. When they did, the intensity was off the charts and the contrast striking. On a mission they constantly dealt with violence and rage. When they saw each other, the emotional pendulum swung the other direction. Heated love and passion. Strong feelings on both sides of the coin.

Jamie wondered when they'd settle into a normal, predictable, boring marriage like most couples she knew. Hopefully never.

Work hard. Play hard. Love hard, was something Curly used to say.

That thought brought back a twinge of sadness. Jamie refused to give it any place and lose the ground she'd made up from the two days of cleansing out those negative feelings. When she thought of Curly, she was determined to think good things. Remember the good times. Thank him for all he did for her. Make him proud of what she did to make the world a safer place. Whatever success she had as a CIA officer, she owed it all to him.

The positive thoughts of Curly and the interaction with Alex warmed her heart.

She pulled up an email on her computer from Jill Vanderbilt, the CEO of Save The Girls, and the feelings went away immediately. Jill had sent her the latest annual report on sex trafficking.

Save The Girls was a Christian nonprofit organized for the purpose of helping girls who'd been rescued from sex trafficking. AJAX funded ninety percent of their annual budget. Jamie had been running missions to rescue the girls for the CIA for several years now. Save The Girls took many of the girls in and gave them a new lease on life.

Over the years of working together, Jamie and Jill had formed a close professional and personal relationship.

The details in the report would spoil anyone's mood. Jamie read it carefully. She was particularly interested in the section on trafficking in the U.S.

The report on America was sobering. And infuriating.

The official government report said that 62,500 people were trafficked each year in the U.S. Seventy percent of them were women. From experience, Jamie would say that number was lower than it actually was in real life. Another study said the number was between 100,000 and 300,000. A different study narrowed the gap and said between 240,000 and 300,000.

Which was it? 57,000 or 300,000? Or two million?

A jolt of anger hit her. Why couldn't they get the numbers more accurate? Why bother even putting out a report? With a range like that, they might as well be guessing!

Truthfully, they didn't know. That was the takeaway.

The report did have some statistics that could be verified.

150,000 sex ads were posted online each day.

75% of victims were trafficked online.

55% of the children trafficked reported that they attended school.

Unbelievable!

Where were the counselors, teachers, parents, and fellow students? Why were the kids afraid to say anything? Even when they were away from their abusers?

Then Jamie read the most infuriating statistics of all.

2041 incidents reported to authorities.

807 people arrested.

"Pathetic," Jamie said aloud. "A drop in the bucket."

She'd just rescued more than two thousand girls in Hong Kong in a little over a month.

The thought occurred to her that she needed to do more in the United States. The problem was that her hands were somewhat tied. Overseas, Jamie could break whatever law necessary to achieve the end goals. Not in the U.S. Privacy laws and rules of engagement limited her ability to work with impunity.

Jamie understood those laws and supported them. That's why she did nothing in America. For years, she couldn't. The CIA was forbidden from operating on U.S. soil by the Constitution. Once she left the CIA and started AJAX, those laws didn't technically apply to her anymore. She could rescue girls in America. She didn't.

Because of the lack of support and coordination between law enforcement agencies. The fact that sex trafficking was a low priority and scant resources were thrown at it was evidenced by the fact that only 807 traffickers were arrested.

The real reason. She didn't want to get thrown in jail. Jamie was too much of a free spirit. Loose cannon was a term some used for her. Overseas, especially in third-world countries, Jamie could rescue the girls, kill the bad guys, dump their bodies in a river, and call it a day. In America, she was merely a civilian. With no mission authority to act on US soil. No ability to arrest anyone or interrogate them.

What would she do with a trafficker if she found one? Call the police. He'd be back on the street by nightfall. That's if the police even responded. She could dump their bodies in the river but then she'd be the one arrested. People had to be read their rights. Overseas, the bad guys had the right to be dead.

Probably best that she didn't do more in America.

A section in the report caught her eye.

An uptick in gang related sex trafficking.

In major cities such as New York, LA, Baltimore, Detroit, Chicago, and others. Law enforcement had seen increased prostitution activity among gangs. That made sense. Girls had to be watched and controlled. Sex trafficking required a veil of secrecy. Also, a large group of people with no morals whatsoever. No regard for human decency or human suffering.

Gangs fit that description perfectly.

The report said that a shift was occurring from individual pimps to gang related brothel keepers. Used to be one man did everything. Recruited the girls, housed them, secured the johns, and provided the girl's ongoing support. And pocketed most of the money. The pimps engaged in turf wars and considered the girls property and claimed ownership on real estate. Specific street corners, abandoned houses, hotels, things of the like.

Once gangs got in the business, human resources increased exponentially. Sex trafficking provided another source of revenue for the gangs. Big money. From drugs and prostitution. They fit together nicely. An obvious expansion of distribution for powerful gangs. It also made it harder for the girls to escape. Instead of having to extract themselves from the clutches of one pimp, they had to free themselves from the power and ruthlessness of perhaps hundreds of gang members.

I really should do more.

Jamie's phone rang, interrupting her thoughts.

Page McBride. Bae's mom.

"Hello Page. Have you heard from Bae?"

"I was hoping you'd heard from her," she said. Jamie could hear the almost panic in her voice.

"I left her a message, but she hasn't called me back."

"I'm worried."

"I'm sure Bae's fine," Jamie said, not willing to reveal the concern she was also feeling. She'd checked her phone several times wondering why Bae hadn't called her back.

"What should we do?" Page asked.

"I'm flying back to Virginia right now. I'll stop off in Richmond and find her. I'll call you when I do."

"Thank you. Let me know as soon as you hear from her."

"Of course."

Jamie hung up the phone and pushed an intercom button that communicated directly with the cockpit.

"How's it going up there, A-Rad?" she asked.

"Beautiful day for flying. We haven't been shot at and I don't expect to be."

Jamie couldn't help but chuckle. A-Rad got his nickname because he was a radical. When she met him, A-Rad was flying hurricane planes for the Air Force. Meaning he made a living flying weather planes into the eye of a storm to get weather readings.

Knowing A-Rad he'd be much more comfortable if they were being shot at.

"I want to make a stop," Jamie said.

"In Cuba?" he asked.

Jamie laughed again. A-Rad once flew her into the eye of a hurricane and she parachuted out of the plane and into Cuba. Something she barely lived to tell about.

"We're not going to Cuba today. Take me to Richmond, Virginia."

"You're so boring."

"Don't worry, A-Rad. I'll take you on a mission where you get shot at real soon."

"You promise?"

"I promise."

"I'll put in a flight plan now. Do you want to parachute into Richmond, or do you want me to land?"

She could see the wide grin on his face as he said it. A-Rad used to be the quietest person in the room. Always a jokester, but shy. Especially around girls. He was coming out of his shell and Jamie was glad to see it.

"Let's land this time," Jamie said.

"Like I said, boring."

"Just get me on the ground safely."

"As always."

Jamie hung up the phone. Her mind was still on Bae.

Where are you, girl?

Jamie's mind suddenly connected sex trafficking and gangs to Bae being missing. That was stupid. Bae was fine. Probably in classes. Studying for tests. With a boyfriend.

For some reason, Jamie had a bad feeling about it.

7

Acton, Kentucky

Rascal bought me breakfast as promised and I amazed him with how much I ate. More than him, even. After breakfast, we got back in the truck, and he drove me across the Kentucky line and stopped at a small town called Acton. That's as far as Rascal was going anyway. He lived there.

"Are there any hotels in town? Low rent," I asked. "A seedy place where I might find some action."

Spending the last few hours together, Rascal knew what I meant by action. I had a plan to leave my motel room door slightly ajar. Perhaps someone would take it as an opportunity to try and rob me.

"I know just the place," Rascal answered. "But why don't you stay with me? I got room."

"No thanks. I need some privacy. Someplace with a shower and a place to brush my teeth."

Normally, going to a strange man's apartment would be exactly what I wanted. Not with Rascal. It'd be a waste of time. There was no danger there. I was convinced Rascal was a good guy after all. If he was going to do anything to me, he'd have already tried it. I needed some time to rethink my plan.

Rascal had mentioned that he got into fights at bars. I was determined to find one.

"Are there any bars in this town?" I asked him.

"Several."

"Which one is the worst?"

"What do you mean? The worst food?"

"No silly. The worst clientele. You know. A place where rough guys go. Where I can go to get in a fight."

Rascal's deep laugh felt like he was mocking me.

"You better be careful, little girl. There's some bad dudes in Acton. And by bad, I mean bad. Not good. They'd just a'soon hit ya as look at ya."

"Perfect. What's the place with the worst of the worst?"

"Whiskey Joe's."

Rascal pulled the truck into the motel parking lot.

"When do they open?"

"Open at eleven for lunch and close at four in the mornin'."

"Thanks for the ride, Rascal," I said.

I stuck out my hand and he shook it.

"You be careful," Rascal said.

"I won't," I retorted and closed the door.

Rascal didn't know that you were never supposed to say 'be careful.' When Alex and Jamie were on a mission, they always said to each other, "Don't be careful." I asked them why.

Curly. He told them careful gets you killed. I didn't understand so Jamie explained it.

"When you're on a mission and bullets are flying, you mostly react by instinct," she said. "If you're being careful, then you are reacting by your thoughts. It takes longer to react to thoughts than to instinct. What Curly was saying was that if you overthink things, that split second hesitation might be enough to get you killed."

That made sense. Of course, Rascal didn't know so I just ignored the comment.

If the front door to the motel was any indication, the motel was exactly what I was looking for. Dilapidated and low rent.

"Can I have a room on the first floor?" I asked a man who looked to be the manager. He reeked of cigarette smoke and alcohol.

The chances of being attacked in the motel in broad daylight were slim to none, but I figured my chances were better on the first floor than on the other floors.

"This is a motel. We only have one floor," the crusty man said groggily. I might've woken him from a nap. Or breakfast. He had jam on his shirt.

"I'm a young girl, traveling alone. So I want a room that's toward the back."

The manager seemed harmless, but I didn't know that for sure. I wanted him to know that I was a vulnerable young woman, in case he was the kind of guy who might try something.

He ignored my comment. I wasn't sure he even looked at me long enough to make any analysis. If he did try anything, he wouldn't be much of a threat. It seemed like he had trouble buttoning his shirt which was not aligned correctly.

I paid with my credit card, and he gave me the room key. Not a key card. A key. I don't think I'd ever seen one of those at a hotel before.

The motel looked perfect. Run down. Seedy almost. It needed a coat of paint and a carpenter to fix the disrepair that was every place your eye could see. Jamie often talked about going dark. In CIA terms, that meant off the grid. Where no one could find you. She gave me pointers. Look for a seedy motel. Off the beaten path. One without a security camera. Pay with cash.

I slapped my forehead.

I paid with a credit card!

There was still a lot to learn. Oh well. It's not like I was trying not to be found. I was just looking for a place where somebody might see me and make a move. There wasn't a single car in the parking lot which made me think it wasn't going to happen at the motel.

Truthfully, my best bet was *Whiskey Joe's*. Tonight. Right after dark. Rascal said a number of bad guys would be there.

Perfect.

I took a lukewarm shower and brushed my teeth. Then turned on the television and watched Twilight Zone reruns. Practiced tamping down fear.

I left the door cracked slightly just in case somebody was looking to steal something from a room or saw me go in.

Maybe I'd get lucky.

8

Virginia Commonwealth University
Richmond, Virginia

Jamie found Bae's dorm and knocked on the door. The hope was that Bae answered. If she did, Jamie had a built-in excuse. She was in the area. Thought she'd drop by. Maybe get lunch and catch up. It occurred to Jamie that if Bae was there, then she shouldn't say anything about her mother calling Jamie to check up on her daughter. The last thing Jamie wanted was for Bae to think the drop in was planned.

Bae was only seventeen but mature for her age. She'd be graduating from college soon. Becoming a young woman. Jamie remembered what it was like to go to college. It was a time to spread your wings. Be out on your own for the first time. Of course, Jamie didn't have any parents looking over her shoulder. Her mom died when she was Bae's age, and she didn't know her dad at the time. The closest thing she had was an aunt who barely had a leash on Jamie. Much less a tight leash.

Between work and school, Jamie barely had time to get into trouble anyway. She certainly would've called her aunt back though. Somehow Jamie needed to fit that into the conversation. Gently chastise Bae for not calling her back. Or her mom. In a way that Bae wouldn't know Jamie had been in touch with her mom.

Jamie was surprised when Bae's roommate, Ruby Blake, answered the door. Jamie met Ruby the last time she visited Bae and didn't like her. The girl was aloof and snobby. A rich southern girl who was nice enough but didn't have time for adults. Not much time for her roommate either, Bae had confided.

Jamie had hoped Bae would have a roommate who would take her under her wing and show her the ropes. Hopefully, the good ropes. That wasn't Ruby. She had her own set of popular friends, and a refugee from North Korea with quirks didn't fit into her clique or agenda.

"Hi Ruby," Jamie said with a smile. "Do you remember me? I'm a friend of Bae's."

"Jamie, right?"

"Is Bae around?"

Ruby looked around the room. That seemed unnecessary. Ruby should know if Bae was there. The dorm room was barely three hundred square feet. Two desks. Two beds and a bathroom with a shower off the main room.

The door was half open. Jamie pushed it all the way open, so she could see for herself. A little risky if Ruby had a visitor. Nearing noon, Jamie didn't much care if she did.

No one was in the room. Or if they were, they were in the bathroom.

"Bae's not here," Ruby finally answered.

"Do you know where she is?"

"No."

Jamie studied her carefully to see if she was lying. She wasn't. She just didn't care where Bae was.

"When was the last time you saw her?"

Jamie felt like she was doing an interrogation. Like pulling teeth.

"Couple of days ago."

"Did she say anything? Was she going away for a few days? Did she meet a guy? Is she staying at his place?"

The questions were coming rapid fire now. Jamie wasn't pausing between questions to wait for an answer, because it didn't seem like Ruby knew anything or would say even if she did know.

Ruby shook her head no. Jamie assumed that was the answer to all the questions but decided to press the issue.

"No, what?" Jamie raised the tone of her voice. "No, she didn't say anything? No, she doesn't have a boyfriend? Or no, you're perfectly clueless and a horrible roommate who doesn't even know where her friend is? Did it ever occur to you that something might've happened to Bae? Does she always disappear for two days without telling anyone?"

The girl rolled her eyes.

Jamie wanted to slap them permanently into the back of her head. This was why she didn't operate in the U.S. If she were in a third-world country, she'd push the girl up against the wall, put her forearm against her throat, and demand information. Actually, she probably wouldn't. Not in this instance. The girl had no clue where Bae was. Obviously hadn't even noticed she was gone.

"Mind if I look around?" Jamie asked, not waiting for an answer. Instead pushing her way past the girl and into the room.

She heard a noticeable sigh from the girl but ignored it.

Jamie began looking through Bae's things.

"Close the door when you leave," Ruby said. "I've got class."

Ruby grabbed a backpack off her bed and was gone in a second.

Jamie rummaged through the drawers in Bae's desk. Then looked in her closet. Noticeably missing was the backpack Alex and Jamie had given Bae for Christmas. Most of her clothes were there, but her toothbrush and other toiletries were missing. Bae had clearly left the dorm with the intention of being gone for a few days.

Not long or she would've taken more things. All of her textbooks were there so it appeared that Bae wasn't intending to go to class over those days.

Where would she have gone?

Jamie could probably rule out foul play. No one carried their toothbrush in their backpack.

Beside Bae's bed table was a Reeder Rich novel. Jamie picked it up and thumbed through it. Several pages had dog ears. Jamie scanned them. The pages marked were fight scenes. On Bae's desk were eight more Reeder Rich novels. All with similar pages highlighted.

Jamie sat down on the bed and stared at the ceiling holding the book in her hand.

She thought she knew where Bae was. Not where she was but what she might be up to.

Stupid girl!

Jamie remembered a conversation the two of them had on the phone a few weeks ago.

I told her it was a dumb idea.

9

Jamie remembered the conversation. Bae had called her. Jamie was at home in Virginia. Between missions. Bae was in her dorm. The same room Jamie was sitting in at that very moment.

"Have you read the Reeder Rich novels?" Bae had asked Jamie.

"I actually have."

"Don't you just love them?"

They were entertaining. Jamie spent long hours on a plane or yacht going around the world. She had a lot of time to read. Reeder Rich novels were something she devoured. That and every kind of spy series. They didn't always match real life as she knew it, but Jamie dismissed those thoughts and allowed herself to be immersed in the action. Reeder Rich wasn't a spy, but she admired his skills.

"I do love them," Jamie answered.

"Wouldn't it be cool to be on your own like that? Traveling around the United States. Searching for bad guys. I'd love to do that."

"I sort of do that now."

Jamie never read the books while she was in the throes of a mission. She had enough real-life drama without having to read about it.

Bae was as excited as Jamie had heard her in a long time. "I know! I want to do it too."

"I thought you were studying to be a doctor?"

"I'm having second thoughts."

"Does your mom know?"

"No! And don't tell her."

Bae's adopted mom was a doctor. When Bae first moved in with the McBride's, the only thing Bae could talk about was being a doctor like her new mom. Then she graduated high school in two years and was on track to graduate college in two years. Soon she'd be starting med school. From what Jamie knew, Bae was already accepted into the program, and the plan was set.

When they first met, Bae wanted to be in the CIA. Alex got Brad to let them send Bae to the Farm for two weeks and let Curly teach her some things, during a time when Curly was between training classes. He put her through the ringer, and Bae loved it, but it seemed like Bae had gotten the spy bug out of her system. She hadn't talked about it lately until she brought up the Reeder Rich novels.

"I won't tell your mom," Jamie said.

Then Bae said something that surprised Jamie.

"Maybe I should take a semester off and travel the U.S. I could be a female Reeder Rich."

"That's a bad idea," Jamie retorted.

At the time, Jamie thought Bae was joking. Looking back, it made perfect sense. It's possible Bae took off on her own. She didn't have a car, so she'd have to hitchhike. Like Reeder Rich. She had money. Credit cards. An ATM card. A cell phone. Things that could be tracked.

Surely not.

Not even Bae would do something that stupid.

Jamie took the phone out of her pocket and called Alex.

"Hello, Love," Alex said. "Did you stop off to see Bae?"

"Are you spying on me?" Jamie said jokingly.

They had location devices on their phones which were always synced. In case either of them ran into trouble. Even if they didn't, Alex was the foremost cyber hacker in the world. He could find just about anyone within five minutes if he wanted to and they were on the grid.

"No. I need the plane, though," Alex said. "I was checking to see if you were about to land and saw that you were in Richmond. At VCU. In Bae's dorm room."

"Can you see what I'm wearing?" Jamie quipped.

Alex laughed. "No. But that's a good idea. I could hack into the security system and check it out. Probably black leggings. White pull over cotton shirt and black shoes with a slight heel."

That's exactly what she was wearing.

"You know me too well."

"In my mind, you're always wearing sexy lingerie. I think I'll stick with that image."

"I've only worn sexy lingerie once in my life! On our honeymoon. At Buckingham Palace. Do you remember?"

"How could I forget? A night with you in the royal suite at the Queen's invitation. I'll never forget that night."

Jamie wanted to change the subject. She didn't mind the banter but didn't have time for it. She needed to find Bae. First, she had to determine if she was even missing. Alex could help her with that, if they could ever get to her request.

"Anyway. What do you need the plane for?" Jamie asked.

"Is it any of your business?"

"Yes. I own half the plane. And half the business. Not to mention that we're married. So what's yours is mine and what's mine is mine."

"You make good points. I need to go down to Sigao Cay. I want to check on Pok."

Sigao Cay was an island they purchased a few months before. Sigao meant hidden in Greek. Very few people knew about the island. Pok worked there along with a dozen or so computer hackers.

Jamie had captured Pok while on a mission to Hong Kong. He was a cyber hacker who Alex had been trying to kill for several years. Alex's nemesis. Everyone thought Pok was dead. Killed in a missile attack on a cyberlab in Iran. Jamie discovered that he was very much alive.

When Jamie showed up in Costa Rica with Pok on their yacht, Alex was shocked. His first instinct was to finish the job and dump Pok's body in the ocean. Jamie convinced Alex that Pok could be useful to AJAX. So, Alex gave Pok an offer he couldn't refuse. Come to work for him or be killed. Pok chose to work for Alex.

Surprisingly, they were now best of friends.

Alex built a huge cyberlab on the island. Pok ran it. Under Alex's careful eye. He liked Pok but didn't trust him further than he could throw him. Pok used to steal money from good guys and put it into the pocket of the North Korean government. Now his tremendous skills were used to steal money from the bad guys. Terrorists. Arms traffickers. Oligarchs.

He hacked into their financial accounts and transferred the money into the AJAX corporation which was used to fund their CIA missions. Jamie's rescuing girls and Alex's fighting cybercrimes.

When Pok worked for North Korea, he stole upwards of a billion dollars a year. The island operation was approaching that figure for AJAX.

"I'll send A-Rad back with the plane right away," Jamie said.

"You're not coming home with him?"

"No."

"What are you doing?"

"Is that any of your business?"

This was part of their constant banter. Since their work involved such serious matters, they tried to keep their conversations as light as possible. Both knew the other was kidding.

"No. It's not," Alex said, ceding the fake argument with little effort.

"I need you to do me a favor," Jamie said.

"You tell me it's none of my business, then you ask me to do you a favor. I feel used."

"You'll get over it."

"What ya need? Is it legal or illegal?"

"Illegal."

"The best kind."

"I need you to track Bae's credit card. Look at recent transactions. I need to know where she used the card last."

"That's not illegal. We helped her get that card. Hold on a sec."

The phone went silent.

"She used it at a motel in Acton, Kentucky," Alex said a little over a minute later. His skills on the computer never ceased to amaze her.

"When?" Jamie asked.

"A few hours ago."

Her gut instinct was right.

"Thanks. Can you go into her phone and put a location tracker on it?" Jamie asked.

"That would be illegal."

"Since when did that concern you?"

"Since they made it a crime punishable by up to twenty years in prison."

"I told you before. I'll visit you if you go to prison."

"The least you could do since I would be there because of you."

"Hold off for now," Jamie said. "If Bae's in Acton, Kentucky, I can be there in a few hours."

"Do you need the plane?"

"No. I think I'll drive."

"If you need to track the phone, I can have Pok do it from Sigao. It's still illegal, but at least I'm not doing it on U.S. soil."

"That won't be necessary. When I see Bae, I'm going to download a location app on her phone. Sync it with mine. That way I know where she is at all times."

"She might not want you to know."

Then I'll do it without her knowledge.

"I'll visit you in prison."

"I look forward to it."

"Why is Bae in Acton Kentucky?" Alex asked.

"I think she's trying to go off the grid and become a female Reeder Rich."

"Who's Reeder Rich?"

Jamie forgot that Alex didn't read fiction. He'd heard her talk about Reeder but must've forgotten.

"He's a character in a book. A vigilante per se. He hitchhikes across the U.S. with nothing but the clothes he's wearing. No money. No credit cards. No cellphone. Off the grid."

"How does he live?"

"He bums rides and meals. When he needs money, he steals it from bad guys."

"Sounds like someone I would like. What does that have to do with Bae?"

"I think Bae is trying to do the same thing."

"Seriously! Do you think she hitchhiked to Acton Kentucky?"

"That's what I'm thinking."

"Looking for bad guys?"

"I hope not. If she is, I'm sure she'll find some. She has no idea what she's getting herself into."

"Bae is impulsive. I could see her doing something stupid like that. Two weeks on the Farm with Curly is not enough training. She could get herself into real trouble."

"I know. That's why I'm going to Acton."

"What are you going to do?"

"Find her before she does something really stupid."

10

Whiskey Joe's

I had never been in a dive bar before. *Whiskey Joe's* was what I pictured when I thought of one. The lighting was dimmed but not dark. Country music was pulsating. Not too loud but loud enough to where you had to talk louder than normal if you wanted someone to hear what you were saying.

Peanut shells littered the floor.

What's up with that?

People ate the insides of the peanuts, then tossed the shells on the floor. Indiscriminately. It didn't appear any of the help was going to make any effort to clean them up. They were busy anyway. Beyond busy. The demand for drinks was almost outstripping the seven girls' ability to keep up. The semi-attractive women wore short shorts. Cowboy boots. White T-shirts tied in front, so their mid sections showed.

Occasionally, they'd all do a dance together. Much to the delight of the drooling patrons who had already had too much to drink, and it was barely nine o'clock in the evening.

The clientele was most interesting to me. That's why I was there. In search of riffraff. The term clientele brought a smile to my face that I could see in the mirror that spanned the length of the back wall. Behind the liquor. Clientele was not the term I'd normally use for a group like this.

Rascal had been right. The bar was filled with roughnecks. I'd never seen so many tattoos in one place. Many were clearly bikers. They wore black leather jackets. With insignias. Not gang emblems. More like logos for motorcycles. Harley Davidson. Honda. Yamaha. Some sported state logos or patches on their jackets. Some state attractions. Things like Yellowstone National Park. Custer State Park. Mount Rushmore seemed to be popular since I saw that several times. Places I'd never seen but had heard of.

As time went on, I began to think the bar might not work after all. The people were nicer than they looked. One of the particularly rough looking guys bumped into me. Spilled my soda and some of the beer in his hand got on my shirt.

I balled my fist and prepared to strike, even though he outweighed me by two hundred pounds.

The bigger they are, the harder they fall, Curly had said during my training at the Farm.

"Do you have to hit them harder than smaller people?" I asked Curly.

"No. You just have to hit them in the right places. Neck. Groin. Kneecap. Shin. Behind the ear. Right below the nose. With the palm of your hand. Like this."

Curly showed her how to hit a man just below the bridge of the nose.

"That'd send the biggest man in the world to the hospital if you hit him in the right spot," he had said.

Even though my fist was balled, I thought better of it. Then he totally surprised me by being nice.

"I'm sorry," the man said. Then he looked down and saw that half my drink was on the floor and a few splashes of his beer were on my shirt.

"That's my fault. I wasn't looking where I was going," he said.

The man had a black beard, full and thick. Bushy eyebrows. The beard flowed down past his neck. Almost to his chest. Was at least six inches in length. His hair was long and covered his ears. He had tattoos on every knuckle. A cross on the back of one of his hands. What looked like a coiled snake on the back of the other. An eagle tattoo was on the side of his neck.

An American flag patch was on one shoulder of the jacket and a confederate flag patch was on the other.

"Let me replace your drink for you," the slightly drunk man said. He smelled of cigarettes. The entire bar did even though smoking wasn't allowed inside. Residual smell from the steady stream of people going outside to smoke, then coming back inside. The multiple ceiling fans spread the smell of cigarette residue throughout the bar.

I wasn't sure what I was going to do. I only brought a couple of shirts with me. I'd have to wash this one out good in the sink and let it dry overnight.

Anyway, striking the man wasn't an option. How do you hit someone as nice as him? Even if he didn't look like he would be nice, he was. Looking around the bar, it seemed like everyone else was like him. Most of them older. They might have been rabble rousers back in the day, but now they seemed to be middle aged men and women having a good time at a local bar.

"That's okay," I said to him nicely. "It's fine. You didn't mean to do it."

"If you change your mind, I'm right over there," he said and pointed to a group of people standing around a table.

I leaned back against the bar and observed the rest of the patrons.

It took several minutes, but then I saw them.

Three men.

A little older than me.

Rough looking. Up to no good. You could see it in their faces.

Jamie always said to study the eyes. You can learn to spot evil in them. I wasn't good at that yet, but it wasn't hard to see one of them take a small package out of his jacket pocket and slip it into the hand of another person, who then filled the man's then empty hand with money.

Clearly a drug deal.

Over the next twenty minutes, the man repeated the procedure with half a dozen more people.

My heart began to race. This was what I was looking for. Bad dudes. People who were breaking the law.

I had to figure out how to get close to him.

The music stopped suddenly. A big cheer went up in the crowd. Everyone got in lines. Then the music started again. People throughout the bar were dancing in sync. A couple of steps. Then a hop. A duck down. Then they went to the right. Dipped their shoulders. Hopped. Then went back to the left. In unison, they went backward. Then forward. Then repeated the same moves. With huge smiles on their faces.

Even the druggies were in a line. I saw an opportunity. I got in line next to one of them. The moves were unfamiliar to me, but it didn't take long to pick up some of them. Drug Dealer guy looked at me and smiled. Then started showing me what to do. I followed his lead. Got most of the steps until they threw some new stuff in.

A tap your heel with your hand threw me off and made me look silly.

Then the lights dimmed, and the music slowed. Druggie grabbed me around the waist and pulled me close to him. I was startled but played along. We started swaying to the music. My hands were around his waist, and I could feel a gun in the back of his trousers. He moved my hands away from it when he sensed I had touched it.

He towered over me. Like most people did. His left hand grabbed my head and held it against his chest. His right hand was on my butt.

I was frozen.

Not in fear, but not sure what to do. Should I knee him in the groin? Not exactly the best position to do so. That wouldn't solve the problem of his drug dealing. I needed to figure out a way to take him out permanently. This was what I wanted but I hadn't thought that far ahead. I was desperate to find a bad guy. Now I was in the arms of one and had no clue what to do.

To my defense, I never thought I'd be on a dance floor with a bad guy groping my behind!

Something flashed in the corner of my eye.

A sudden movement.

Then a strong hand.

On my shoulder.

A woman.

"What are you doing dancing with my man?" the woman said in a rough and raspy voice.

Druggie released his grip, raised his hands in the air, and backed off.

I turned and faced her.

"I didn't know he was your man. Besides, he asked me to dance."

We were face to face now. She was only slightly taller than me, so we were almost eye to eye. He hadn't really asked me to dance, but now wasn't the time for semantics. I wondered if the woman even knew what the word meant. That almost made me laugh in her face.

"Well, he's mine. So keep your hands off of him."

"First of all, I don't see your name tattooed on his forehead. Or a ring on his finger. Second of all, why would he want to dance with a skank like you when he could dance with me?"

I didn't know what a skank was, but I'd heard Jamie call a woman that one time in a restaurant and they came to blows. I should say, blow. One blow. Jamie knocked the woman out with a single punch after the woman took a swing at her first.

Jamie used that as a teaching moment for me.

Don't ever swing first unless you think your life is in danger. Always give the person a chance to walk away. Most of these people aren't worth the trouble.

So, I waited for the jealous woman to swing first. Then I was going to knock her out. She hesitated. I needed to egg her on. I was so close to hitting someone I could taste it.

The woman was vulnerable. Totally out of position. Her right knee was in front of her left. But her right fist was balled. She was out of balance. Any swing would lose its power by the time it connected with me. If it did. I could easily duck or move out of the way of it. It'd take too long to get to me.

She was telegraphing it anyway. I could read a chapter of a Reeder Rich book in the time it took for her to rear back and throw a punch at me.

I, on the other hand, was in perfect position. Facing straight on. Feet slightly past my shoulders. Planted firmly on the dance floor. I could strike her with either hand. Elbow if I wanted. Kick her with either foot. I could even grab the back of her head and bring it down on my knee. That'd knock her out. She'd lose some of those yellow stained teeth.

"Take it outside," Druggie said.

"Fine by me," I exclaimed. "I'll whip you out there or in here. Your choice."

"Outside. Now," she demanded.

Then brushed my shoulder on the way past me.

Rascal was right. The bars were the place to go.

This was going to be fun.

11

Whiskey Joe's Parking Lot

The woman and three men walked out the door and motioned for me to follow them, which I was happy to do. They led us out to a small clearing in the parking lot, with little grass and poor lighting. It seemed like something they'd done before.

A small crowd followed us out as word apparently spread that a fight was about to take place.

The three men stood behind the woman, and the crowd gathered on the side to my immediate right. I stood in front of the woman about eight feet away from her.

A buzz filled the air. An excitement I'd only seen one time before.

Alex and Jamie took me to an MMA fight a little over a year ago. It had that same feel. This time, without the referee. In an MMA bout, the ref stopped the fight before anyone got hurt. The woman should wish someone was there to stop it. I was going to take out my years of frustration on her.

First, I had to give her a chance to back out. I wasn't going to make the first move. Jamie said it was a requirement unless my life was in danger, meaning the person had a gun on me or was about to harm someone else. As far as I could tell, the woman was unarmed and unsophisticated in the art of fighting.

She seemed confident. Smug even. Probably because of my size, and she'd probably beaten up a lot of girls over the years. I had no doubt she was tough. Just not tough enough for someone with my skills.

"Are you sure you want to do this?" I asked.

Jamie had told me exactly what to say. If I had the time to say something.

The woman's eyes widened. "What? Are you chicken? You come in and put your hands all over my man and then think you can just walk away. Are you dreaming? I'm going to mess you up."

She pushed her long sleeves up her arms for effect.

I stood there calmly. "When you're in the hospital tonight, remember that you had a chance to walk away. About three minutes from now, you're going to wish you had."

I had to bite my lip to keep from laughing out loud. When Jamie said it the first time, it cracked me up. It sounded even funnier now. Jamie had given me other lines.

You should walk away. While you still can. If you don't, you're going to be eating your meals through a straw for the next six months.

Did your mom drop you on your head when you were a kid? 'Cause fighting me is a stupid thing to do.

The woman stuck both of her fists in the air in front of her in a boxing pose before I had a chance to decide which line I wanted to use.

I still remained perfectly still. Like a statue. That confused her, given the twisted lips, and she dropped her hands, unsure what to do.

That gave me the time to say a line I remembered.

"I'm breaking one of my rules of fighting," I said.

The woman furrowed her eyebrows further in confusion.

"What's that?" she asked.

"Never fight an ugly person. They have nothing to lose."

That's all it took. The woman became enraged. Just what I wanted. She lunged at me and took a wild swing. I ducked away but maintained my footing. As her fist passed my head in the air, the woman had her back and side facing me. I twisted my hips to the left, raised my elbow, and brought it down on her right kidney.

She let out a yelp and fell to the ground. A kidney punch was extremely painful and a vulnerable area in a person. I took something off the punch, so the blow wasn't too debilitating. It had been four years since I'd actually hit someone. I didn't want to ruin the feeling by ending the fight too soon. With just one blow. I wanted her to be able to get back up so I could hit her again.

I stood over the woman. The crowd was laughing and cheering.

Then I saw a movement.

From behind.

What's that?

I barely had time to realize my mistake. When I did, I let out a groan. I hadn't watched my back. Didn't even think about the possibility of the three men who were now standing behind getting in the fray.

I saw the punch coming out of the corner of my eye but had no time to react. I heard the swish, then the crunching sound of knuckles against the side of my head.

For a moment, everything went black.

Then I saw stars.

Staggered. But somehow managed to stay upright.

Then he kicked my legs out from under me, and I fell to the ground. My hands broke some of the fall, but my head bounced off the ground and my vision blurred even further.

He kicked me in the ribs.

I could feel the air leave my lungs.

He was on top of me now. Flailing away at my head.

I forgot all my training and several of the blows made it through my defenses.

Curly said I had failed this part of the training. What to do when you were hurt. That was the most vulnerable time. The point when a fight was won or lost. I was clearly losing and didn't know what to do.

So, I started flailing my arms. Throwing punches in the air. They weren't connecting. I was doing nothing more than wasting energy. Which would run out soon from the lack of air from the kick to the ribs.

The woman was standing now.

She grabbed my hair and started pulling on it.

Dragging me across the ground.

I raised my hands and grabbed my hair to minimize the pressure.

That left my midsection and lower body vulnerable.

All three guys were kicking me now.

I tried to kick them back.

Excruciating pain.

My head. My ribs. My neck.

My skull felt like it was on fire.

I was in deep trouble.

Then I saw another movement out of the corner of my eye.

The sound of a crack. On a skull.

The boyfriend was no longer on top of me. He slumped to the ground at my side.

I could feel the movement of the air as a bat connected with the woman's back. She let out a scream and released my hair.

I could feel chunks being pulled out.

My eyes focused.

Rascal.

The throng of people were almost delirious.

Women were screaming.

Rascal stood over me with a bat in his hand. Bertha!

Two of the guys tried to get an angle on him. One in front and one in back. Rascal kept swinging the bat in each direction. Holding them off.

"Ya want some of this?" he said to the other two.

When he got close enough, Rascal jabbed Bertha into one of the men's midsection, sending him to the ground. The other man took off running.

So did the crowd. I heard the sirens.

"Let's get out of here," Rascal said.

He reached out his hand and pulled me to my feet. I still felt punch drunk, but he steadied me and helped me to his truck. Then went around to the driver's side, started the truck, and sped away, peeling out as we left the parking lot.

I looked back and saw the police cars arrive. At first, I thought they might follow us, but they didn't.

"I told you to be careful," Rascal said.

"How did you know I'd be at *Whisky Joe's*?" I asked.

"I figured you were dumb enough to go there. Yous was lookin' for trouble. When you're lookin' for trouble, it's going to find you. I was stupid for tellin' ya about *Whiskey Joe's*. It's a rough crowd. I came down there in case you got in trouble."

"I didn't need your help!" I said. "I had everything under control."

"Yeah, right."

Truth was, I did need his help and was thankful for it. I'd made a stupid mistake. Not watching my back. I was embarrassed. I had my first test and I had failed it. If not for Rascal, I could've been hurt badly.

"Thank you," I said. "Maybe I did need your help."

"Is your stuff at the motel?"

"Yes."

"Let's go get it."

"Why?"

"You're stayin' with me tonight."

"I'll be okay."

"The cops'll be by thar. Maybe those other two boys. They've got friends. It's a small town. You'll be safe at my house."

That sounded like a good idea.

My head hurt. So did my ribs. I'd have bruises. He'd probably have ice that I could put on it. He was also right about the cops. They might come looking for me at the motel. For that matter, it was a small town. They'd probably come looking for me at Rascal's house. If anybody was willing to talk.

I mentioned that to Rascal.

"Won't they come looking for you? People at the bar probably know your truck."

He shook his head no.

"This is the south. Ain't nobody going to tell on nobody. They'll keep thems mouth shut. You'll be safe at my house. In the morning, I'll drive you back the way you came. You need to go home."

That wasn't going to happen. I made a mistake. I knew that. Tonight was a learning experience. But I loved it. The thrill. The adrenaline rush. It was in my blood.

I'd go to his house. Put some ice on my wounds. Get something to eat or drink.

As soon as Rascal went to sleep, I'd sneak out. Head on down the road.

West.

With a new resolve.

I had to redeem myself.

Find more bad guys.

Next time, things would be different.

12

Jamie arrived in Acton, Kentucky, around nine o'clock that night. Later than she'd intended. After leaving Bae's dorm, she told A-Rad to take the plane back to D.C. so Alex could use it to go to the island and check on Pok. She caught a taxi from the college to the Richmond International Airport where she intended to rent a car and make the five-hour drive to the small town right past the Kentucky border where Bae had used her credit card at a motel.

Turned out some kind of big convention was in town, and all the rental car companies were out of cars. Jamie had to wait for someone to turn a car in before she could get on the road. That didn't happen until after four o'clock.

Jamie pushed the pedal and made the five hour and thirty-nine-minute drive in a little under five hours. Including a stop for a bathroom break and a power bar and energy drink and a hot dog she scarfed down at a truck stop.

By the time she got to Acton, she was fuming. Her concern for Bae had turned into full-fledged frustration. Why would she do something so stupid without talking to her first? At least return her phone calls. Instead of irresponsibly leaving college and hitch-hiking across country like she was Reeder Rich in search of bad guys. If Bae were looking for them, she'd no doubt find them.

The bad guys Reeder Rich encountered were fictional. The ones Bae would find would have real guns and be ruthless and vicious. She was no match for them. Jamie wouldn't even consider doing what Reeder Rich did in the books.

When Jamie saw the motel Bae was staying in, her anger intensified. Jamie had seen better accommodations in southeast Asia red-light districts. The building should be condemned, razed, and the parts sold for scrap. According to the credit card charge, Bae paid sixty-five dollars for a room that wasn't worth thirty. Actually, someone would have to pay Jamie to stay there.

With no other hotels in the area, Jamie wasn't sure where the two of them would stay once she found Bae. Not in that dump.

Of course, she couldn't actually make Bae leave with her if the stubborn girl bowed her back and refused.

Well... she could make her. Jamie had the height, weight, reach, and skills over Bae to force her to leave, but that wouldn't be wise. Bae would resent it. She'd need to use her skills of persuasion and talk her into it. The problem was she'd drilled into Bae to be a strong woman. Independent. Stubborn. Unyielding. The same traits she had on steroids. That's why she'd even agreed to send Bae to the Farm and spent so much time with her. The girl had potential. She just wasn't ready to face real live threats. People with guns. Bigger bodies who could snap Bae in two like a twig.

Jamie walked into the motel office with a picture of Bae in her hand. The man behind the counter was either drunk or stoned. Possibly both. He rose from his chair slowly after Jamie rang the bell on the counter several times. It looked like he'd been sleeping.

"Is this girl staying here?" Jamie said in a stern tone.

She saw the look of recognition on his face.

"I don't think so."

The registration sign-in book was on the counter, and Jamie grabbed it and stepped back two steps, so it'd be out of the man's reach. The last entry was signed by Bae Hwa. The number nine was written beside the name.

"I'm supposed to meet her here," Jamie said after sitting the book back down on the counter. "I'm her mom. I need to check in. Can you give me a key to room nine?"

"She only paid for a single room."

Jamie wanted to make an issue of the fact that ten seconds ago he said she wasn't even staying there, but let it go. Making a point with this loser wasn't worth the time. If she had to, she'd just pick the lock.

"How much for a double room?" Jamie asked.

The man's eyes lit up.

"Forty-five... I mean... fifty dollars."

"She already paid you sixty-five."

"Fifty more."

"I'll give you twenty."

Easier to pay him than come behind the counter and take a key from him. Easier than putting him to sleep with a chokehold.

"Twenty-five," he countered.

Jamie took the cash out of her pocket and handed it to him. The man gave her a key.

It took a minute to find room nine since the number was upside down on the door and looked like a six.

Jamie knocked on the door and called out Bae's name. No one answered after several louder knocks. Though nighttime, it didn't look like the hotel had any other patrons to worry about waking. Convinced Bae wasn't there, Jamie used the key to unlock the door and entered the room. She knew immediately that Bae had been there. The backpack they gave her for Christmas was sitting on the bed.

Other than that, the room looked unused. Jamie checked the bathroom and found more evidence Bae had been there. A towel hung over the shower rod, and Bae's toothbrush and toothpaste were on the sink. The towel was damp which told her Bae had used it several hours ago. Probably earlier that morning.

Jamie went back in the main room and sat down on the bed then immediately bolted back to her feet. The bedspread was sticky and reeked of unidentifiable smells and Jamie refused to sit on it. Her initial plan was to wait in the room for Bae to return, which she eventually would do, to at least get her stuff. But Jamie didn't want to spend one minute longer in that room than she had to and decided to wait in the car.

Then she remembered why Bae was even at that motel.

I want to be a female Reeder Rich.

If her hunch was correct, Bae was on the prowl for some bad guys. That's why her backpack was still in the room. Jamie had taught her to travel light on a mission. Keep your hands free. Only carry essentials. Cash. Credit Card. Driver's license. Passport if you're overseas. A backpack was cumbersome in a fight.

A fight!

Jamie hoped her imagination was just running wild, and Bae wasn't actually looking for a confrontation.

Where would the girl go if she were itching to hit someone?

A bar.

The town had to have one.

Jamie pulled up her location on her phone's GPS.

The town had four bars. Interesting, considering the population was only 8,543. Or at least that's what the sign on the road leading into town read.

Jamie drove to the first bar. More of a diner than a bar. It didn't look promising, but Jamie went in anyway. Perhaps Bae was hungry and went there for dinner.

"Have you seen this girl?" Jamie asked the hostess, after she made a quick walk-through and confirmed Bae wasn't there.

"No honey. Haven't seen her."

"Thank you."

Jamie got the same response from the second bar. These were the two closest to Bae's hotel which was why Jamie went to those first. As far as she knew, Bae didn't have transportation and had to walk wherever she went. Or hitch a ride.

When Jamie drove up to the third bar, her heart sank two levels in her chest. Blue strobe lights illuminated the parking lot. An ambulance was driving away.

She slammed on the brakes, threw the rental car in park, jumped out, and practically sprinted to where a policeman was standing.

"What happened?" Jamie asked the officer.

"I'm not sure. That's what I'm trying to piece together. Some kind of fight."

"Someone was injured. Was it a girl?"

"Nope. A man. Local boy. He's got a cracked skull. Someone hit him over the head with a baseball bat."

"Do you know who hit him?" Jamie asked.

He shook his head no. "Got a hundred people in the bar, and no one saw anything. Just that woman over there. But she ain't talkin'."

He pointed to a woman sitting on the steps leading into the bar. Jamie guessed the woman to be twenty-two or twenty-three going on forty. Haggard. Smoking a cigarette.

Jamie walked up to her and asked, "What happened?"

The woman turned her head away. Took a long drag from her cigarette and blew a large puff of smoke into the wind.

The woman was clearly in pain as she winced when she changed position on the steps.

"Did you get in a fight with someone?" Jamie asked.

"Who are you?"

"I'm looking for a young girl."

The woman's eyes widened.

Jamie showed her a picture and saw the flash of recognition immediately.

"I never saw her before in my life," the woman said bitterly.

Jamie knew just what to say.

"So, this young girl beat you up. Was it her who sent your boyfriend to the hospital?"

Jamie was taking a wild but educated guess. If Bae did get the best of the woman, she'd respond and challenge Jamie's version of events. She'd never admit that a girl the size of Bae had beaten her and her boyfriend up. The boyfriend part was a shot in the dark.

"She sucker-punched me. In my back. The slut was hittin' on my man."

Nice. A kidney punch. Good job Bae.

Jamie couldn't imagine a scenario where Bae would be interested in this girl's boyfriend.

"What happened to your boyfriend? The cop said she hit him over the head with a baseball bat."

"She didn't. Rascal did."

"Who's Rascal?"

"A local. He's always looking for a fight. We didn't have no bone to pick with him. He snuck up on Ralphie and smacked him on the head with a bat. Knocked him out cold."

"Where can I find this Rascal?"

"Over off Crowley's Ridge. He lives in a trailer just on the other side of the railroad tracks."

"I suppose you and your boys are going to pay him a visit."

"Yeah. Right after we find the girl. I heard she's over at the motel. Some of my boys are headed there now. We're going to teach her a lesson. She ain't from around these parts. She's gonna wish she's never been born."

Jamie practically sprinted back to her car.

She had to get to the motel as soon as possible.

***

Jamie was too late.

Five of the woman's friends were already at the motel.

Banging on Bae's door.

Jamie hesitated.

She could take off and try to find Bae or she could deal with the threat. She chose the latter. If she didn't take out these five guys,

Bae might have to if they found her before Jamie did. A chance she wasn't willing to take. Bae would be no match for the five guys.

Jamie was concerned as well. Curly always said one guy was no problem. A person of Jamie's ability could easily handle two. In fact, Curly said there weren't two guys in the world who could best Jamie in a fight. Three put the odds at 75-25. In Jamie's favor. Four was fifty-fifty depending on their abilities.

Five was problematic. No way to cover every angle and take them all out before at least one got a punch off. If they had weapons, the odds shifted in their favor. Nearly impossible for even the most skilled operative to shoot five people before one of them got a shot off.

For Bae, the odds were slim to none, and *slim had left the building,* as Curly sometimes said.

Jamie had no choice.

She took a deep breath. Touched the gun at her side. Opened the car door and approached the five men.

13

The men pounding on Bae's motel room door still hadn't seen Jamie. She got out of her car, walked around to the front of it and leaned against the grill. One of the men was yelling at the top of his lungs for Bae to open the door.

"The girl's not there," Jamie said, during a pause in the din.

She wasn't sure if Bae was there or not, but Jamie wanted to let the men know that she was associated with the girl they were looking for.

The man pounding abruptly turned around to see who was speaking. "Where is she?" he asked roughly.

"I don't know."

"Then how do you know she's not there?"

Good point.

So, Jamie ignored it and kept her casual stance with her arms crossed still leaning against the rental car.

"Who are you?" the man asked. More inquisitively than con-frontationally.

"The girl who's about to put the five of you in the hospital if you don't get out of here and promise to never come back."

The man twisted his lips into a smug smile. The right side slightly above the left. His right eyebrow followed suit and was lifted while the other remained lowered. Jamie always wished she could do that. Even practiced it in front of a mirror. Could never get one eyebrow to move without the other one following.

She assessed the five men. Young men really. Not as tough as they thought they were. She wanted them to know that she was prepared to fight them. They'd be reluctant. The next step would be to egg them on. Challenge their manhood. They'd be hesitant to attack a girl with such an unfair advantage. An innate sense of fairness that even the lowest of the low possessed.

"And how are you going to do that?" Smug guy asked. "There are five of us and only one of you."

Jamie began clapping her hands together. "I'm impressed. I didn't think you knew how to count."

"Do you think this is a joke?"

"I think you're a joke. Acting all tough. Like I'm supposed to be scared of you. One of the members of your little gang of morons has already been beaten up by a girl once. Do you want to make it twice?"

Calling them morons would probably do the trick. Mocking them for getting beat up by a girl would get under their skin. According to the cop, Bae wasn't the one who put their friend in the hospital, but Jamie didn't know how much they did or didn't know.

One of the men started to take a step toward Jamie, but the man in the middle of the formation— the apparent ringleader— held him back.

The movement was enough to cause Jamie to stand straight up, no longer leaning against the grill. The men were in a less-than-ideal configuration from Jamie's perspective. Curly taught her a number of ways to win a fight when she was outnumbered. The preferred way was if the men were in a crescent formation. Half-moon. With space between them. That's normally how a group of fighters would approach a situation like this. They'd want to surround the victim. Cut off any potential escape routes.

If they were in that formation, Jamie would simply unexpectedly charge the one on the end. Either end. In Jamie's case, the one on the left, since she was right-handed. She'd take the end guy out with one punch. Efficiency of blows was paramount in a situation like this. You couldn't waste time hitting a person twice.

Not enough time.

The hope was that if the other four saw a devastating blow to their friend and watched him collapse to the ground in a painful heap, they might think twice about acting. At least hesitate enough for Jamie to hit a second guy. They would also then be in a straight line. One behind the other. That lessened their advantage.

Another proficient strike to the second in line, and in less than six or seven seconds, before they even knew what was happening, the advantage had changed to three against one. Curly gave Jamie a seventy-five, twenty-five percent advantage in that situation. With these guys, Jamie put it more like ninety-five percent to five percent.

One of them could always get off a lucky blow. She could trip on the gravel. One or more of them might have a gun. That evened the odds considerably. Jamie had one as well, but it took her about the same amount of time to shoot three people as it took one person to draw a gun.

Fifty-fifty. Maybe slightly her advantage because of her shooting skills under pressure. Also, Jamie didn't want to kill the men. She just wanted to send them a message.

Leave Bae alone.

The men took two steps toward her. Her words had clearly riled them up. They were cutting off her angles of escape. Not that she intended to run. The threat needed to be handled here and now. So Bae wouldn't have to do it. Jamie was certain Bae wasn't at the motel. Otherwise, she would've looked out the window. Once she saw Jamie, she would've come out to help. Bae was probably brash enough to come out anyway to confront the men. She doubted Bae was cowering inside the room.

From the looks of the men's eyes and the fidgeting with their fists, they were itching to get the fight started. In this instance, Curly would tell Jamie to charge the man in the center. The leader.

Clothesline him or give him a blow to the neck or midsection. That would also change the configuration. But then Jamie would temporarily have her back to them. The men could close in on her. If one pulled a gun, she might not see it.

Jamie had a different plan. One Curly would be proud of her for thinking of.

"What are you idiots waiting on?" Jamie asked. "Are we going to fight or sit here and look at each other all day?"

"We don't have a bone to pick with you," the leader said. "We just want the girl. But if you don't shut up, we're going to mess you up something bad like."

What Jamie did next was totally unexpected to the men. Curly always said to make your first move a surprise. Something your opponent would never anticipate. They'd hesitate. That'd give you a slight advantage. But you'd better make the most of the opportunity.

Jamie calmly walked around to the back of the car.

"Yeah, that's right. Smart girl. You'd better walk away," the leader said mockingly.

He turned like he was going back to the motel room door to bang on it some more. Jamie reached down and picked up a rock. She reared back and threw it at him, hitting him square in the back.

He let out an expletive and turned around.

"Get her!" he said to the others. His eyes were burning with rage.

At that point, the men had a decision to make. The car was between her and them. The men hesitated. Looked at the leader. Not sure what to do.

Jamie knew exactly what she was going to do.

"Come on, fellows," Jamie said. "I'm ready. Are you afraid of a girl?"

They did what Jamie hoped. Two went one way and three the other. Once they were committed, Jamie bolted to the side of the car with the two men. They had changed the odds to her favor.

Two against one.

One hundred percent to zero in favor of Jamie. Not Vegas odds. Curly's odds. He knew better. No two men in the world who Jamie couldn't beat in a fight. Especially when she had the element of surprise.

Efficiency of blows was still tantamount. The three men would be around the car in a matter of seconds.

The two men stopped in their tracks when they saw Jamie charge them. The first man was slightly ahead of the other. His eyes widened and his mouth gaped open. Just as Jamie smashed the palm of her left hand into his jaw. Directly under his chin. That caused his neck to snap back like a whiplash one would get in a car accident. It sent him tumbling to the ground. Backwards into the other guy who instinctively tried to catch him which made him vulnerable.

In one motion, Jamie swept her right leg wide and kicked the second man in the thigh. On the side, right into the sciatic nerve, with enough force to paralyze the leg. The man cried out from the intense pain a kick like that inflicted on the leg.

Within seconds, the second man was on the ground clutching his leg and writhing in pain.

Three against one.

Advantage Jamie. Seventy-five to twenty-five.

She kept moving. To the other side of the car. Keeping the car between her and the three men. They kept coming after her. She kept moving away from them. Playing a game she used to play as a kid.

The men were clearly frustrated as every other word was an expletive.

An observer might think Jamie was taking the coward's approach. Curly said there was no such thing. Whatever it took to even the odds. That's what you did. The men were the cowards. Attacking a woman. Five against one.

Jamie forced them to make a second decision. She picked up another rock and threw it at them. The idiots didn't learn from the first decision and split up again. One came one direction and two the other.

Perfect.

One against one. He never had a chance.

Jamie clotheslined him. Sending him to the ground. His head cracked as it hit the gravel.

Oops.

The adrenaline was flowing through her like she'd been hit with a stun gun. She smacked him harder than she had intended.

Oh well.

Two against one.

Odds: Hundred percent Jamie. Curly would agree.

Both of the men pulled out knives.

Okay. Maybe ninety, ten.

She might've acted too soon. Keeping the car between them would've still been a good plan.

The men were several feet apart now. Knives extended in front of them. Circling around trying to improve their angles. Jamie didn't retreat but made them keep circling by moving closer, then back, then closer again. The men were more cautious now. Having seen three of their friends taken out with one blow, they must've realized that she posed a serious threat to them.

"You shouldn't have taken out the knives," Jamie said. "Now I'm going to have to kill you."

Still circling.

"You're the one who's dead meat," the leader said.

Jamie reached to her side and pulled out her gun.

"Whoa! Whoa! Whoa!" the leader said and backed up.

Jamie kept moving toward them. Alternating the gun from one to the other.

"Drop the knives or I'll shoot," Jamie said.

The men had both hands in the air out in front of them. The knives in their right hands.

The leader blinked first and dropped his knife. The second man followed.

Jamie holstered her weapon. Then charged the leader. He slipped on the gravel but caught himself with his hand. That made him vulnerable. Jamie kneed him in the head, sending him flying backward.

Out like a light switch.

The other man took off running. Jamie gave chase.

She tackled him.

Turned him over.

He tried to struggle.

Jamie rabbit punched him behind the ear.

She pinned his arms to the ground.

"You tell your friends that if they come anywhere near the girl, that I'll kill them. I'll start with you. Is that understood?"

He tried to throw a punch at Jamie's head.

She caught his wrist in the air, twisted it, and snapped it.

He let out a yell.

She stood up and kicked him in the ribs. She could hear a cracking sound as she made a direct hit.

"You tell them that they are messing with the wrong person," Jamie said roughly.

She brushed herself off.

Checked on the other four to make sure the threat was over.

Jamie pulled out her phone and dialed 911.

"What's your emergency?" the operator asked.

"There are five injured men at the Acton Motor Lodge. In the parking lot."

"What is your name please?"

Jamie hung up. Her phone was encrypted, and the number couldn't be traced.

She walked over to Bae's motel room door, took the key out of her back pocket, and opened the door.

Empty.

The backpack was no longer on the bed.

Bae was gone.

14

The entire scene at the motel played out right in front of me. Jamie took on five guys and beat the living daylights out of them. I'd come back to the motel with the intention of sneaking into one of the rooms and crashing for the night. My head was pounding from the fight earlier in the evening. The lady had jerked on my hair, and my entire scalp was tender to the touch.

When I saw the five guys in the parking lot pounding on my motel room door, I realized I was going to have to come up with a different plan. Confronting them wasn't an option. My head was still fuzzy from when the girl's boyfriend coldcocked me from behind. A cheap shot. He should be ashamed of himself. I should've been more careful.

I was just getting ready to leave when a car drove up. Imagine my surprise when Jamie Austen got out.

How did she find me so quickly?

Then she confronted the five guys. I was close enough to hear her challenge their manhood. It almost caused me to laugh out loud. When the men headed toward her like they were ready for a fight, I was prepared to jump into the fray if she needed me.

She didn't.

Jamie made quick work of the five guys, and they were all lying on the ground unconscious or writhing in pain before I could even react.

Jamie was amazing! I was invigorated by watching her in action. I'd only seen Jamie spar in a gym. Never actually been around when she confronted bad guys. Her skills were beyond what I'd imagined them to be.

Curly had said that Jamie was the best he'd ever trained. Alex said that Jamie was the best female operative in the world. The world's deadliest female assassin. I could see why. Going to the other side of the car was brilliant. At first, I thought she was going to run away. Then I realized she was leading them into a trap. I don't remember, but my mouth was probably gaped open in amazement.

Jamie had forced the five men to make a decision. When they did and went different directions to try and trap her, she pounced on them like a cougar on a lame deer. When one of them pulled a knife, she reacted with lightning-quick speed and pulled her gun.

Fight over.

Excitement welled up inside me like a wellspring of water comes gushing out of the earth. It made me realize that I was doing the right thing. This was my calling.

I wanted to be Jamie.

Take on five men and live to tell about it.

Rid the world of the riff raff.

Like the men who had killed my parents in North Korea. Actually, those men were on a different level. They were professional terrorists. Iranians. I wasn't ready to take on those bad guys. Jamie was. I would be soon enough. For now, I needed to stick with lowlifes like the ones lying in the motel parking lot, beaten like an old mule.

The ache in my head reminded me that I had a long way to go to be as good as Jamie. When I put my hand to my head and touched my tender scalp, I winced. I'd made several mistakes at the bar that night and I intended to learn from them. Jamie faced five guys. I'd only faced three. While I beat up the girl easily enough, I didn't watch my back and paid the price.

Jamie got in her car and drove off.

I wanted to flag her down and let her know how great she did, but I resisted the urge. She'd make me go home. My mother had probably sent her to find me. I could hear Jamie's words in my head.

"Bae, you have to finish school."

"Bae, you aren't ready to take on bad guys."

"Bae, you almost got yourself killed at the bar tonight."

Blah. Blah. Blah.

I loved Jamie, but she wouldn't understand. This was something I had to do. But I had to do it better. For one thing, I had to make sure Jamie couldn't find me. Obviously, she either tracked my cell phone or my credit card.

Stupid.

Jamie had taught me how to go dark. Dark meaning off the grid where you couldn't be found. I'd forgotten everything she taught me. Broken all the rules. *Don't use your cellphone or credit card. Those can be traced. Pay cash for everything. Don't use your real name. Create a cover. Stay out of public places. Make yourself unmemorable. Do everything you can to blend into your environment.*

I pulled out my phone, took out the sim card, and threw it into the bushes where I was hiding. I'd keep the phone itself in case I wanted to get another sim card later.

Then I ran across the street and searched the five guys lying on the ground in the motel parking lot and relieved them of all their cash. I had an ATM card and plenty of money in my account, but Jamie could track it. With cash, she wouldn't be able to find me.

I counted it quickly. Between them, the bad guys had more than two thousand dollars in their pockets. Dirty drug money, I presumed. That would last me for a while. With the cash, I could check into hotels and pay for food. That'd get me to the next destination.

Then I heard the sirens. They seemed to be headed toward the motel. I had to get out of there. Out of Acton, Kentucky. As far away as possible. Jamie wouldn't stop looking for me. The police probably had a description of me from the fight at the bar. I hoped Rascal wasn't in trouble. Nothing I could do about it if he was.

With the money in my pocket, I took off running.

The pounding in my head got stronger with each pained step. My lungs burned after what I estimated was only a half mile of running. I realized I hadn't been controlling my breath like Jamie taught me to do in a stressful situation.

I said a quick prayer for Jamie, hoping she wasn't in trouble with the law. I'd purposefully headed the opposite direction from her. West. Not sure where I was going but anxious to get there. Jamie always said that when things didn't go well in a mission, the best thing to do was to go on another one right away. Get back in the saddle again, she said.

That's what I intended to do.

Find someone to fight as soon as possible.

First, I had to get over this headache.

Actually, first, I needed to find a ride. I stuck out my thumb, and the first car that came along stopped. Quickly, I started running again, to the side of the car where the window was rolled down.

"Where you headed?" the girl in the passenger seat asked. I could tell that another girl was driving. They appeared to be my age and harmless.

"Where are you headed?" I asked.

"Chicago," the girl said.

"That's where I'm going!"

"Do you go to DePaul, too?" she asked.

"Sure."

"Hop in. You can ride with us," passenger-seat girl said with a warm smile.

"I sure appreciate it."

I climbed into the backseat. The vehicle had a new-car smell. Clearly, the girl driving had money. Or at least her parents did.

"What's your name?" passenger-seat girl asked. She was cute with red hair and freckles. Had an unassuming smile. A southern accent. Not like Rascal but clearly deep south. I'd met a hundred girls just like her at my college.

"Marcia," I answered. I wasn't going to tell them that Bae was my real name. I was in full operational mode now. Building a cover. Even though I hadn't thought it through, I was prepared to come up with one on the fly. Then I realized that I should've come up with a fake name that started with the letter B. Curly said to keep your lies as close to the truth as possible. Too late now. I'd have to go with Marcia.

"I'm Connie and this is Julie. We're roommates." Connie was the one driving and hadn't said anything.

"Nice to meet you," I said. "Thanks for the ride."

"No problem. What are you doing on the side of the road hitchhiking at this time of night?" Julie asked.

"My car broke down. They said it couldn't be fixed so I left it in Acton. The garage paid me a few hundred dollars for it."

I realized I was talking too much. Jamie said not to make your cover too elaborate. The more lies you told, the more you had to remember. That made it hard to keep them all straight. The fewer details the better.

"I have money though," I added, changing the subject. "I can pay you for a ride."

"Don't worry about it," Connie said, as I heard her sweet-sounding southern drawl for the first time. "We're happy to have the company. Besides, it's dangerous out there. A young girl alone in the dark. A girl can't be too careful."

I didn't want to be careful. No use trying to explain that to them. The thought occurred to me that I might be of use to the girls if they ran into any trouble.

"At least let me fill up your tank with gas the next time you stop," I said.

"That's a deal," Connie said. "We just filled up though, so we're good for a while."

"How far a drive is Chicago?" I asked. I knew where it was on a map but had no idea in relation to Acton Kentucky.

"Six hundred miles. About ten hours," Connie said. "We plan on driving all night. We'll take turns."

"I don't mind driving if you want me to."

"Don't worry about it. Relax. Get some sleep if you want," Connie told me.

Sleep sounded good. My head was still screaming at me.

"Is Chicago a dangerous place?" I asked.

They both laughed.

Julie turned around and said, "I saw on the news that there were fifty-seven murders in Chicago this past weekend."

Perfect.

15

A little after two in the morning Jamie's cell phone pinged, startling her and shattering the silence in her car.

A message from Alex.

Call me! Marked urgent in all caps.

Her heart started racing again. She'd just gotten it under control after the confrontation with the five thugs in the motel parking lot a couple hours before. Then another confrontation at Rascal's house when she went there in search of Bae.

Rascal thought Jamie was an intruder, and she thought he was lying to her and actually knew where Bae was. After she relieved him of the baseball bat he swung at her head, they both became convinced that each had Bae's best interest at heart. Rascal had been genuinely surprised when they went into the room where Bae was supposedly sleeping only to find a note on the pillow thanking Rascal for everything. Along with a short explanation that she needed to get back on the road in search of bad guys.

It's my life's calling.

Signed, *The Female Reeder Rich.*

Why did Alex want her to call him? He had to have some information on Bae. Jamie assumed the worst and called him immediately.

He answered without saying hello.

"You won't believe what I found!"

"Bae?"

"No! I was hoping you had found her. I see you're in Acton, Kentucky. Did you get our girl? Obviously not."

"No sign of her. What did you find?"

"A grey hair!"

"What?"

Alex had called her in the middle of the night because he found a grey hair? It took a second for that information to process.

He sounded distressed. "Right in the middle of my chest. A big ol' curly grey hair as long as a guitar string. I'm too young to have grey hair."

Jamie felt her blood boil. She was already on edge. Angry at Bae for making her traipse around the country while she was foolishly thinking she was some kind of Joan of Arc with a special calling to save the world. Now Alex was scaring the living daylights out of her with an urgent message that turned out to be about a grey hair.

She was ready to unload on someone. Then took a deep breath to temper her words some. Not much, but some.

"You sent me an urgent message about your stupid grey hair!" Jamie said in a more exasperated than angry tone.

"No," Alex said hesitantly. Like he was confused. "I sent the urgent message because I found Bae's cell phone."

"Oh."

"I'm with Pok and we traced her cell phone. She was at the motel. Then went to a honky tonk called *Whiskey Joe's*. Then went to a house across the railroad tracks. Then went back to the motel."

"I've already figured all that out. Thanks though. I'm sorry I yelled at you! I'm really tired. I *am* in Acton. So is Bae. She was at *Whiskey Joe's*, but she left before I got there. Apparently, she got in a fight with a skanky girl over her boyfriend. Then that same guy—the boyfriend—jumped Bae from behind. A good ol' boy named Rascal saved her with a baseball bat. Put the bad dude in the hospital. Five of his friends came looking for Bae at the motel. I had to take them out. Let's just say the hospital is overflowing with kids in leather jackets at the moment. Then I went to Rascal's house. Bae wasn't there. Anyway. It's a long story, and I don't have the energy to go into all of it."

"Did you find Bae or not?" Alex asked.

"No. And I've looked all over for her. When I find her, I'm going to wring her neck."

"Hold on."

Jamie could hear Alex talking in the background. Probably to Pok. He was on their island.

He came back on the line.

"It looks like our girl has ditched her phone. She took the sim card out. Probably so you couldn't track her."

"That stupid, stupid girl! She's as stubborn as a mule and fearless as a bobcat. A bad combination."

"Sounds like someone else I know."

"What's that supposed to mean?"

Jamie had pulled off the side of the road and was sitting in her rental car. She'd spent the last hour driving around Acton looking for Bae. Eventually, she decided Bae had left town and she needed to do the same. The local police were out patrolling. Looking for whoever put the six guys in the hospital.

"It just means that she takes after you," Alex said, almost apologetically.

It didn't soften her anger. If she'd thought about it, her frustration should be aimed at Bae. Alex was the one in the crosshairs and made it convenient to take the frustration out on him.

"She's nothing like me," Jamie retorted. "I'd never do anything this stupid."

"You mean... like jump out of a plane into the eye of a hurricane."

Admittedly, the dumbest thing she'd ever done. She was lucky she was alive to tell about it. That didn't mean she was going to cede the argument.

"You're one to talk! The only reason we know Bae is because you got the bright idea to sneak into North Korea and infiltrate Pok's cyberlab."

"My point exactly. We're wired differently than most people. We do stupid things. Bae's got that same gene. She's a risk taker. Like us."

"We're trained to do this, Alex. Bae's a kid. She's seventeen years old. Hasn't even finished school yet. She doesn't weigh a hundred pounds wearing five layers of clothes. Two weeks with Curly and a couple of sparring sessions with us is not enough training."

"You've taught her a lot. She knows how to handle herself."

"She knows just enough to get herself killed."

"She'll be alright. Let her get it out of her system. She'll be back home before you know it."

If the steam inside of her could actually come out of her head, the windows would all be fogged up.

"Why are you arguing with me about this?" Jamie said roughly. "Can't you just agree with me for once?"

For the first time, Alex started to sound angry. "So, you want me to be your yes man? Always agree with everything you say? Oh, I'm sorry. I didn't know." Now he was being sarcastic. "From now on it's, 'Yes, dear. No, dear. You're always right, Dear.' Is that what I'm supposed to do for the next fifty years?"

"Yes! That's what you're supposed to do. Now that we understand each other..."

She needed to diffuse the situation before it got out of hand. They were arguing over nothing. Alex laughed, letting her know he got the joke and was ready to move on as well.

"Whatever you want to do, honey? I'll support you." The words were dripping with sarcasm.

"Now you're patronizing me," Jamie said in a softer tone.

He ignored the comment. "The most pressing issue is... what are we going to do about my grey hair?"

That caused Jamie to laugh, easing the tension inside her. She'd seen the grey hair when they were in bed a couple of nights before but didn't have the heart to say anything.

"I think it's cute," she answered, glad he couldn't see the huge grin on her face. "Men with grey hair look distinguished. Women, on the other hand, look like old hags. I'm dreading the day I find my first grey hair."

"I don't want to look distinguished."

For some reason, that retort cracked Jamie up, and she burst out laughing.

"Don't worry. You don't," she said, barely able to get the words out between the intense impulse to laugh hysterically.

Euphoria was another side effect of the adrenaline rush she got after a fight. Extreme danger had a strange effect on the body and caused all kinds of amped-up emotions. Hilarity being one of them. She also got that way when she hadn't slept. Jamie started the car and started driving. She needed to find a hotel to get some sleep. Searching anymore for Bae was pointless. She was probably long gone down the road to who knows where.

"I'm serious," Alex said. "I don't know what to do about it."

"There's not much you can do. Shave it off."

"I pulled it out! It hurt like the dickens."

Jamie laughed again. She could picture Alex plucking the hair right out of his chest. It probably did hurt.

"Problem solved then," Jamie said.

"Won't it come back?"

"Probably. You can dye it. Or keep your chest shaved. Honestly, I've got bigger problems to concern myself with at the moment. Can you tell me how to find Bae?"

"Without her cell phone, we can only track her if she uses the credit card."

"I don't think she will. Bae must know I'm here. That's why she ditched her phone. She doesn't want me to track her."

"Then let her go. Go back home and wait for her to call. She'll turn up eventually."

Clearly, Alex wasn't as worried as she was. Jamie had a sixth sense about these things. Following her gut had always served her well in the past. Bae was in over her head. If she was looking for trouble, she'd find it. She'd only been gone for a day and had already gotten into a fight at a bar. If it hadn't been for Rascal, Bae might've been seriously hurt.

Not only that, but Bea's thinking was irrational. Like she was some kind of vigilante. On a mission to save the world. Rascal said Bae was angry with him because he hadn't attacked her. She clearly wasn't thinking straight.

Time for her to get off the phone and find a place to sleep. She'd regroup in the morning and come up with a different plan.

"I'll be in touch," she said as sweetly as she could muster.

"Love you."

"Alex," Jamie said in her most serious tone.

"Yes, dear," he said sarcastically.

"Honey. If you find a grey nose hair, call me immediately. I'll talk you down off the ledge."

"You're not funny!"

Jamie hung up. Feeling much better.

16

FBI Field Office
Chicago, Illinois

A heated exchange had broken out in the conference room of the FBI offices between two members of the Strikers Task Force. Rita Navarez was the only female in the room and felt like she was holding her own against the unanimous consensus of her six male colleagues who didn't like the plan she'd presented.

Hector Friday being the most focal.

"It's too risky," Hector argued.

"I'm the one taking all the risk," Rita retorted.

"You know that's not how it works," Agent Scully interjected. He'd been mostly silent up to that point. As the director of the task force, he had the final say but rarely forced his own opinion on the group.

"We're a team. If you're at risk, we all are," Scully added.

"I'm undercover!" Rita shot back. "Are you forgetting what that means? Of course, I'm at risk."

Rita had been tasked with infiltrating a gang called the Strikers. One of Chicago's most notorious and ruthless criminal organizations. The Strikers didn't have the money or brains of the mafia but made up for it with their risk taking and willingness to flaunt their activities right in front of law enforcement.

They also operated on Chicago's south side where the FBI was hesitant to operate in the open. Too dangerous for even local law enforcement to control.

The Strikers had recently branched out into human trafficking which was why Rita was brought in. She held dual roles with the FBI. One as an important member of the STIF, the Sex Trafficking Investigative Force. The other team—the one meeting at that moment—was formed to investigate and ultimately bring down the Strikers and their drug operations.

"You're on the outside," Hector argued. "What you're proposing is going inside and working directly with Shiv?"

Shiv was the leader of the Strikers. A known entity they'd been trying to nail for more than a year.

Rita seethed even though this was one of the dynamics of a task force. Iron sharpens iron. Holding each other accountable and questioning actions were necessary to keep them productive. Also keep her alive.

This was dangerous work.

"My plan's a good one," Rita argued. "It *will* get me on the inside. That's the goal of undercover work. I might be able to find out where Shiv is running his drug operations. I think it's down at the docks somewhere."

While the men cared about the sex trafficking aspect, they were more interested in their jobs of drug enforcement. She focused more on her aspect of the mission.

"I don't think recruiting hookers is the best approach," Hector said.

The second time he'd called them hookers. The first time, Rita let it slide. She wouldn't do so again.

"If you call them hookers one more time, Hector, I'm going to come across this table and slap you so hard, you'll be picking your teeth up off the floor!"

She said it with the vitriol of someone who meant it. Hector was sitting right across from her on the other side of the large conference room table.

Everyone in the room knew Rita *could* do it if she wanted to. She graduated at the top of her training class in the areas of firearm efficiency, evasive driving, fitness, and hand-to-hand-combat. Her skills were widely known in the department. As was her temper. Rita had the reputation of being someone you didn't want to get on the wrong side of.

Which made her perfect for dealing with lowlifes like the Strikers. Along with her stunning good looks, Rita was the ideal candidate for her job in sex trafficking. If she did run into trouble, she had the ability to fight her way out of it, even against insurmountable odds. She also had the personality to talk her way into and out of any situation and the fearlessness to do so regardless of the risk.

"I hate to point out the obvious," Hector said more cautiously than before, "but they are indeed, hookers."

"They're victims!" Rita nearly shouted.

"I thought you were only recruiting girls who were already in prostitution," Scully interjected again. An obvious attempt to diffuse the situation that had gone from heated to confrontational in tone.

Rita took a deep breath to compose herself.

"I am. That doesn't mean they aren't victims. You have no idea what these girls have been through," Rita said, her voice cracking.

She was passionate about helping those girls. The men needed to see her determination. She despised the word *hookers*. It was disrespectful, even if the girls called themselves the same thing.

Rita formed her argument carefully and with emotion. "These girls come from broken homes. Most of them have been abused. Physically and sexually. By family members. Friends. Pastors and Priests. Men they trusted. Or should've been able to anyway. I've never met a girl who was selling her body who didn't have some trauma in her past. Unimaginable horror. That's why she thinks she deserves that lifestyle. She deserves for men to keep abusing her."

Rita bit back a tear then continued her soapbox argument.

"Make no mistake. Even the girls who are doing it voluntarily are being abused. That's why it's illegal. Don't think it's about the money for them. Yeah. These girls make more than they would waiting tables. But the damage to their souls is immeasurable. They often don't know anything else. They're called hookers because they are hooked. Like a fish with a hook in its mouth."

The words were coming now with bitterness and resentment. Not toward her colleagues but toward the men like Shiv who so easily abused the women.

She continued. "These women are reeled in like a fish into a boat. By disgusting, filthy scum of the earth men like Shiv. Who think they are better than the girls. These girls sell their bodies because they don't respect themselves. If we don't respect them and call them hookers, then how are we going to get them to see their own worth? That's why I have to help these girls. That's why I hate the term."

The passionate speech shut them up temporarily which was the desired effect.

"So don't call them that," Rita said angrily. "Call them girls. Women. Victims. Whatever."

Agent Scully changed the subject or at least redirected it.

"We all appreciate what you do for these girls. Help us understand how recruiting them into the Strikers is helping them."

Rita could see the group's point.

Rita's plan involved finding girls who were already working in prostitution and recruiting them into the Strikers. Her pitch was protection. While convincing the girls to work for a violent gang might seem counterintuitive, they were actually safer than working out on the streets where Rita found them. Gangs protected their assets. Especially those who created income for them. They screened the johns. A gang member accompanied the girls on tricks to make sure they got paid and stayed safe.

Working for the Strikers was obviously not the ideal situation for the girls. A matter of geography though in Rita's mind. The ends justified the means. Recruiting the girls into the Strikers gave her street cred with the gang. They had been skeptical of her at first when she showed up on their doorstep. After bringing them more than a dozen girls, the Strikers were convinced she was as dirty as they were.

No FBI agent would ever recruit girls into their organization. At least, that's what she assumed they were thinking. Rita wouldn't under normal circumstances. She was doing so now because she felt like she was doing the girls a favor, as small as it was.

It put the girls in a position to be rescued by her when the time was right. They were now on Rita's radar. She knew the girls. Where they lived. How she could help them. When the task force made their move and took down the Strikers, Rita hoped to rescue as many of the girls as possible.

Her sister, Julia, worked in a women's shelter for abused women. Rita intended to funnel as many of the girls to her sister's organization as possible.

In the meantime, her efforts had ingratiated her with Shiv and the Strikers. She'd brought them several quality girls who had increased their income substantially. That presented a unique opportunity for Rita to get into Shiv's inner circle.

She explained this all to them again.

Hector and the others didn't approve of her methods and continued to voice their concerns. To the point that Rita was getting tired of the conversation.

She couldn't think of any other way to get close to Shiv. It had worked. No question, it came with risk. If Shiv found out her real intentions, he wouldn't hesitate to kill her on the spot.

A risk she was prepared to take.

Rita decided to soften her tone so her words wouldn't get lost in the rhetoric.

"I have intelligence that Shiv is not just dabbling in prostitution," Rita continued. "He's also involved in human trafficking. Some girls are being held against their wills. According to my sources, Shiv has five houses where he holds the girls. He's keeping them locked in the basements of those houses. Like slaves. One of the houses is on Dexter Street. I think I can get Shiv to take me there."

"Why would Shiv take you to his hideouts?" Scully asked.

"Because he's convinced that I'm one of them. That I can help him."

Scully shook his head like he didn't agree with her. "I agree with Hector," he said. "It's too dangerous."

"I'll be careful. I just need more time," Rita said. "I'm getting close. You have to trust me."

"Don't do anything rash. Wait until we have more info. What do you need from us?" Scully asked.

"I need $12,500."

"What?" Scully said.

"You heard me. I need some money to renovate the houses. That's my way in."

"Are you crazy?" Hector asked.

Rita glared at him.

She hated that word *crazy* almost as much as hookers. Rita and her two sisters worked in mental health. Her sister Anna was a high school guidance counselor and Julia worked with abused and battered women. They all had psychology degrees. Crazy was a word that was not in their vocabularies. Even in that context.

"Hear me out," Rita said. "I'm going to set up a meeting with Shiv."

"No way," Scully said. "Not alone."

Rita ignored the command. Technically, Scully wasn't her boss. While he was in charge of the Strikers task force and had some control over her, her main boss was Meryl Baker, director of STIF.

"Like I said, I'm going to meet Shiv," Rita said dismissively. "I'm going to get him to show me his five houses."

"Why would he do that?" Hector asked the same question Scully had asked that she'd already answered. Rita let out a sigh and then answered again. She didn't need their permission but wanted their support.

"Like I said, Shiv trusts me," Rita said. "If I'm going to bring him girls, I want to see where he's keeping them. I want to use the money to fix up the houses for the girls. Make their lives more comfortable for the time being. That'll give me access. At the right time, I'm going to help them escape."

"I can't authorize that kind of money to fix up gang houses," Scully said.

"Then I'll pay for it myself!" Rita said angrily.

She abruptly stood and walked out of the conference room leaving the men sitting in their chairs with their mouths agape. Meryl had signed off on her plan. She told Rita to inform the Strikers task force. She'd done so. She didn't need their approval but did need the money. But she wasn't surprised that she didn't get it. Meryl had turned her down as well.

Didn't matter.

Rita would pay for it out of her own savings if she had to.

She got back to her desk and pulled out the cell phone she used for undercover work. Her contact inside the Strikers was a man known in Strikers' circles as Bulldog. Reginald Demario was his real name. A man with a rap sheet as long as her arm. For whatever reason, he had pulled Rita into his inner circle. He was her ticket into a meeting with Shiv. He liked her. She was making him look good with Shiv. Her girls had doubled his income in a short period of time.

She dialed his number.

"Did you talk to Shiv?" Rita asked when she heard the grunt on the other line.

"Yeh."

Reginald was a man of few words. Not educated, but streetwise.

"When can we meet?" Rita asked, as she suddenly felt her heart racing.

"How 'bout tonight?"

"Perfect. Tell me when and where."

Reginald gave her the instructions.

Rita hung up the phone slowly. Knowing what this meant. She was in. This had seemed too easy. She didn't expect to get a meeting this soon.

That gave her pause.

Scully's words screamed inside her head.

It's too dangerous!

You can't meet with Shiv alone!

Are you crazy?

Actually, she might be.

17

Later that night.

Rita was keenly aware of the precarious position she put herself in.

The meeting with Shiv was playing out like a scene in a thriller movie. Only in this instance, the six bad guys standing next to Shiv had real guns with real bullets and were less than ten feet away from her position.

They were in an abandoned warehouse near the docks which was important information in and of itself. It confirmed to Rita the intelligence that Shiv ran his operations in that area. With the amount of scrutiny Shiv was getting from law enforcement, Scully and the task force doubted he strayed far from his hideout.

The warehouse was empty except for the black Lexus Shiv arrived in along with a black SUV with darkened windows that followed it in, and the black SUV she had arrived in. Two armed thugs exited Shiv's vehicle, and four got out of the SUV like they were secret service agents protecting the President.

Reginald, one of Shiv's higher ups, drove Rita to the warehouse in a separate black SUV. They didn't bother to cover her head which told Rita they didn't use the warehouse for anything more than clandestine meetings and didn't care that she knew the location.

Reginald stood next to her which was somewhat comforting. Hopefully, no one would fire a gun at her with one of their own nearby.

Rita tried to keep her face friendly, but confident. Not wanting to give the least hint of the anxiety that was pulsing through her veins like a waterspout. Undercover work was harder than anything she'd ever done before. It required nerves of steel, complete control of her emotions, and the ability to lie through her teeth without giving anything away in her voice, tone, mannerisms, or words.

The slightest mistake could get her killed. Even if she didn't make a mistake, these men would kill her without compunction at the drop of the hat and not lose a minute's sleep over it. Had she made a mistake even being there? Her conclusion was yes.

Too late. She was face-to-face with Shiv.

That's what she wanted. Get further into his inner circle if possible. Find the location of the five houses. Rescue the girls.

Stay alive.

Shiv motioned to one of his guys to approach Rita. Presumably to search her. Rita reached into the back of her skirt and pulled out her gun and carefully lifted both arms in the air, holding the gun out from her with her fingertips. As expected, the sudden movement caused all of Shiv's men to draw their weapons in unison.

Rita held her breath, hoping and praying that one of them didn't have a nervous trigger finger.

They shouted angrily at her to drop the weapon.

Shiv was unmoved. He didn't even flinch.

She wasn't about to drop it. One, she wanted them to know they couldn't control her. Two, guns had been known to go off when they hit the ground.

Rita skillfully maneuvered the gun, so it was facing down and not a threat and handed it to Shiv's man. He took it from her but kept his gun pointed at her head.

He handed Rita's gun to Reginald. Then gripped his weapon with both of his hands and gave Rita his most menacing look.

She shrugged her shoulders in disgust. Probably a response they didn't expect. Shiv probably expected her to be shaking in her boots. High heels as it were.

"Is this necessary?" Rita asked.

The man holstered his weapon and came closer to her. He reached his hands toward her like he was going to pat her down.

"Do you want a broken arm?" Rita asked roughly as she glared at the man and took a step backward.

His eyes widened in surprise, and he stopped and looked back at Shiv. Like he wasn't sure what to do. Another move from Rita designed to keep them off balance. The sooner they knew she wasn't afraid of them, the sooner they'd either kill her or give her the respect she was demanding in her attitude.

Rita wasn't about to let the man search her. She had a gun hidden in her thigh. She also didn't want his hand groping her in that area. He'd take any liberties she'd give him. Some goons thought it was sport to frisk a woman inappropriately.

That wasn't going to happen. She couldn't let them think she was like the other girls they controlled. She might not ever be their equal, but she wasn't a woman they could kidnap and hold in a basement. She'd die first.

They might kill her, but she'd die with her dignity intact.

She stared at Shiv to see if her actions had the desired effect. The last thing she wanted to do was get into a physical confrontation with the man. Actually, she'd love nothing more than to inflict pain on him. Just not in the plan at the moment.

Rita bowed her back and put her chin in the air for added emphasis.

The show of strength and creating boundaries would hopefully work to her advantage. Men like Shiv respected strength.

Or at least she hoped he did.

Either way, she almost preferred a shootout to the man's hand between her legs. Fortunately, the man was stopped in his tracks. It appeared they were at a stalemate. Rita was waiting for him to get within striking range. He was waiting for Shiv to give him permission.

"You brought a gun to a meeting with me?" Shiv asked, with a sly grin on his face.

"You brought six men with guns to a meeting with me!" Rita retorted. "I'm one woman. Are you that worried about me for some reason? I thought we were here to discuss a partnership. Based on mutual objectives. If that's not the case, tell me now. I'll get back in the car and leave."

"I just wanted to make sure you're not armed or wearing a wire."

Rita laughed. "How do I know *you're* not wearing a wire?"

Shiv laughed.

"Exactly!" Rita said. "I'm no more the Feds than you are. So, let's get on with it. You have me outnumbered. I get that. But I didn't come here for a confrontation I can't win. But make no mistake. Your man is *not* touching me. If he does, it'll be one of the last things he ever does."

The other goons started to mock the man. Made all kinds of men's locker-room-style banter.

Shiv's man looked confused. Not sure whether to take the challenge. Rita was counting on him not acting without Shiv's permission. Shiv had no reason to escalate the situation. She'd voluntarily given him her gun, and Rita was right. She was outnumbered and little-to-no threat to Shiv.

She saw Shiv making that calculation in his mind. Confirmed when he said to his man, "Leave her alone. Just keep an eye on her."

The goon took two steps back. His shoulders sagged like he was hurt. Rita wanted to mock him but thought better of it. She'd pushed her luck as far as it could be pushed. At least to that point.

Shiv had been leaning against the car but stood and walked toward her.

"I like you," he said in a complimentary tone.

"I don't like you," Rita replied. "At least not yet. I thought this was a business meeting. You're not making a good first impression."

Shiv stopped about five feet away from her and looked her up and down. Not in a sexual way, but in a scope-her-out sort of manner. Like he wasn't sure he could trust her. Something she expected. Shiv didn't get to where he was by not being cautious. Gangs had certain rituals. Rights of entry. No one was allowed in without jumping through considerable hoops. Ones that usually involved violence. Proof that you were worthy to be in their gang.

Rita's point of entry was providing the girls. Another fast way to prove your worth was to bring Shiv money. That's the only reason she had gotten in his presence.

She was surprised she'd gotten this far. More than likely, Shiv had come out of curiosity as much as anything else.

She'd soon know how much further she was going to get. She needed to tone it down a bit. No need to risk overdoing the bravado.

Another tightrope.

One of several more ahead of her. After she was past the testosterone challenge, she had to carefully negotiate a deal. Not seem too anxious to make one but be savvy enough to get what she wanted.

Access to the houses where the girls were being held. The only reason she was taking such a risk.

Neither of them said anything for a good minute.

Just stared at each other like a couple of junior-high kids in a staring contest. A game of chicken almost. To see who would blink first. A game she couldn't afford to lose. Fortunately, no guns were pointed at her.

Eventually, Rita decided she needed to change the dynamics. She shuffled her feet back and forth in a show of impatience and looked away.

"How do you like my girls?" Rita finally asked.

"I like them," Shiv said.

She'd recruited a dozen or so girls into his organization. Rita estimated that her girls had already made him ten grand or so. Shiv would owe her money at the end of the month.

"I knew you would," Rita said. "I can get more."

"Why would you?"

"I thought you knew why."

"Explain it to me."

Shiv was still playing his cards close to his vest. Rita studied him closely. Looking for any sign that he was on to her. If so, she'd have to try and talk her way out of the situation. If that didn't work, she had the gun in her thigh and the one hidden in the front of her skirt which would be easier to draw.

She put her odds at slightly over ten percent to survive a gunfight. She couldn't kill six men at once, even with the element of surprise, which she didn't have. Shiv's men had their guns in their hands. She tamped down her fear. At this point, she had no reason to believe that Shiv wasn't just feeling her out. Something she was doing as well.

The tension in the room was the most disconcerting thing. Everyone was on edge. It'd help if they all relaxed some. Rita couldn't think of anything funny to say that might accomplish that goal.

So she decided to keep Shiv talking. As long as they were discussing details of a deal, their minds would be distracted from the obvious mistrust between them.

"Your man approached me about working together." Rita pointed toward Reginald.

That wasn't exactly true. Rita only made Reginald think it was his idea. He was more than willing to be manipulated. She was making him look good in Shiv's eyes.

"I was under the impression you called this meeting," Shiv said. "That you wanted to meet me. So, here I am. What do you want from me?"

"Nothing! With all due respect, I don't need you. You don't need me either. I'm here because I think we can help each other. My girls need protection. Which I can't provide. At least... not to the extent that you can. They also need a steady stream of paying customers. You have both. I have the girls. Seems like a good symbiotic relationship."

Rita watched Shiv closely to see if he understood the word. Scully and others had argued that Shiv had to be educated to run the Strikers as effectively as he did. He didn't blink twice at the word. Nor show any sign that he didn't know what she meant.

Shiv didn't say anything. He just kept staring.

She was starting to get an uneasy feeling and finally said, "Apparently, you don't feel that way. It's no sweat off my back. I'll be on my way."

"I didn't say that." Shiv continued to stare.

"This is obviously a waste of time," Rita added. "Let's go, Reginald."

Shiv's behavior was strange. Almost like he was toying with her.

Rita turned and walked back toward the car. Halfway expecting a gunshot to ring out. The last thing she'd hear on this earth.

She felt him follow her.

Reginald opened the back door of the car.

Shiv was close now.

Rita turned.

He was practically on her. "Go ahead," he said, pointing to the back seat of the car. "Let's discuss this in the car."

That statement threw Rita off guard.

What did it mean? Was Shiv on to her? Did he just want to discuss the deal? Did he intend to kill her? Was he going to try and rape her?

All kinds of thoughts raged in her mind, sending her into a panic. She wasn't in a position to run. Nor in the right proximity to commandeer the vehicle and drive away.

She had no choice but to get in the car.

Shiv got in behind her as Rita scooted to the other side of the back seat.

Reginald closed the door behind them.

18

Somewhere in Ohio

I was awakened from a deep sleep by the car lurching to a sudden stop. A bright light shined through the window into my eyes. I struggled to focus. A sudden panic came over me as I tried to process where I was and what was going on.

I quickly remembered. I was safe. I'd hitched a ride with two college girls from Chicago. Connie and Julie.

"Hey, sleepy head," Connie said from the passenger seat. "You were out like a light."

I shook my head to try and get the cobwebs out. Was confused when my eyes came into focus. I thought I remembered that Connie had been driving and Julie was in the passenger seat. Or at least I thought she was.

"What are we doing?" I asked.

"Getting gas," Julie said. "And a coke so I don't fall asleep at the wheel."

"What time is it?"

"Four o'clock," Connie said as she opened the door.

"I thought you were driving," I said, my brain still in a fog. My headache was better, but I still felt like I'd been hit by a truck.

"I was," Connie said. "We switched places about an hour ago. You slept right through it."

That wasn't good. I was in operational mode. I should be aware of my surroundings at all times. Then I remembered Curly's words. *Sleep and eat when you can. You never know when you might get another chance.*

Good advice. I should grab something to eat and drink as well.

"I'll fill up the gas tank," I said to Connie after I exited the vehicle. She was about to stick her credit card in the fuel pump dispenser.

She pulled her hand back.

"You don't have to," Connie said. "I mean. We have to, like, drive to Chicago anyway."

"I insist. You guys are the best. Giving me a ride. It's the least I can do. Can I get you something to eat and drink?" I asked.

"Coke and a bag of chips," Connie said.

I reached into my pocket and pulled out my credit card then hesitated. Jamie could track me. It also had my real name, Bae Hwa. It might raise suspicion if the girls saw it. So, I needed to pay with cash. I had two grand in hundred dollar bills I'd pulled off those lowlifes back in the motel parking lot. I'd use that.

I felt proud of myself as I walked to the entrance of the convenience store. I felt like a real-life spy. Dark. The term Jamie used when she talked about going off the grid on a mission. Making herself impossible for anyone to find. It felt good to finally be doing things the right way.

A crusty old fellow with deep bags under his eyes stood behind the counter. I pulled out a hundred-dollar bill and sat it in front of him.

"I need to fill up with gas." I looked out the window at Connie who was still standing by the pump looking my way. Obviously waiting for the man to turn it on.

He pointed at a hand-written sign on the cash register.

Sorry. No bills over $20 accepted after dark.

"I only have hundreds. Can you give me change?" I asked.

"No can do."

I wanted to slap him.

He stood there with one hand on the register and the other on the counter. Looking totally disinterested in having a conversation with me.

"Company policy," he added.

"Company policy is stupid," I said. "The gas is going to cost forty dollars or so. We're also getting snacks and drinks. We're going to spend fifty or sixty bucks in your store. Are you willing to lose our sale? Do you want us to go to another station?"

He shrugged his shoulders and kept staring at me.

I looked out at Connie who appeared to be getting impatient. Julie had gone in the direction of the back of the store. Maybe in the restroom. Maybe getting her coke. I wasn't sure.

Another man got in line behind me. Now I really felt rushed. I reached into my pocket and pulled out my credit card. Hesitated. Stared at it. Considering my options. There were none. I had no other choice. If I used the card, Jamie could track me, but I'd be long gone by the time she got to the convenience store. She wouldn't know that we were headed for Chicago. It seemed safe to leave that much of a trail.

It actually caused me to smile to think that Jamie would be on a wild goose chase. Then I thought about how angry she'd be when she did find me. Too bad. It was her own fault. I was a grown woman capable of making my own decisions. Jamie shouldn't be following me anyway.

I made a mental note to get change for the hundred so I could stay off the grid as much as possible. Going dark was harder than I thought it'd be.

The man took the card and swiped it and handed it back to me.

"Thank you," I said sarcastically and twisted my face in some kind of annoyed contortion for his benefit. He barely noticed. Then I realized he'd have to swipe it again when I got the drinks and snacks. I probably should be nicer to him. He was working in a convenience store in the middle of the night. I wouldn't be in a very good mood either.

The beverage dispenser was in the back. I went there and filled up two oversized cups with ice and coke. I didn't fill mine up completely. I got an energy drink off the counter and poured it into my drink. A concoction I'd learned from Jamie. A mixture designed for optimal energy and focus when on a mission.

I took a sip and also grabbed a bag of chips off the counter along with a package of peanut butter crackers. Then walked back to the counter with my hands full, careful not to drop one of my drinks or snacks.

As I was doing so, I noticed that a man outside approached Connie. It stopped me in my tracks. He was the same man who'd been behind me at the counter.

The man took a step toward her. Connie had taken a step back and was now behind the pump. I couldn't see what she was doing.

Was she in danger?

I looked around for Julie but didn't see her.

The situation wasn't ideal. My hands were full. Another person was at the counter and there was no time to set them down. I could see the man reach out his hands toward Connie, but I still couldn't see her.

I made a beeline for the door and pushed it open with my shoulder. The cold drinks were pressed against my chest as were the snacks which were getting crushed.

"Hey!" the shopkeeper shouted. "You haven't paid for those."

I ignored him and walked as quickly as I could toward the car. The man was still partially out of view behind the pump.

"What are you doing?" I shouted.

He had his hands on Connie's shoulder.

I kicked the back of his leg. A glancing blow since I couldn't get any leverage. He didn't go down. Curly always said to make your first strike so debilitating that the person couldn't fight back.

I reared my leg back to kick him again.

He pivoted so he was facing me and lunged forward. Right into me. The ice-cold drinks suddenly chilled my chest as the cups disintegrated and the liquid soaked my shirt. I backed away and put my hands out as the drinks and snacks fell to the ground.

I balled my fists.

The man took two steps toward me. His hands were also balled into fists and his eyes filled with rage. I noticed him favoring the leg I had kicked. Good information. A weakness I could exploit again with another swift kick. His midsection and groin were also wide open for a strike.

"What are you doing, Marcia?" Connie said sharply. Then she stepped between us.

Why did she call me Marcia? Then I remembered that was the name I had given them. My operational name. Not Bae Hwa. Marcia. I don't think I gave them a last name. Jamie always said to make your cover name start with the same letter as your real name, so you remember it. I'd forgotten to do that in the spur of the moment, but now I could see why that was important.

"Who is this man?" I asked roughly.

My shirt was dripping wet. I wondered if the man could see through it. Because he was staring at me. The drinks were splattered on the concrete.

"This is Michael," Connie said. "He's a friend of ours from school."

I suddenly felt foolish.

I stammered.

"I'm sorry. I saw his hands on you. I thought he was trying to hurt you or something. Strange guy out in the middle of nowhere. What are the odds you'd run into a friend?"

"I can see where you could make that mistake," Connie said. "But Michael is harmless."

"You know this girl?" Michael asked. He was now holding the back of his thigh where I kicked him.

"Yes. She's with us. We're giving her a ride to Chicago."

The man behind the counter stood at the door holding it open. He shouted at me.

"You need to pay for those drinks, or I'll call the police," he said.

"I'm coming! Don't get your panties in a wad," I said. I'd heard Jamie say that before. It sounded even funnier when I said it. Connie laughed. Michael didn't. He was still glaring at me and holding his leg.

I skulked back inside the convenience store.

"What did you have?" he asked roughly.

"I had two large cokes, a bag of chips, and peanut butter and crackers."

"That'll be ten dollars and twenty-four cents."

"I shouldn't have to pay for the drinks. They spilled on the concrete. That man knocked them out of my hands."

"I don't care who pays for them. Somebody has to." The man was acting belligerent now.

Julie walked up to the counter about that time. "What happened?" she asked. "Why's he mad?"

I explained it to her.

"That's so sweet that you were trying to protect Connie."

"I didn't know Michael was your friend. The old geezer here is trying to make me pay for the spilled drinks. Even though it wasn't my fault."

"I'll pay for them," Julie said.

"I can't let you do that," I said. I pulled out my credit card and handed it to the clerk. He ran the card, and I signed the receipt. Then slapped my head.

"What's wrong?" Julie asked.

"I also bought an energy drink. I forgot to pay for that."

The man ran the card again.

I laughed, easing the tension somewhat. "I still have to buy the drinks. And a shirt."

He'd have to run the card a third time.

I looked over at the clerk. "Do you sell T-shirts?"

"Don't pay for a shirt," Julie said. "I have an extra shirt in the car you can borrow."

Before I could object, Julie was out the door and rummaging through the back of her car.

I watched her hug Michael. She obviously knew him as well. Seconds later, Julie walked back to the store with a T-shirt in her hand. I went back in the restroom and changed. My pants and socks and shoes were soaked as well, but I didn't want to say anything. I was already beyond embarrassed.

The shirt was two or three sizes too big but would have to do. It said DePaul University with Chicago written in the center of a circle.

I made two more extra-large drinks and decided to forgo the energy drink. My hand was already shaking, and my heart was beating out of my chest from the adrenaline rush that came with the confrontation. I didn't think I needed any more stimulation.

The man at the counter rang up two drinks.

I could feel the scowl on my face from having to pay for the drinks again. While it wasn't his fault they spilled, it wasn't mine either.

He continued to ignore my attitude.

I reached for a hundred-dollar bill then remembered the sign that was staring me in the face.

Handed him my credit card, and he swiped it for a fourth time.

I picked up the two drinks and walked toward the door.

"Thanks for nothing," I muttered under my breath.

Then I saw him.

A man was in the middle of the road. I'd seen the man sitting outside the store when I first walked in. He looked drunk.

The man staggered. Then fell to the ground.

A car was off in the distance. Headed straight toward him.

I took off running as fast as I could. Still holding the two drinks which was slowing my progress.

Without thinking, I ran right into the street. The headlights were close now. The car didn't appear to be slowing.

I dropped the two drinks and helped the man to his feet. He couldn't stand under his own power. Fortunately, he wasn't that big. Almost emaciated from the years of probable drug and alcohol abuse.

I heard one of the girls scream.

I strengthened my grip on the man's arm. The adrenaline rushed through my body like a powerful wave.

The car honked.

Then swerved.

We dove to the side of the road and went tumbling to the ground. I could feel the breath knocked out of me as the man landed on top of me. He reeked of alcohol and bad breath.

Michael was the first to reach us. He helped me to my feet and then helped the man.

"Are you okay?" he asked the man.

What about me? I wanted to say. My elbows and knees were scraped. As were the palm of my hands.

The man's speech was slurred.

He started to walk back toward the road.

I jumped to my feet and grabbed his arms and led him back toward the convenience store. He resisted but was easy to control in his drunken state.

"You saved that man's life," Julie said.

"That was amazing!" Connie chimed in.

"I thought that car was going to hit you," Michael said.

I appreciate the sentiment but focused on leading the man toward the store and into safety.

When we walked in, the store clerk took one look at the man and said, "You can't bring that drunk in here."

"What am I supposed to do with him? He was in the middle of the road. He could've been killed."

"I don't care! Get him out of here."

"You were happy to have him in here when he was buying your alcohol."

I didn't know for sure that's where the man had gotten his booze but took an educated guess. Confirmed when the store clerk didn't dispute it.

"I'm going to call the police," he said.

"You're a world-class jerk. You know that. A heartless cold S.O.B."

"Get him out of here! Now!"

I led the man outside. Sat him on the ground. Michael, Connie, and Julie gathered around him.

"Maybe we should call the police," Julie said. "At least he'll be safe there."

I nodded in agreement.

I allowed myself a moment to catch my breath and assess my injuries which were minor. Then I realized my throat was parched.

The drinks.

Dang it.

I had to go back into that store. And buy more drinks. Which I did. The store clerk swiped my card for the fifth time.

I walked out the store and quickly gave Connie her drink so I wouldn't spill it.

The girls said goodbye to Michael. I simply gave him an obligatory wave.

Once we were in the car and on our way, I felt a wave of satisfaction come over me.

"You're a hero," Julie said. "That man wouldn't be alive if it weren't for you."

That's right! I'm a female Reeder Rich.

19

Chicago South Side

Strange as it seemed, Rita felt safer outside the car staring down six guns than she did inside the car sitting next to Shiv. The man was a Goliath. An imposing figure when he'd been standing ten feet away. Now that he was next to her, she felt like a Woolly Mammoth had invaded her space and was preparing to kill his prey.

As soon as Shiv sat down, he sucked all the oxygen out of the car. Or at least it felt like it since she suddenly struggled to find a complete breath.

At a quick glance, Shiv's neck appeared to be as wide as Rita's waist. His forearms and thighs were massive. His knuckles were scarred from the untold number of fights he'd no doubt been in. Considering his state of health and good physical condition, Rita presumed Shiv had won all or most of them. She also assumed that if Shiv got in a fight, it wouldn't be over until the other person was dead.

Rita still had the two guns on her but no confidence that she could draw them in time. Shiv was close enough to her that he could reach out and snap her neck with his bare hands before she could even reach them.

If that was his intention.

Which made the situation even more unnerving.

Why did Shiv get in the car with her?

Was he on to her? Playing her like a fiddle? Still sizing her up and feeling her out? Or was he waiting for her to make a mistake? Toying with her like a lion would a prey?

Was that what she was? His next victim. It felt like it. His face had the look of a killer. Angry. Vicious. Unforgiving. Ruthless. A thesaurus didn't have enough synonyms to fully describe the man who seemingly could decide on a whim if she lived or died.

Shiv's FBI file estimated that he'd been responsible for hundreds of murders. None that could be pinned on him though. Rita suddenly realized why. Shiv could murder her that very second, toss her body in the river or on the side of the road, and no one would have any proof he was behind it. He was shrewd in that way. Making himself almost untouchable to the Feds. She hoped to change his luck.

If he didn't kill her first.

How did I get myself in this position?

A better question, *how do I get out of it?*

Rita's mind was out of control. It took every bit of self-will to rein it back in.

Then it dawned on her.

What if he didn't intend to kill her? What if his intentions were sexual?

She'd rather die!

Not quite. But almost.

That caused a smile to come across her face. If Shiv noticed, he didn't say anything.

When nearly thirty seconds had passed and he hadn't said anything, Rita didn't know what to think. Rita braced for the worst. Felt herself instinctively reach for the door to steady herself. She scooted a little closer to the door. Further away from him which also allowed her to turn her entire body to face him. She was looking for every possible angle that might give her an advantage.

She'd always believed in her hand-to-hand combat skills and chances against any one man in a confrontation. Now she wasn't so sure. Any confidence that she could best Shiv was gone. Still... she wouldn't go down without putting up a fight.

Exiting the car wasn't an option. The car door was probably locked anyway. Even if it weren't and she managed to get out of the car alive, the six men outside the car would finish the job.

She was trapped in that car like a caged tiger in a zoo.

Her breathing was shallow. Labored. Her heart felt like it was beating two-hundred beats per minute. She might die of a heart attack before Shiv put his hands on her.

She fidgeted nervously.

Changed positions several times.

Cleared her throat.

Then decided to seize the moment. "I want a piece of all your action," she said with as much bravado as she could muster.

His eyes widened. She instinctively braced for a backhand across the side of her face.

Then she realized how that must've sounded to him and quickly backtracked.

"I don't mean the drugs. The girls."

"Strikers don't sell drugs," Shiv said.

He seemed slightly nervous. She had caught him off guard. That probably didn't happen very often.

"Right! My bad," Rita said, sarcastically.

"I don't understand," Shiv said. "You already get a piece of every girl you bring to us."

"I want to manage your girls as well."

Rita wasn't sure she was even supposed to know about his girls. Reginald was a chatterbox. She'd gotten all kinds of actionable intelligence from him. He'd confirm in a roundabout way that Shiv was trafficking girls. He'd divulged almost everything about the operations except for the girls' location.

Which was why she was in this predicament to begin with.

"Why would I give you a piece of girls you didn't bring to us?" Shiv said, with a hint of anger. Raising the level of tension in the car if that was even possible.

Even so, Rita could feel her confidence grow.

"Because you aren't maximizing your income," Rita answered. "Men will pay more for women who aren't servicing them voluntarily. You charge less for your girls than I charge for mine. I think you can charge more for them."

Shiv's eyes widened again. Like he was surprised she knew about the girls much less what he charged for them.

Rita kept talking. Not wanting to give Shiv a chance to object. It came natural to her. When she was nervous, Rita talked too much anyway. Her trainer with the FBI said she needed to learn to control it. She'd long since given up trying to do so.

In this instance, Rita was afraid of a lull in the conversation. As long as she was talking, it meant she was still breathing. If she controlled the conversation, it made her feel a slight bit of security. As dubious as it was.

"You keep those girls in the basement of a house," Rita added. "In deplorable conditions."

Shiv looked out the window at Reginald. She'd probably gotten him in trouble. Shiv was clearly not happy that Reginald had told her about his operations because she saw his fists ball and his jaw clench.

"I can get you more girls," Rita quickly said, trying to turn Shiv's attention away from Reginald and back to the profit motive which was what the conversation should focus on.

"I come across runaways all the time," Rita explained. "Girls find themselves on the streets for whatever reason. They're looking for someone to help them. Some are best suited for straight prostitution. You know. They have their own place. Transportation. Clothes. That sort of thing."

Rita took a deep breath.

"But some are desperate. No money. No friends. No place to turn. Those girls can be trafficked. No one will ever know if they disappear. I can get you more of those girls. But I want a piece of all of it. I want to manage all of the girls. Even the ones you already have in your possession. I'm sure they're a pain for you anyway."

Shiv nodded in agreement, but stared off in the distance, like he was thinking.

"What percentage do you want?" he asked.

A good sign. Negotiation meant a sale was possible. Shiv was considering it. It also meant that he wasn't on to her. The concern for her safety might've been overblown.

"Fifty percent," Rita said confidently.

Rita got twenty-five percent of the total take on girls she brought to Shiv. He got twenty-five percent and the girls got fifty. The rate they'd negotiated for girls who worked for them voluntarily.

"You get twenty-five percent now," Shiv argued.

"The girls we are talking about obviously don't get anything," Rita countered. "That saves you fifty percent. I want twenty-five percent of the fifty."

She wondered if she was pushing her luck. What difference did it make what she made? She'd never see a dime of it. Her plan was to get the girls out of the houses as soon as possible and not subject them to their plight for any longer than necessary.

"I have to house them and provide them with food," Shiv said.

The negotiation felt right. It gave her more credibility with Shiv. Helped build her cover and make it more believable. So, she continued making the argument.

"What you're providing is inadequate," Rita said. "With all due respect," she added. "I want to totally renovate the basements. Get the girls new clothes and basic necessities. I hear that some of the girls have run out of basic supplies. Like shampoo and toothpaste. I intend to make these girls more desirable to the men. Why would men pay top dollar for an inferior product?"

"The men don't have much in the way of expectations. They know these girls are doing it against their wills."

"I want to exceed their expectations. Like I said, you don't charge enough. We can get more for the girls. But we have to make them more desirable. I can do that. You'll see."

"How much will that cost?" Shiv asked.

Rita waved her hand dismissively.

"I'll pay for it out of my fifty percent."

Scully had turned her down when she asked the FBI for money. She'd have to pay for it herself. Shiv might agree to pay it, but the conversation was going so well, she didn't want to push her luck by creating an objection that didn't matter anyway.

She'd already decided to take the money out of her savings account.

If things went well, the girls weren't going to be around long enough for it to matter anyway. Once she had access to the basements, she intended to free the girls and bring Shiv down.

Perhaps Scully would reimburse her then, if she had scored a big arrest that he got credit for.

Rita forced those thoughts out of her mind. She didn't want her face to give anything away. Shiv was staring her down again. Sizing her up. Which caused her to start to fidget again. She caught herself clasping her hands together and nervously rubbing her palms against her skirt. She changed her position again so the bulge in her waistband didn't show. The last thing she wanted was for Shiv to see that she had a gun.

Actually, the last thing she wanted was to have to use it.

Shiv held out his hand.

Rita hesitated.

What did he want?

She put her hand in his. Hoping he just wanted to shake on the deal. She felt herself wince inside. She fought hard to keep it from showing on her face.

"So, we have a deal?" Rita asked.

"We do," Shiv said.

He kept a strong grip on Rita's hand and pulled her toward him.

"Just don't ever betray me," he said with malice.

"I won't."

Their faces were within inches of each other.

"If you do, I'll kill you," he said matter-of-factly. Like he'd said it a thousand times before.

Shiv gripped her hand so tightly it hurt. Anger rose up inside of her, but she tamped it down and strengthened her grip. It's fine that he knew she was intimidated. She wouldn't let him see that she was petrified of him.

"Don't betray me either," Rita said. "I'm loyal to a fault. Some men think they can take advantage of me. Don't underestimate me. I'm tougher than I look."

That caused Shiv to smile. Then release her hand.

"I like that. I wish some of my men were as tough as they look."

Shiv let out a sigh.

Rita matched it.

He abruptly opened the car door and stepped out. Then closed it behind him.

Rita wasn't sure if she should get out or stay put. Then decided she was safer in the car.

Shiv went straight to Reginald. They had an animated conversation. When it was over, Reginald walked around the car and got in the driver's side. He started the car. Then looked at himself in the rearview mirror. At himself first, then at her.

"This is yours," Reginald said. He had her gun in his hand and reached back over the seat to hand it to her.

Rita took it.

Reginald put the car in drive and hit the gas. He did a u-turn and drove to the entrance of the warehouse which was more of a loading dock and ramp than anything else. Two men opened the large doors that were big enough for a semi to drive through.

Rita finally allowed herself to breathe freely. Even though her heart was pounding in her chest, it was still beating. And that felt good to her.

"Where are we going?" Rita asked.

"Shiv told me to take you to the house and introduce you to the girls."

Rita felt the jubilation rush inside of her that felt like a champagne bottle was just uncorked and spewing expensive bubbly everywhere.

She was in.

20

Rita was glad Reginald was driving and that the car they were in had dark-tinted windows. They had left the warehouse down near the docks and drove to the south side of Chicago into one of the roughest and most dangerous parts of town to a small house with white siding on Dexter Street.

They came in on a road from the back and entered the house via the back door which led into the kitchen. A half a dozen or so Strikers were sitting around a table drinking beer and eating pizza. Dishes were piled up in the sink, and the house smelled of mold, stale cigarettes, and body odor.

It could use a good cleaning which gave Rita an idea.

Right off the kitchen was a door with huge padlocks on it. Obviously, the door leading into the basement where the girls were being held. A pang shot through her heart as fast as a bullet could be shot out of a gun. She knew women and girls lived in virtual slavery which was why she did what she did. It still broke her heart every time she saw it firsthand.

Reginald unlocked the door and motioned for Rita to go through it. A paranoia shot through her body replacing the pity for the girls. What if it was a trap? On the drive over from the warehouse, Rita had allowed herself to relax. Realizing she had succeeded in her goal to get deep into the inner circle of the Strikers and into the basement where the girls were being held.

Now she was wondering if it had been too easy. It wouldn't be hard for Reginald to lock the door behind her. Then she'd be trapped along with the girls with no way of escape.

She tamped down the fear. That scenario didn't make sense. Why go through the ruse? If Shiv wanted her dead, he could've killed her a dozen times over. Reginald had also given her back her gun as soon as they left the warehouse. He wouldn't have done that if he intended on locking her up with the other girls. They wouldn't want her in the basement with a weapon.

Unless the bullets were removed from the gun.

She hadn't thought to check it.

Rita's imagination ran wild, and she tried to bring it under control. Still, she hesitated when Reginald motioned for her to enter the makeshift dungeon. Not that she had a choice. She was committed. No way she wasn't going downstairs to see the plight of the girls and confirm her worst fears. This was what she'd wanted. If she hadn't thought it entirely through, then so be it. These were the risks of the deadly game she played. Impossible to take all of the risk out of her efforts.

Reginald had a confused look on his face. His lips twisted with impatience. She couldn't wait any longer, so she had to make her move. Any more hesitation and she risked blowing her cover. Even if Reginald had removed the bullets from her gun, she had two others which they presumably didn't know she had. With the element of surprise, she might be able to fight her way out of the basement.

Hopefully, it wouldn't come to that.

Rita walked toward the door and then stepped through it with a purpose, starting the descent down the basement steps. The room was dimly lit.

Five girls were sitting on mattresses on the floor. They cowered back against the wall when Rita walked in. Reginald followed her in and closed the door behind them. Or at least she thought he did. She'd only felt his presence. Her focus was dead set on the girls.

This was a critical moment. Her face couldn't show her breaking heart. As far as Reginald was concerned, Rita was as coldhearted and ruthless as they were. Any deviation from her cover would raise suspicion.

So, she walked around the enclosed area like she owned the place and went from room to room. There were only three. A closet, a bathroom, and the main living area. Reginald had been right. The room was mostly empty of any supplies. It smelled worse than the upstairs. The living conditions were deplorable. As vacant as the eyes of the girls who looked at her with fear which only slightly masked the deep pain.

Seeing the girls nearly broke her heart, and she had to force back the tears that had welled up in her eyes. She kept her head turned away from Reginald so he wouldn't see them. Sometimes, when sitting in a sterile FBI field office, she found it unfathomable that people would treat other human beings this way. Then she'd get in the arena and be reminded that it was more pervasive than their statistics showed. More heinous than they could even imagine or explain to someone who hadn't seen it with their own eyes.

She forced herself back into a professional and icy cold demeanor. Her tone was strict and demanding.

"Is there a security camera down here?" Rita asked Reginald. She'd looked around but hadn't seen one. Important information. If so, she couldn't speak freely with the girls and had to maintain her cover even if alone with them.

He shook his head no. That's what she thought but had to be sure.

"You girls stand up," Rita said sharply. "Don't worry. I'm not going to hurt you. As long as you do what I say."

The girls slowly stood to their feet.

"I want this place cleaned up. It looks and smells like a pigsty! When you're done here, I want you all upstairs. We're going to clean this house from top to bottom and keep it that way."

She needed to get the girls out of the basement for an extended period of time. While they might not appreciate it now, going upstairs and seeing the sunshine and smelling some fresh air would do them all good. Give them some semblance of normalcy. Rather than feeling like caged rats.

"Is that clear?" she said to the girls.

They all nodded. One had her shoulders back in defiance.

Good for her.

"You can go Reginald," Rita said. "I'll take it from here. I'm sure you have better things to do than babysit a bunch of pathetic girls. I'm going to whip them into shape. The next time you see them, you won't recognize them or this place. There's a new sheriff in town, and things are going to be run differently around here."

"Do you understand that I'm in charge now?" Rita said to the girls with a raised voice.

She walked by each one of them like a drill instructor inspecting a set of new recruits.

"Lift your chin up," she said to one of them.

"Wash your hair," she said to another. "It's all matted."

"You girls are here to please the men. If I were a man, I wouldn't touch any of you with a ten-foot pole."

Reginald started laughing. Rita realized how that might've sounded to a man. Like an off-color joke. Locker room humor. Rita smiled at him. Inside she hated him and everything he stood for. She wished she could pull the gun from her skirt and shoot him in the head.

As if he realized he'd overstayed his welcome, Reginald abruptly turned and went back up the stairs.

"Leave the door unlocked," Rita shouted after him. "I'll lock it up when I leave."

As soon as the door was closed and Rita was certain he was gone, she changed her entire demeanor.

She whispered even though no one upstairs could possibly hear her.

"My name's Rita. I'm here to help you. I'm so sorry for what you are going through. I'm going to get you out of here."

One of them started to cry.

Rita took her in her arms. The woman reeked of suffering. Rita held her close.

"You can help us escape?" the defiant girl asked.

"Not today. But soon. I promise. I won't leave you here. I'm also going to get you some supplies. Clothes. Sheets for your mattresses. Shampoo. Toothpaste. Basic necessities. You may be slaves to these low life scums, but you don't have to act like it."

"Why can't we leave now?" defiant girl asked.

A good question.

One which Rita did not have a good answer for. As far as these girls were concerned, they were pawns in a bigger picture. The right thing to do was to march them upstairs and out the door at the first opportunity. Rita couldn't do that. And bring Shiv down which was the ultimate goal. While not fair, the girls had to continue to play their role until the opportunity presented itself to free them from their slavery. They might not understand, and she didn't bother trying to explain. The less they knew the better.

While Rita had made it into the one house, according to Reginald, there were four more out there. That he knew of anyway. There might be more. She had to gain access to all of them before she could free one. As soon as she made her move, her cover would be blown. Hopefully, it'd be soon. In the meantime, they'd just have to trust her.

Rita took out her phone and began videotaping the girls.

"Tell me your full names and where you are from," Rita said.

Each girl said her name and Rita captured it all. Evidence against Shiv, but also proof they could use to contact the next of kin.

After they were done, Rita walked around the room again. She spotted a dresser against the wall and pulled it out.

"Do you have anything to write with?"

One of the girls nodded her head.

"I want each of you to write your names on the wall. Just first name and last name initial. When the girls were rescued, Rita wanted there to be some physical evidence that the girls were there. Also, their identities in case things didn't go according to plan. While Rita intended to help them, the girls were still in grave danger. Would be until safely away from the house and in the FBI's custody.

They each scribbled their names on the wall. When they were done, Rita moved the dresser back in front of the names so they couldn't be seen.

"Everyone, get dressed," Rita said, trying to maintain a firm but kind tone. "I wasn't kidding about cleaning the upstairs."

The girls let out a groan.

"I know it sounds like hard work and it will be. But I want to get you out of this basement. Help you feel normal if only for a few hours. You'll thank me in a few hours."

The girls hesitated.

"Go on now. Get dressed. Shorts and tee-shirts. Sneakers. When you get upstairs, don't speak unless spoken to."

Rita wanted to go and get the supplies from the store but decided to wait. She didn't want the girls alone upstairs with the Strikers. She didn't think they'd bother them, but she wanted to be there to be sure. Once the girls were done cleaning, she'd help them clean up the downstairs and then go get the supplies.

Once they were dressed, she did another makeshift inspection.

Satisfied, Rita said, "If I sound harsh with you, realize it's only an act. I'm on your side. I'm here to help you. Play along, and we'll all get out of this thing alive."

At least that's what she hoped would happen.

21

Bricks, Ohio

It took Jamie about three hours to drive from her hotel in Kentucky to a convenience store just across the Ohio border. She'd gotten up early with a sense of urgency to go somewhere; she just didn't have a clue where. Not until Alex called her with information about Bae.

"Did you find an ear hair?" Jamie had quipped when she answered the phone. The last time they talked, Alex had called her in panic mode about a grey hair he found on his chest.

"Ear hair? What are you talking about?" Alex asked.

"Since you're calling me this early in the morning, I figured you must've discovered a hair growing in your ear."

"Hairs don't grow in ears," Alex said.

"They most certainly do. Curly used to complain about it all the time."

"I never heard him say anything about growing hair in his ears. You're making that up!"

"I am not."

Jamie sat up in the hotel bed. She'd been a little groggy dozing in and out of sleep when he called. Now she was fully awake and enjoying the banter.

"Do you have hair in your ears?" Alex asked.

"Women don't get them, but men do. As they get older."

Silence on the other line.

Then she heard movement. A rummaging around.

"What are you doing?" Jamie asked.

"I'm looking in the mirror as we speak. But I don't see any hairs in my ear. I think you're joshing me."

Alex had always been vainer than her. He took longer in the bathroom than she did. His hair had to be meticulous before he'd go out in public. He got his hair cut every two weeks. She went in every eight weeks for hers. Only because she had to keep it trimmed for work.

Alex even ironed his shirts and shorts. Fortunately, he didn't ask her to do it for him. He preferred to do it himself so it would be "done right."

He used to shave his chest hairs but quit that habit after they were married. Which was probably why he hadn't discovered the grey one before now. Alex was a jock in high school and college. The starting quarterback for Stanford. Even played in the national championship game. They would've won, but the defense gave up a late touchdown to Alabama. To this day, Alex refused to watch the game.

Jamie found Alex's obsession with his looks amusing.

Growing old with him was going to be fun.

It wasn't that Alex was doing it to attract attention to himself. He couldn't have cared less about what others thought of his looks. He did it for his own compulsions. It's probably what made him a great CIA operative, an exceptional businessman, and the best computer hacker in the world. His ability to zero in on a task and attack it until he succeeded never ceased to amaze Jamie.

The current conversation reminded her of why she loved him so much. He was unpredictable. Would come up with the weirdest things at the weirdest times.

Her affection and respect for him didn't keep her from teasing him at every available opportunity. Although, she realized she'd gotten enough mileage out of this banter. And she wanted to know the real reason he called. Probably had something to do with Bae.

"Anyway, if you weren't calling about finding strange hairs on your body, why are you calling?" Jamie asked.

"Bae used her credit card. In Bricks, Ohio."

Jamie formed a mental image of a US road map in her head. As she was falling asleep the night before, she tried to get into Bae's mind and figure out which direction she might go. Jamie finally decided that Bae would go north. While she could've kept going directly west, there wasn't much that way. Nashville. Memphis. Little Rock. Oklahoma. Bae could go south to Atlanta, New Orleans. Maybe Dallas.

But Jamie had an instinct about her while on a mission. Technically this wasn't a mission, but it felt like it. Bae would go to the closest big city. Somewhere up north. In the rust belt. That's where the action would be. Detroit. Cincinnati. Chicago.

Maybe.

A bit of excitement came over her when she heard that Bae had used her credit card again and in Bricks, Ohio. That meant she was going north. It also was an unexpected break. Jamie didn't expect Bae to be so careless. She had taught Bae how to go dark. In other words, get off the grid so she couldn't be found. Using a credit card was the last thing you wanted to do if you didn't want to be found. That and use a cell phone, which Bae knew enough to discard.

Of course, when she taught Bae how to go dark, Jamie hadn't expected her to use those skills to avoid her.

"Text me the address and name of the convenience store," Jamie said to Alex as the annoyance for Bae's actions suddenly returned with a vengeance. While she had a lead, she still had a lot of work to do to find the little brat.

"Will do," Alex said. "There's something else that's kind of strange."

"What's that?" Jamie asked.

"Bae used her credit card five times in a span of ten minutes at the same convenience store."

"What? That is strange."

"That's what I thought. The first charge was at 3:43 this morning. Her time. She spent $53.14 on gas and snacks. I didn't know our girl had a car."

"She doesn't. She's hitchhiking. Otherwise, she'd have a receipt for a rental car. She probably offered to pay for the gas, and the driver let her. I wonder who she's with."

Jamie said that last statement as much to herself as to Alex.

Alex continued. "Eight minutes later, she charged another $8.14. For snacks."

"Okay," Jamie said hesitantly. "Not totally unheard of, but unusual. There could be any number of explanations."

"Less than a minute later, she charged another $2.53. For snacks. She used her card two more times. Each time for snacks."

"That's weird."

"Bae's weird."

"Can't argue with you there. Any chance her card was stolen?" Jamie asked.

"The signature on the receipt matches Bae's signature."

"How did you see the receipt already?" Jamie asked. "It wouldn't be on the credit card statement yet."

Before Alex could answer, Jamie said, "Never mind. I don't need to know how you did it. How's Pok doing?"

She figured Pok was helping Alex. Between the two of them, they could pretty much find any information anywhere on earth. Hidden or otherwise. They were the two best computer hackers in the world. Now that they were working together, no telling what they were up to when it came to Bae. She'd just sit back and be the beneficiary of their efforts.

Alex didn't mention Bae anymore. He spent fifteen minutes filling Jamie in on the cyberwar that was never ending. She felt slightly guilty about pulling Alex away for something as trivial as chasing after Bae. Not that they considered Bae's life trivial. It's just that they both had better things to do than keeping her from doing something this stupid. A point Jamie intended to make with Bae as strongly as possible when she caught up with her.

After she hung up with Alex, Jamie showered, packed her bags, checked out of the hotel, and got on the road, not even bothering to dry her hair. Alex would've taken twice as long to get ready if he'd been with her.

Jamie drove the three hours mostly ignoring the speed limit. She pulled into the convenience store in Bricks, Ohio and filled her car with gas even though she still had more than a half a tank. She knew Bae was long gone but hoped the clerk or store owner would have some information for her. They'd be more willing to help if she were a paying customer.

When she finished filling the tank, Jamie pulled the car into a spot in front of the store so other customers could get gas. She hated it when empty cars were in the spaces and a line of potential customers formed. People who didn't do so were rude by her estimation.

The man behind the counter looked tired. Old and tired. Hopefully, he'd been on the night shift. Otherwise, she'd have to wait around all day for the person who worked the night before to come back to work.

A thought that caused her anger toward Bae to rise up inside of her again.

Jamie waited for the only customer in line to leave.

"I'm looking for someone," Jamie said to the man. She flashed a picture of Bae in front of him. "Have you seen this girl?"

She saw the look of recognition on his face.

"Who wants to know?" he asked.

Jamie looked around the store.

"I'm the one asking about her. So, I guess I do. I thought that was obvious. Has more than one person been in here looking for her?"

Sarcasm was not the best way to get him to cooperate, but sometimes she just couldn't help it.

"I don't know nothing," the man said.

"I didn't ask if you knew anything. I asked if you've seen her. It's a simple question. A yes or no answer is all that's required. You can even use your head if you want. You don't even have to speak. Nod once if you recognize her. Twice if you don't."

He crossed his arms. "Nope. Haven't seen her."

"Did you work here last night?"

He nodded his head.

"Alone," she asked. "Did anyone else work here with you last night?"

He shook his head no.

"This girl made five charges at this register. So, you did see her. Why are you lying to me?"

He shrugged his shoulders.

"There's a ten-thousand-dollar reward for information on her whereabouts."

His eyes widened and he leaned toward Jamie.

"Are you serious? Yeah. I saw the girl. She was in here last night."

"I don't believe you. You just want the money."

"I swear. I saw her last night. A pickle of a girl. With an attitude. She about got in a fight with one of my customers. Then she wanted to pick a fight with me."

All the confirmation Jamie needed. Bae had been there.

***

Jamie bought a Coke and an energy drink and mixed them together. She had a power bar in the car which she scarfed down. A few sips of the drink and she already felt energized. More so because she had some good information. Once she mentioned the reward, the clerk became very helpful. Told her a tall tale of a feisty little girl who came in his store with two other girls.

After some questioning, Jamie learned that one of the girls was wearing a DePaul shirt and had given Bae one when she spilled a coke all over herself. That confirmed with a degree of certainty that they were headed for Chicago. Jamie could also relax some. Bae was with two college girls. Perfectly safe. For now.

Jamie would drive to Cincinnati, turn in the rental car, and catch the first plane to Chicago. Hopefully arriving before Bae did.

She put the car into reverse, looked both ways and began to back out. As she was doing so, Jamie saw a car appear out of nowhere.

She slammed on the brakes.

Their bumpers touched. Slightly. Barely a tap.

What in the world?

Jamie got out of the car and walked around to the back. An older model Chevy Caprice was catty-cornered to her car. Their bumpers were touching. No damage that she could see other than a scratch on his bumper.

A man stumbled out of the car. Tall guy. Maybe six foot four or five. Early thirties.

Jamie wondered if he was drunk.

He was clutching his neck with one arm and his back with the other.

"Why don't you watch where you're going?" the man said roughly. "You backed into me."

"I'm sorry. I didn't see you there."

Jamie was trying to replay the scene. It seemed to her like he came out of nowhere. Like he had done it on purpose.

He slumped to the ground.

Jamie knelt beside him.

"What's wrong?"

"My neck. I hurt my neck when you crashed into me. And my back."

"What are you talking about? Our bumpers barely touched."

"I got a whiplash when I had to stop suddenly. I'm calling the police."

Jamie didn't need this now. She had a plane to catch in Cincinnati. This might delay her by a few hours. Not to mention that the guy was clearly lying. He was no more injured than she was.

He let out a huge moan as he pulled out his phone.

"Do you want to settle this without me calling the police?" the man said.

"What do you mean?"

"I mean, pay me a thousand dollars, and I'll let the whole thing drop and not call the police."

"Oh, for heaven's sake!"

"I'm serious," the man said. "I'm willing to settle this without causing you a lot of problems."

Jamie had a thousand dollars in her wallet. And several billion dollars in her AJAX accounts. The prudent thing to do was to pay the man the money and head on down the road to Chicago and track down Bae. But Jamie wasn't wired that way. The principal of the thing wouldn't let her let the man get away with it. If she paid the money, he'd feel emboldened to do it to someone else.

While Jamie was contemplating the next move, her phone rang, interrupting her thoughts.

Alex.

She ignored the scammer and answered the phone.

"I know where Bae's headed," Alex said.

"To Chicago," Jamie replied.

"Shoot! You're too good. I was hoping that for once I knew something before you." She could hear the disappointment in his voice.

"Better luck next time."

"I guess. Are you on the road again?"

"Actually, I'm not. I have a question for you. I need some advice."

"Real or hypothetical," Alex said, as the excited tone in his voice returned.

"Real."

"Go ahead."

"If a man crashed his car into yours on purpose, then pretended to have a pain in his back to scam you out of a thousand dollars, what would you do?"

"I'd make the pain in his back real."

"That's a good idea."

Jamie said goodbye to Alex and hung up the phone.

22

DePaul University
Two days later

Turns out, there's not a bad guy on every corner.

In one of his books, Reeder Rich said there were. Maybe that's true in novels, but not in real life as I was finding out firsthand.

Reeder Rich made it look so easy in his books. He rolled into a city and found trouble before nightfall. I'd been in Chicago for two days and hadn't had one sniff of a bad guy. Unless you include a man who was stalking Julie. Sort of. No one had seen him since we'd gotten back to campus. Julie thought he might've moved on to someone else but wasn't sure.

She gave me a description of him, and I looked all over campus but didn't have any luck finding him. A stalker shouldn't be hard to find. By definition, he ought to be in close proximity to the target of his obsession most of the time.

A major disappointment and a colossal waste of time.

Not that the last two days hadn't been fun. Connie and Julie let me stay with them at their sorority house, which was a godsend. Kept me off the streets of Chicago. Every night, I watched the local news and realized I needed to avoid certain areas. The south side of Chicago, for instance, which was overrun with gangs. Not even I was a match for a local gang with a hundred-armed men.

The sorority house was filled with several girls, and every night we had a blast even though I might as well have been back in Richmond on my own college campus, going to classes, walking around looking for bad guys in my spare time. If I were going to hang out on a college campus that wasn't my own, there needed to be some purpose to it. I needed to find out what that was, or I was going to hit the road again.

Connie let me borrow her cell phone, and I called my mom to tell her I was in Chicago and not to worry. That conversation didn't go well. It also gave away my location. I'm sure my mom called Jamie as soon as we got off the phone. A tactical mistake on my part. Not ideal from an operational standpoint but something that needed to be done.

Jamie would come to Chicago if she wasn't already there. But the Windy City was a big place, and she'd never look for me on a college campus. For the reason I just stated. Why would I leave my college to go to another one? I'd developed a perfect cover. Jamie would never think to look for me at DePaul. I felt a certain satisfaction in knowing that I'd fooled one of the foremost CIA operatives in the world.

I was getting good at this.

Except that I told Connie and Julie my real mission. To be a female Reeder Rich.

I know.

Missions were supposed to be covert. Undercover. Under an assumed name. I told them my real name was Bae Hwa. Not Marcia. I even told them some of my exploits. About North Korea. Escaping and crossing the DMZ in the dark of night. They were impressed. I told them about Alex and Jamie, although I left out some of the details to protect their covers.

Keeping my big mouth shut was one of the things I still wasn't good at.

I couldn't help it. The way the girls gushed over me was worth the trade-off. They viewed me as a hero. A sort of superwoman vigilante. After some of the other girls in the house heard the story about how I saved the life of the drunk man in Ohio, I became a legend on campus with their friends. Some of whom came to the house just to meet me.

I ate it up and put on a show. Even showed them some self-defense moves to their amazement.

Still, I was at a crossroads. I had to do something or else go back to Richmond. I left college so I wouldn't be bored. So far, Chicago was even more boring.

Jamie never seemed to be bored on a mission. She was like Reeder Rich. Finding bad guys came easy to her. Every time she went on a mission, she was fortunate enough to get shot at. She almost always got to beat up somebody.

I wondered what I was doing wrong.

Maybe the problem was that I was looking in the wrong places. Jamie rescued girls from sex trafficking. Brothels weren't hard to find. Big cities had red light districts. Streetwalkers. Websites that promoted prostitution.

Massage parlors.

The thought hit me. Why couldn't I focus on sex trafficking? If I found a business of ill-repute, I'd find a bad guy running it. Probably someone with a gun. Also, a bunch of Johns who deserved to be taught lessons they wouldn't forget.

Jamie mentioned that she could operate in those locations without the local police getting involved. Who was going to call them? The person running the illegal brothel? One of the girls performing tricks? The men who went there expecting anonymity? Not a chance. They wouldn't want the police involved any more than I would.

It made sense that I should change my strategy and focus on rescuing girls. That'd also make Jamie proud of me. Maybe lessen the sting when she did track me down. Some mission successes under my belt might calm her down if she were angry with me. I'd already saved one person's life in Ohio. A few more and she might actually endorse what I was doing.

The library had free computers to use, so I went there and logged into one. In an area off in a corner so no one else could see the screen. My heart rate was elevated. It seemed like I was doing something wrong. Mysterious even. The unsuspecting people around me would have no idea that I was on a mission.

I knew just where to look. Jamie told me about a website where men rated sex establishments. By city. I pulled up Chicago. Hundreds of places and thousands of reviews roared onto the screen like a movie in an IMAX theatre. Scrolling through them took me nearly two hours.

The website contained a wealth of information. Locations. Names and addresses of all the establishments. The names of girls to ask for. Prices. Quality of the experience. The men were even graphic in describing the services offered. I felt myself blush several times. I knew what prostitution was, but I had no idea the extent women went to please men.

I was angry when I realized that nearly half of the men weren't pleased and left the girls bad reviews. For some reason, I couldn't help but take their criticisms personally. The women had degraded themselves in disgusting ways so the scumbags could get their kicks and most of them didn't even appreciate it.

It made me spitting mad.

I couldn't wait to get my hands on some of them.

Not in the way they would be expecting.

I decided to stick with massage parlors. The local news had a story about a street prostitute found dead in a dumpster. One of more than a dozen that year who'd been murdered. It seemed like working out of an actual business might be safer. A map on the website showed me the closest locations to the campus.

One in particular caught my eye.

Korean massage.

126 reviews.

Mostly four and five stars. A girl named Starr garnered the best ratings. The men liked her. I let out a noticeable gasp when I read what they said about her. A couple of people looked my way which was why I knew my internal shock had made it into a verbal sound noticeable to those in close proximity to me.

Satisfied I'd found my next mission, I logged out of the computer and walked straight to the strip mall where the massage parlor was located, along with half a dozen other Korean retail businesses. A grocery store. A hibachi express. A dry cleaner with a laundromat next door. A dentist's office. The parking lot was more than half full. People going about their busy days, rushing in and out of the various establishments, probably having no idea the depravity going on in the massage parlor next door.

The massage place had a *Help Wanted* sign in the window.

Excellent. I had wondered how I would approach the business. The sign gave me the perfect excuse.

It took me more than ten minutes to get up the courage to go through the door. The fact that people started to notice me loitering around the parking lot was the impetus to finally make my move.

Cook or take the pot off the stove, Curly said to me on more than one occasion during my CIA training at the Farm. He told me that he had cleaned up the saying for my benefit, since I was only fifteen at the time. I tried to get Alex and Jamie to tell me the real saying, but they wouldn't.

Now that I was becoming their peer, maybe they would start treating me like one. That thought emboldened me to the point that I walked right into the massage parlor with no more hesitation.

The door opened into a lobby with half a dozen red chairs. A coffee table with magazines strewn on it was in front of a small couch. A small fountain in the shape of a buddha sat on the counter. Which I thought was funny. North Koreans had no religion other than the worship of the emperor. Buddhism was highly prevalent in South Korea. Along with Christianity which I had converted to. Thanks to Alex and Jamie and my American mom and dad.

A tiny woman opened a door that probably led to the back and walked into the room and stood behind the counter.

"Anyoung haseyo!" I said to her in Korean. Hello or good morning. Interchangeable.

She returned the greeting, and I instinctively bowed. As a sign of respect for an elder. Although I had no respect for what this lady did for a living and what she put the girls through.

"I saw your sign. I want to apply for the position," I said, assuming that she spoke English.

She did, but it was broken.

"How old you?"

"Twenty-three." I lied. I was seventeen and certain I was already doing something illegal.

The old woman pursed her lips and made a slight spitting sound even though nothing came out of her mouth. The gesture meant she didn't believe me.

"You go school?" she asked.

"Yes. The college. I'm older than I look."

"Where you from?"

I gave her the name of the town I was from in North Korea. Her eyes widened in surprise. Very few people escaped the clutches of the dictatorship and lived to tell about it. The woman was obviously from South Korea and had immigrated to the United States. I could tell she was impressed as her demeanor changed.

"You do men in Korea?" she asked.

"Yes. Since I was thirteen."

She wouldn't have any reason to doubt it.

"You work in America?"

"In Virginia. For two years. I'm good at it."

"We don't pay you."

I didn't understand what she meant. She pointed to a rate sheet on the wall. Forty dollars for half an hour body massage, sixty for full hour, the sign read in big letters. I already knew the going rate from the website. In reality, I probably knew more about what happened behind the closed doors than she did.

138

"We get that. You work on tips. I get half of tips," the lady said. She pounded her chest with her fist as she said it. "Take it or leave it."

"That's fine," I said. "When can I start?"

She looked me up and down. Then shook her head no.

"That won't do. You need clothes. High heels. For men. Nightie."

"I can buy something."

She shook her head no again. "I have some. Might be too big. Have to do."

She opened the door she had come in from and motioned for me to go through it.

"What's name?" she asked.

"Marcia."

"I'm Carolyn."

We both knew those weren't our real names.

She led me down a long hall. On each side were rooms. The doors were open, and I could see a massage table and a dimly lit lamp on a small table against the back wall in each. Each table also had a scented candle on it and what looked to be various bottles of lotion. The entire hallway smelled like a candle store.

At the end of the hall was another door. Carolyn opened it and we went through it into a kitchen. A girl was sitting at the table eating something. A beautiful Korean girl. Rich black hair. Innocent features. Scantily dressed.

"This Marcia," Carolyn said. "She new girl."

"I'm Starr," the girl said in perfect English as she held out her hand for me to shake it.

"Nice to meet you." I felt like I already knew her. Based on all the detailed reviews I'd read on-line.

Carolyn left the room and returned a few seconds later. She laid a sexy, lacy, partially see-through lingerie similar to what Starr was wearing on the table, along with a pair of high heels. She showed me where the restroom was so I could change.

Once I donned the new clothes, I immediately felt self-conscious. Even though I was mostly covered, it felt strange to be in sexy attire. I also almost fell over trying to walk in the heels.

When I walked out of the restroom, Carolyn was already gone.

Starr said, "You look cute."

"Do you ever get used to heels?" I asked.

"Don't worry. You won't have them on for very long," Starr said with a sly grin on her face.

I wasn't sure what she meant and was too embarrassed to ask. Starr was experienced. I had given Carolyn the impression that I was as well. I didn't want to blow my cover with Starr in the first five minutes by asking.

"What's it like working here?" I asked after I had sat down across from her. The heels were already killing my feet.

"It's the best place I've ever worked. The money's good. Carolyn stays out of my business. I stay out of hers. Do your job well and everyone's happy."

I asked at least a dozen more questions. I wanted to see if Starr was someone who I could rescue, but she didn't act like she was being held as a slave, so I didn't pursue it.

"How much do you make? If you don't mind me asking," I said.

"Six figures. More than a hundred grand."

My mouth almost flew open.

"I've got a lot of regulars," Starr said. "The key is to be good at what you do. Guys don't mind paying for good service. I charge more than most. But can get away with it."

"How much do you charge?" I asked. "For tips?"

"Sixty dollars for hand. Hundred for oral. Two hundred if they want all of me."

She blurted out the numbers like she was telling me the price of cars on a used car lot. Unemotional.

"I never discount," she said. "If you do, word will get around then you have to give everyone a discount."

That made sense.

"There are some things I won't do," Starr said soberly.

I remembered reading that in some of the reviews. The only negative comments she got.

Then I saw it.

The slight hurt in her eyes as she winced. The shame which her eyes couldn't hide. Jamie talked about it a lot. Every working girl had that same look. Slave or not. I recognized it now. It didn't matter if the girl charged a thousand dollars for one hour or ten dollars on the streets of Miami. They all felt the same guilt, shame, and condemnation.

Impossible to hide even behind the confident air.

I suddenly felt sorry for Starr. And hatred for the men.

Before I could say another word, Carolyn appeared in the door-way.

"You're up," she said and pointed to me. "Room four." She left the room before I could say anything or ask any questions.

I stood to follow her.

Starr stopped me. "Give her a minute to get the man in the room."

I sat back down.

The door was still open, and we heard footsteps and talking. A large man was lumbering down the hall. Starr's mouth gaped open when she saw him. He had to weigh four hundred pounds.

"Don't let him get on top," Starr said to me in a serious tone. "He'll crush you."

I didn't know what to say.

A panic came over me.

I wasn't ready for this.

23

One hour later

I felt like I needed to take ten showers.

Even then, I wasn't sure I'd get the vile smell out of my nostrils. It certainly wouldn't cleanse my mind of the image of the four-hundred-pound man lying naked on the massage table that was now permanently seared into my memory.

Starr must've seen the disgust on my face when I walked into the back area, because she said, "What's wrong, Marcia? What happened?"

I'm glad she mentioned my cover name. I'd forgotten for a minute that I wasn't Bae.

"Nothing!" I said with contempt. "He only wanted a massage."

"I'm sorry. That happens. Not often. But sometimes."

Her voice trailed off as she said it. Starr was sitting on a couch in the lounge. Reading a book. I was really growing to like her.

I wasn't through venting though.

"The guy was a jerk," I said with disdain. " 'I prefer a deep tissue massage,' he said to me. He didn't *just* want a massage. He kept saying, 'I like it hard. Harder! Harder!' He was talking about the massage. I tried to rub him harder. I really did. There's only so much I can do. I only weigh ninety pounds. My hands were killing me after ten minutes."

I shook them out. They were still cramping and sore.

"Did you ask him if he wanted more than a massage?" Starr asked. "If a guy says he only wants a massage, I try and tempt him to buy at least a happy ending."

I was familiar with that term from reading the reviews. If nothing else, this trip had been educational.

"I tried to sell him some sex," I said. "But I think I screwed it up. I couldn't remember the prices you told me."

I paused. I was sounding like an amateur and risked exposing my cover.

Oh well.

Part of me didn't care. I wanted to take off my stupid outfit, gather my things, and get out of that place as fast as possible. But then I would've failed. Curly always said to never give up. Jamie had lots of missions go sideways, and she made the best of them. I had to do the same.

I was replaying the last hour in my mind like a movie. As soon as I walked into the massage room, I lost all perspective. Became frozen like a deer in headlights. Especially when the man said, "I want you to start with my glutes."

"What are glutes?" I asked.

"My butt," he said.

My mouth must've flown open a mile wide.

He didn't see it because he was lying face down on the table. I wanted to punch him right then and there. Of course, my mission at the massage parlor would be over before it started, so I stiffened my back and tried to play along.

As soon as my hands touched his rear end, I wanted to throw up.

I realized immediately that I hadn't really thought things through. A business establishment wasn't a good idea. On the streets, one-on-one in a car or hotel room would be a better plan. If alone with the John, I could do whatever I wanted to him without getting caught. More dangerous for me as well, but I'd have more control, and no John in the world had my skills.

Too stinking late now!

I was proud of myself for at least trying to make the best of it.

The conversation came rushing back into my mind like a raging river.

"Don't you want sex?" I had asked him.

"No thank you. Just a massage."

I pressed the issue. That's where I got confused and began to stammer around. Forgot the things Starr had taught me.

"I'll do me for a hundred," I said. "If you want my hands, it's two hundred. Sixty for..." I had forgotten what the other was.

Now that I was out of the room and in the back with Starr, I suddenly remembered what the prices were.

I slapped myself on the forehead.

"I forgot how much you charge," I said to Starr after she looked at me inquisitively.

My mind immediately returned to what had transpired.

"Just a massage," he replied after I botched the menu of options and prices.

Of course, I never intended to do any of those things. The man was lucky he said no. Jamie taught me a move a few years back. The Death Touch, she called it. Dim Mak was a Cantonese term for it. A pressure point move. Applied to the back and side of the neck against the carotid artery. It cut off the oxygen to the brain and can cause instantaneous death if applied properly.

I didn't intend to kill the man. Jamie showed me how to apply just enough pressure to knock someone out. That was my plan. Once the man was out, I intended to go through his wallet and take his money. Find his address. Take pictures of him in the compromised position. Warn him. Threaten to send those pictures to his girlfriend or wife. Or the police.

I hadn't anticipated the possibility that he might turn down the offer of sexual favors. It never occurred to me that I would be expected to give someone a massage for an entire hour! How could

I threaten him if he turned me down for sex? I was the one who would look bad to the cops if they were called.

At some point I realized that even if he didn't call the cops, he'd complain to Carolyn, and I'd be out of a job. This mission was doomed from the outset and could never last for more than one massage.

The decision was made.

I was quitting.

This was a waste of time.

I started thinking of ways to say goodbye to Starr. She was the only thing I'd miss from that god-forsaken place. The only reason I wasn't rushing out of there.

"How do you do guys like him?" I asked her. "He was disgusting."

"You get used to it," Starr said with resignation. "Sometimes you just have to close your eyes and pretend you're someone else. Most of the guys who come in here aren't a Chippendale model. Although... those guys can be a pain in the neck as well. They think they're God's gift to women. Like they are doing me a favor by having sex with me. I almost prefer geeky guys to them. They're usually nicer. Nice is good in our line of work."

"He kept grabbing me!" I said to Starr.

She pursed her lips. "Oh. He's one of those. He says he doesn't want sex but tries to cop a feel. Get some for free. I've had some of those. From the size of the man, he probably can't do the deed anyway."

My entire body shuddered just thinking about it. I had a new appreciation for what Starr went through every day.

The man had his arms hanging off the massage table. He kept brushing his hands against my leg. A few times he reached up and touched my rear. I knew he did it on purpose. I swatted his hands away several times. Even scolded him. That seemed to embolden him.

When he got more aggressive, I tried to apply the death touch to his shoulder area. He started moaning. Like he liked it. I couldn't find the right spot through all the layers.

"Harder," he said.

I changed tactics and karate chopped him across his back.

"I like that," he said in a seductive tone. "Do it again."

I did. The next time, harder.

He acted like he liked it even more. Then I hit him too hard, and he told me to stop. That's when I ended the massage. After only forty minutes. Rushed back to the kitchen. He was probably wondering what happened to me or if I was coming back.

I let out a noticeable sigh and plopped down in the chair across from where Starr was sitting on the couch. My feet hurt from standing in those heels for all that time.

"I think I handled it okay," I said to Starr. I was trying to regain some professionalism in her eyes. I didn't want her to think I was totally incompetent.

Carolyn opened the door and walked in. She handed me three dollars.

"What's this?" I asked.

"Your tip," Carolyn said.

Starr giggled, but then put her hand to her mouth to stop herself.

"I did all that for three dollars!"

I was mad.

"He no like," Carolyn said. "Pay six dolla tip. Want someone else next time."

I raised my hands in the air in exasperation. "Fine by me. I don't want to do him either."

"You do better next time or fired!" Carolyn said.

"I think she handled it well," Starr said. "I don't think I could've done any better. The man wanted something for nothing. Marcia did just fine."

I smiled at the compliment as it warmed my heart. I couldn't believe that I was appreciating accolades of this nature.

What have I gotten myself into?

"You're up in five minutes," Carolyn said to Starr. "Room five."

Carolyn left the room and disappeared down the hall.

"Thanks for sticking up for me," I said.

"No problem."

"I have a question. A sign in the room said, No Sexual Services Provided. Maybe that's why the man didn't want any."

Starr shook her head. Then lowered her voice. "Carolyn put those there. That's in case we're raided by the cops. That's Carolyn's way of covering her, you know what. We're the only ones who would get in trouble."

"Doesn't she know we offer sexual services?"

"Of course. She gets half the tips. Who pays a two-hundred-dollar tip for a sixty-dollar massage? Nobody. You need to do better next time though, or Carolyn will cut you loose. I could tell she wasn't happy about the six-dollar tip."

There wasn't going to be a next time. As soon as Starr left the room, I was going to get out of my stupid and ridiculous nightie, and the high heels, and get out of there as soon as possible.

"I guess I'd better get to it," Starr said. She sat the book down on the couch and stood up.

I immediately recognized the book by the cover.

Reeder Rich.

I couldn't believe it.

I had to stay now. Until Starr finished with her guy. I had to tell her that I was a female Reeder Rich. My cover would be blown, but she needed to know I wasn't some rank amateur. I was a bad dude like Reeder. Starr would be impressed.

Starr hugged me as she walked out of the room. "Hang in there," she said. "You have to sift through some bad apples to get to the good ones. Comes with the territory. Wish me luck."

"Good luck," I said.

When she was gone, I took her spot on the couch and started reading through the book even though I'd read it three times.

Ten minutes later, Carolyn appeared in the doorway.

"You're up again, Marcia. Five minutes. Room eight. I go to store. Be back in hour."

I started to object, but as fast as she appeared in the doorway, she disappeared.

Perfect.

I suddenly realized it was a good thing. I could redeem myself. Things would be different this time. I'd use my Reeder Rich skills on the next guy. Show Starr who I really was. Carolyn would be gone so she couldn't stop me. I'd be gone before she returned.

I waited a couple minutes, then walked into room eight. A man was lying on the table, covered by the white sheet. All his clothes were laying on the chair against the wall including his underwear, so I assumed he was naked.

"What did you come in for today, honey?" I said in a seductive and sweet-sounding voice.

"A massage," he answered.

My heart sank.

"What else?" I asked. I didn't think I could do another hour massage for three dollars in tips.

"What do you charge? For other services?" he asked.

That was a good sign.

"Sixty for hand. Hundred for oral. Two hundred for all of me." I wasn't going to forget this time.

"How about one seventy-five for all three?"

I remembered what Starr said. Never discount your fees. All the guys will expect it. But what did I care? This was the last one anyway.

"Sounds good," I said.

The man stood from the massage table, startling me.

He walked over to where his clothes lay on the chair. I hadn't realized how tall and buff the man was. He was definitely good looking. Over six foot. Two hundred pounds. At least. Muscular. Maybe a former football player. Not as big as Jamie's husband, Alex, but nearly as big.

The bigger they are, the harder they fall, Curly had said.

The man pulled his wallet out of his pants and handed me two one-hundred-dollar bills from it. Not the least bit self-conscious that he didn't have any clothes on. I tried to keep my eyes focused above the waist.

"I don't have change," I said.

"Don't worry about it," he replied. "Hopefully, you'll be worth it."

"Great. Let's get started."

He moved toward me like he was going to kiss me. Held out his hand like he was going to put it behind my head.

I slapped it away.

His eyes widened in surprise.

"So, you like it rough," he said. "So do I."

He moved in closer. I could smell his aftershave and the mouth-wash he'd obviously used a few minutes before.

"I'll show you rough," I said.

I brought my knee up swiftly toward his groin area. As I lifted my right leg off the ground, my left ankle rolled slightly because of the instability of the high heels. My knee only glanced off his thigh. I barely kept my balance.

When I straightened, I saw an angry look on his face as his eyes had turned to coals of burning embers. He backhanded me across the cheek and I fell to the floor before I realized it.

I tasted blood.

My knee landed hard on the floor taking the full brunt of my body weight. A loud thud sent pain up my leg and through my spine.

Aftershave guy was on me in a second.

I tried to resist, but he was too strong. Fortunately, he was behind me.

I tried to wiggle away, but he had me in a bear hug. I was kicking my feet in the air. A waste of energy. So, I brought my right foot up in the air and brought it down on his foot. The sharp high heel smashed on the top of it, and he cried out in pain. He released his grip and began to hop around, holding it.

I ran for the door. He stopped hopping and came after me. As quick as a cat. He probably was an athlete. This time he threw me to the ground. My head hit the table and then the floor and then I saw stars.

This wasn't good.

I had to do something quickly.

I tried to call out to Starr but realized she was still with her client and probably wouldn't hear me.

What would Jamie do?

Aftershave man's face was suddenly buried in my neck. He tried to get us in a position where he was on top of me, but I kept scooting away until I was against the wall. Sitting up slightly to make it more difficult for him.

With my right hand, I grabbed the back of his shoulder and squeezed tightly. The Death Touch. I squeezed with all my might. He let out a yelp. Within seconds he collapsed on the floor, on top of me. I was pinned against the wall. He was out or dead. I wasn't sure which.

Starr must've heard me scream because she burst in the room. She grabbed the man by the hair and pulled him off of me.

I lay on the floor. Stunned. Bleeding from the lip. My hands were shaking.

"What happened?" she asked.

"He attacked me. Slapped me across the face. I thought he was going to kill me."

"Go in the back and get yourself changed and cleaned up," Starr said.

"Is he dead?"

The adrenaline was flowing. I might've squeezed too hard.

Starr felt for a pulse.

"No, he's not dead. Go!" she shouted. "Now. Before he wakes up and before Carolyn gets back."

I rushed to the back of the building and into the kitchen. Gathered my things and went in the bathroom and changed clothes. The nightie was torn. The mirror didn't show much damage to my face. My lip was bleeding slightly and might bruise, but I was okay.

A smile formed on my face. I'd gotten the best of a two-hundred-pound athlete.

"That'll teach people to mess with me," I said to my image in the mirror.

When I came out of the bathroom, I heard Carolyn's voice down the hall. Shouting at the man. Telling him to get dressed and to get out of there before she called the police.

I picked up Starr's Reeder Rich book off the couch. Opened the inside flap. A pen lay on the table beside the couch.

I wrote in the book, *Thanks for all your help. B.H. A female Reeder Rich.*

Then I rushed out the back door.

After I got a distance away, I realized that I owed Carolyn a hundred dollars.

I don't care.

24

Central Inn
Chicago

Jamie grew angrier at Bae by the day.

She'd been looking for the little twit for three days now and still didn't have a clue where she was. Bae had gone off the grid, making Jamie's search for her more difficult. Ironic, since Jamie was the one who taught her how to go into hiding without being found. Bae seemed to be doing everything right. She had ditched her cell phone and wasn't using her credit card, so Jamie had to resort to good, old-fashioned detective work.

Bae had to sleep somewhere. Jamie figured she'd follow the playbook. Seek out a motor lodge or inn. Some place that didn't have security cameras. It had to be a place that didn't require a credit card deposit or driver's license to check in. By definition, someplace seedy. Where all kinds of nefarious transactions took place. Only a hunch, but Jamie figured Bae would be staying at one of the thirty-six motor lodges, motels, or inns in and around Chicago that fit that description.

Jamie had spent the last two days going from location to location. What a colossal pain in the neck Bae was being. Jamie had half a mind to get on a plane and go back home and let the chips fall where they may. Bae obviously thought she was old enough to make her own decisions and was avoiding Jamie. At the same time, she considered Bae like the little sister she never had. Other than Alex, Jamie had no family.

That thought caused a tear to well up in Jamie's eye. She couldn't bear the thought of losing Bae as well. She had to keep pressing on. If she found Bae, and the girl refused to come home with her, then at least she had tried.

Jamie pulled into an alleyway across from the Central Inn of Chicago and began to scope it out. Eventually, she'd go into the manager's office and flash a picture of Bae. No worker would ever give up that information except for money or if under duress, but Jamie was trained to tell when someone recognized a photo. Even if the employee didn't recognize the picture, it didn't mean much. Bae could've checked in when the person wasn't working. Or could've been wearing a disguise. Or simply snuck into one of the rooms.

Which made Jamie's job harder. At some point, she might need some luck. Bae was like the proverbial needle in a haystack.

Alex could be of some help, but he was knee deep in another mission. He was still on their island in the Caribbean working with Pok. The two of them were chasing Somali pirates around the Indian Ocean. Not literally, but in cyberspace. Pok had found a bank account belonging to one of the leaders of a large pirate organization. He emptied all the money in that account and transferred it into an AJAX secret account.

Then followed the money trail to dozens of other accounts. Which he promptly stole and deposited in AJAX's coffers. At the rate they were going, they could put a serious dent in the organization.

Pok was a master at navigating banking transactions and breaching firewalls. It's what he did for years stealing money for the North Korean regime. Now he was using those skills effectively to bring down nefarious groups around the world.

This was Alex's first foray into pirates, and he was loving it. He was obsessed with bringing down the entire organization.

She understood. Saving one girl from sex trafficking was one thing. Shutting down an organization was another. Those were the big wins. Stealing money from one pirate and emptying his bank account was a big deal. Crippling his organization so he couldn't operate was tantamount to winning the Super Bowl in Alex's mind.

Jamie simply couldn't ask Alex to spend time helping her when he had bigger fish on the line. One of several points she'd make to Bae in the strongest of terms when she found her.

The only lead Jamie had was that Bae was seen in Bricks, Ohio with some girls wearing DePaul University shirts. Jamie had conjectured that Bae might be headed to Chicago. Confirmed when Bae used one of the girl's cell phones to call her mom and tell her she was okay.

Alex said he'd find the name of the girl and her exact location when he got a chance. Jamie was still waiting on that intel.

She spent a few hours at the campus but didn't see Bae anywhere and hadn't expected to. Why would Bae leave one college campus to hang out on another? Jamie wished that's where she was. Knowing Bae, she was likely going to end up in South Chicago at some point. One of the most dangerous areas in the United States. More dangerous than many of the third world cities Jamie operated in.

In fact, most countries run by dictators were quite safe. Regimes typically ruled the countries with iron fists, cracking down on all illegal activities including things like drugs and prostitution. Citizens weren't allowed to own weapons. Punishment was swift and harsh. Often cruel. Even petty crime could come with serious retribution. Fear was how the dictators controlled the people. That generally made the streets safe to walk.

The only ones allowed to be corrupt in those countries were the leaders. If an area was dangerous, it's because the leaders had lost control. Like Chicago's south side. Where gangs were able to operate with impunity. Violent crime was rampant. Gun control laws restricted citizens from protecting themselves. From Jamie's perspective, the best deterrent to violent crime was citizens being allowed to carry guns. A bad dude thought twice about robbing someone if that person might be carrying a concealed handgun.

Jamie could only hope Bae wasn't stupid enough to venture into that part of town. She tried to get into the seventeen-year-old's head. Not easy to do considering Bae was impulsive and a wide-eyed optimist. Bae thought there wasn't anything she couldn't do. Jamie loved that in Bae. She was fearless. But reckless.

A combination that could get you killed.

What kept Jamie from getting on that plane and going home.

She had to find her before it was too late.

Now she had a different worry.

The Central Inn was unlike anything she'd ever seen before. Definitely a one-star establishment in a seedy part of town. The inn was one story with thirty rooms. All in a row. The doors were on the outside, and a car could drive right up to the room and load or unload.

All of that was unremarkable.

The strange part was that the parking lot was more than half full. Even stranger, several of the rooms had a man standing outside the door. Like he was guarding it. Not just any man. An armed man. A bad dude. Hardened. Rough looking. With gang-like characteristics.

Over the course of several hours, Jamie observed more than a dozen men drive up—Johns likely—park their cars in front of a room, go inside, and come out thirty minutes to an hour later, get in their cars, and leave. After they were gone, the guard no longer stood in front of the room and went to a room at the front end of the building nearest the office and hung out there with the other guards.

Jamie thought about going to the front desk and flashing a picture of Bae to the clerk and seeing if he recognized her. She didn't for a couple of reasons. One was that she didn't want them to see her face yet. The other was that the guards would likely stop her and question her. She didn't have a good reason for being there.

While she tried to wrap her head around all the activity, another car pulled up. A large bodyguard-type man got out of the driver's seat. He looked around like a secret service agent scoping out the area.

She didn't think he could see her, but she instinctively slumped back in the seat of her car.

A few seconds later, the man opened the back door to the car he'd just stepped out of, reached his arm inside the back seat, and pulled out a young girl.

Jamie sat straight up.

The girl looked to be no older than sixteen or seventeen. The man gripped the girl's arm like he was clutching something valuable. She struggled to pull away from him, but he must've outweighed her by a hundred pounds, and her efforts were in vain.

The girl looked around the parking lot. Like she was looking for someone to help her. Her face was gripped in fear. Jamie had seen that look hundreds of times.

The goon pulled the girl along like she was a rag doll to one of the rooms and knocked on the door. A man opened it. A John. Jamie had seen the man go into the room about ten minutes before. The girl resisted, but the bodyguard forced her inside. The guard shut the door and stood out front, leaving the girl alone inside the room with the man. Obviously against her will.

Jamie knew the signs of a sex trafficking operation. This was unlike any she'd ever seen before. Some girls were coming in and out of the rooms freely. Allowed to get in cars and drive off. They'd return a few minutes or hours later.

They were clearly working girls but not sex slaves. The bodyguards stood in front of their rooms only when they had men in them. Probably providing security for the girls.

This was a well-run organization. Coordinated. Most likely a gang.

A big fish.

Bae was not on Jamie's mind now. She was considering the possibilities that she had stumbled upon a large sex trafficking organization in Chicago. No telling how many girls had gotten caught up in it.

While Jamie was considering her options, a late-model, four-door sedan pulled into the parking lot. A well-dressed woman stepped out of the car. She looked Cuban. Black hair. Beautiful features. Stunningly gorgeous. Two girls got out of her car as well. Dressed like prostitutes. Cuban lady led them to the front part of the inn and opened the door to two rooms.

It seemed like the girls who were there voluntarily worked out of the rooms nearest the office. The rooms in the back, farthest away from all the activity was where the sex slaves were forced to service the Johns. Which made sense.

Who was the Cuban lady?

She acted like a Madam.

At the same time, she also had the look of law enforcement. She carried herself like someone who was highly trained. Jamie knew how to spot that look. Something about the way she walked let Jamie know she wasn't an ordinary madam running a sex-trafficking organization.

Less than five minutes later, the woman got back in the car and left. Jamie memorized the license plate number and took a picture of the car and then texted it to Alex to see if he could find out who owned it.

She wasn't sure what to do next. What she wanted to do was rescue the girl that had been forced into the room. But what would that accomplish? This was a big operation, and she had no doubt lots more girls were being trafficked. Bringing down the organization should be the focus.

That'd take time. Surveillance. Intelligence gathering. Threat assessment. She might even need to bring law enforcement.

But Jamie couldn't quit thinking about the young girl in the room. Forced into doing despicable things.

She couldn't help herself.

The girl needed help.

Jamie exited her vehicle, crossed the street, and went around the side of the inn so she wouldn't be seen. Came from around the back. It was around nine o'clock at night and the moon was behind the clouds, so she had the cover of night to protect her. The inn wasn't well lit either for obvious reasons.

Once around back, she was able to come to the front of the inn on an outer walkway that connected the two buildings. She pressed her back against the wall around the corner from where the guard stood.

Jamie was carrying her weapon but didn't pull it. She wanted to have both hands free. The guards were no doubt carrying weapons as well, but she had the element of surprise. She also hoped to get in and out without being seen.

Jamie took a deep breath and measured her heart rate. Elevated, but in a good range.

She waited until she heard the door open. Peered around the corner. The John exited the room, got in his car, and left.

Jamie waited for the girl to appear.

When she did, she stepped out of the shadows and onto the walkway which led in front of the rooms. The guard was looking in the room and didn't notice her. She was still in the dark. The only light was coming from the room.

Jamie walked toward the man. She was within six feet of him, and he still didn't know she was there. So, she called out to him.

"Hey," Jamie said. "Can you tell me where room 8 is?"

Jamie was wearing all back, so it'd be difficult to see her. The guard could easily mistake her for one of the working girls. At least that's what she hoped happened.

The man turned his head away from her and pointed down the walkway.

When he turned back toward her, his face met her elbow. She brought it forward with such force, the entire right side of the man's face cratered as she heard the familiar sound of cracking bones.

The man collapsed to the concrete sidewalk in a heap. Fortunately, only making a slight thud.

The girl let out a throated yelp. Thankfully not a scream.

"I'm here to help you," Jamie said to the girl who seemed frozen in fear. She bent over the man and searched his pockets looking for an ID.

"Close that door," she said to the girl roughly. She didn't want the light on them.

Jamie found the ID and slipped it into her pocket.

"You're safe now, honey," she said to the girl. "Help me drag him around the corner."

The girl hesitated.

Jamie grabbed the man's arms and began to drag him across the sidewalk back in the direction she had come. The girl suddenly bolted and took off running. Before Jamie could react, the girl was around the corner and out of sight. She decided not to follow. At least the girl was free.

She dragged the man around to the back of the inn and deposited him in a row of trees. Checked for a pulse. She hadn't tried to kill the man but hit him hard enough to cause serious brain damage. He had a pulse and was breathing, so she figured he'd survive until someone found him.

She backtracked to her car. Watched to see if anyone had spotted her or noticed the guard missing.

When she had a chance to collect her thoughts and catch her breath, she was satisfied. She'd freed one girl. That was something. And her cover wasn't blown. It couldn't be tied back to her. Hopefully, the girl would find safety somewhere. Maybe go home. Learn a lesson and not get herself back in the same predicament.

She wasn't as angry with Bae now. At least some good had come out of it. Jamie had a sex-trafficking organization in her crosshairs. An operation she might be able to bring down. This was right in her element. She was determined to investigate it and either take it down herself or notify the authorities once she had more information.

Jamie maintained her position in the alleyway. A perfect place to watch the activities without being seen.

A few more cars came and went. Fortunately, no one noticed the man missing or went looking for the body.

Another car pulled up.

Same kind of bodyguard type got out and forced a young girl out of the car. Took her to a room where a man was waiting. The guard stood outside. Same M.O. as before.

This time Jamie stayed in her car.

She didn't want to risk being discovered and wanted to gather more information. The girls had to be held at some location near there. When done, the man would likely drive her back to where they were holding the girls. Jamie wanted to know that location. She could rescue all the girls at once rather than one at a time.

As soon as the guard's body was discovered, the gang would likely go into panic mode and might move the girls. Jamie needed to act before then.

After nearly an hour, the John came out. As much as it pained her to do so, she kept her position. When the girl exited the room, the guard forced her back into the car and pulled out of the parking lot.

She followed it.

***

I thought I heard a commotion. Or felt it. Sounded like a girl let out a yelp.

I looked out the window of my room. Room 4. Central Inn. Didn't see anything.

"You're just hearing things, Bae," I muttered to myself.

So, I went back to my bed and laid my head down on the pillow. The Hispanic woman named Rita told me to wait in the room. That they'd bring me a John sometime later tonight.

I couldn't believe my luck.

I'd stumbled upon a large prostitution ring. Jamie always said it's better to bring down an operation than to just rescue the girls.

This was my chance to do something bigger than Reeder Rich ever did.

I can't wait.

25

I flipped on the television and then immediately flipped it off and turned my thoughts to the events of the day. The fortuitous route that had brought me to the Central Inn where I was within a few minutes to a few hours of encountering my first John.

After the fiasco at the massage parlor, I went back to the college library to look for locations that might be conducive for street walking. Standing on a corner picking up tricks seemed better to me than working in a massage parlor. There I'd be one on one with the Johns. Either in their cars or at a hotel room.

Curly said during my training that if I couldn't beat up a girl my own age regardless of her size, then he hadn't done his job. He said that more than two years ago. I was more proficient now. Proven by how easily I'd taken out that cad at the massage parlor.

Actually, it hadn't been easy. But he was twice my size. An athlete. I still bested him. I wasn't naïve enough to think I'd win every fight with ease. I would win them though. I figured that if Curly were assessing the situation now, he'd say there wasn't a John I couldn't beat up in a fight regardless of size.

After choosing a general area known for prostitution, I scouted out a location. One that wasn't in the worst part of town but was a place Johns knew to go to find working girls. I found just the place and caught a taxi down there. The location was perfect. Bustling with a number of retail stores in the vicinity. About a dozen or so girls worked the area. Cars were clearly cruising the boulevard evident as I saw the same cars over and over again with nervous men behind the wheels.

The other working girls didn't seem happy that a new girl was infiltrating their territory, and they gave me constant lip about it.

"It's a free country," I argued and ignored them. Not really worried about their false bravado. If I could best any John alive in a fight, I could certainly take down any of those drug ravaged skanks.

Then I remembered Jamie's words. *Every one of these girls has a story. They ended up on the streets for a reason. No little girl grows up wanting to be a prostitute. They see and experience unthinkable things that no woman should ever have to go through. Many of them were abused as children. Imagine the horror of being so desperate that you would sell your body to disgusting men so they can get their kicks. Have compassion. These girls are victims. They may not act like it sometimes. That's only because they don't know anything else.*

So, I took Jamie's advice and said a prayer for them and tried to be as nice as I could. The girls weren't usually around long enough to have a real confrontation anyway. The routine was set. A car would pull to the curb. With the passenger side window down. The girls would take turns approaching it. They'd state their price. Half the time, it was accepted, and the woman got in the car. The other half, the men drove away and stopped at another corner.

Before I got a chance to approach a car, an unusual woman showed up. A Latin American or Hispanic lady. Well-dressed. Confident demeanor. Stunningly gorgeous. A different class than the girls working the street.

She began talking to the girls. Then got around to me.

"My name's Rita," she said.

Pretty Woman held out her hand, and I shook it before I had a chance to assess whether I should or not. Firm handshake. The woman was fit. Muscular in a feminine sort of way. I didn't think she could possibly be a working girl. Her face didn't have that withered and worn look. I wondered if she could tell the same about me.

I didn't give her my name.

"How would you like to make some real money?" she asked.

My defense alarms went off in my head like sirens inside of a firehouse.

"I do okay here."

A lie. I hadn't gotten close to getting in a car with a John. Of course, this woman wouldn't have any clue my real reason for being there or the skills I had. She'd never understand it. Probably hadn't even heard of Reeder Rich.

She should be warned though. If she got in my crosshairs, I'd take her down with one blow to her pretty little head.

"I mean some real money," Rita said. "Without having to stand on the corner all night. Aren't your feet hurting yet?"

She had a point. I was wearing sneakers, but my feet still hurt. I'd been on my feet most of the day. My hands were still sore from giving the man a forty-minute massage.

"I don't know what you want from me," I said.

"I manage a lot of girls. I provide them with security and a place to stay."

A place to stay sounded good. I was planning on leaving the sorority house first thing in the morning.

"What does it entail?" I asked.

"How old are you?" the woman asked.

"I'm twenty-one," I answered.

She turned her head to the side and twisted her lips. Clearly, she didn't believe me.

"I'm seventeen," I blurted out before I had a chance to stop myself. For some reason I trusted this woman. The urge to tell her everything was strong inside of me. I was also curious about the opportunity. The woman ran an organization. A group of women. This might be an opportunity to take down a prostitution ring.

"Come with me," she said. "I'll take care of you. It's dangerous out here on the street."

"I can take care of myself."

"I'm sure you can," the woman said. "What's your name?"

"Bae," I said without thinking.

"Hi Bae. It's nice to meet you. I think we're going to get along really well."

Reluctantly, I got in the car with her. Not sure where she was taking me. Although thrilled about the possibility that she might be leading me into some real action. The entire day had been disappointing.

The woman drove me to a motel called the Central Inn of Chicago. The first thing I noticed was all the activity around the seedy establishment. The parking spaces were more than half full. Several men were loitering around. Bad guys. With guns. They looked like gang members.

"Who are they?" I asked. Not scared, just curious.

"They belong to a gang called the Strikers," Rita said, confirming my hunch. "They will provide your protection. I told you I'd take care of you. Whenever a John comes to the inn, a guard will be outside your door at all times. If you need anything, you just call out, and they'll come to your rescue in a second."

"What do I need to do?"

I saw a pained look cross her face. Almost a grimace. I wasn't sure what to make of that. Maybe she was ashamed of what she was doing.

"Just do what you do best," she said almost soberly. "The men will come to you. You get fifty percent of the take. The Strikers get fifty. Don't skim any off the top. Even the tips. Report all of it. Give the Strikers their share. You don't want them mad at you. These are not people to mess with."

Neither am I, I wanted to say but held my tongue.

I wasn't even sure I was going to hang around. This was like the massage parlor. An organization. My plan had been to attract a John from the street corner and get alone with him. Then use the *Death Touch* or some other form of physical force to subdue him.

Use the opportunity to teach him a lesson he'd never forget. More importantly, make him afraid to ever pick up a working girl again.

That wouldn't work at the inn under the scrutiny of Rita and the Strikers. I went in the room anyway and didn't voice my concern to her. I would at least use the opportunity to gain intelligence.

The motel room was nice enough. It had clean towels and clean sheets. The furnishings were simple but adequate. Supplies for freshening up were in the bathroom. A box of condoms sat on the table beside the bed. Everything a working girl would need.

It might be ideal for prostitution, but not for what I had in mind. When a guy came to my room, I could beat him up. Apply the death touch. Knock him out. Then what? I could only do that once. There'd be no way to explain my actions to Rita or the guards. I was energized by the fact that it was an organization, but as much as I wanted to take it down, I wasn't sure how to do it.

Not from the inside anyway.

I plopped down on the bed and considered my options.

An idea came to me.

The room had a window on the back wall that led to an area behind the inn. I checked it. It was bolted shut. Much to my chagrin. I struggled and strained but couldn't open it. I looked around the room for something to pry it open with but couldn't find anything.

My idea was to sneak out the back window and hide in the shadows behind the motel. Take out the guards and the Johns one at a time. Without them knowing I was there. Once all the thugs were out of the way, I could talk to the girls and convince them to leave the place. Consider another line of work. Some would, some wouldn't. At least they'd get the chance.

A better plan than hanging around the room waiting for a John to come to me. I'd be in the same situation I was in at the massage parlor. With no good options. After considerable work, I finally loosened the window enough to raise it about six inches. Probably enough for me to squeeze my tiny frame through if I held my stomach in.

Before I could escape out the window, I heard a noise coming from outside the door. A gruff voice. Sounded like my guard.

The door opened and a man walked in. A John. With a lustful grin on his face.

The guard held the door open and said to me, "Just call out if you need anything. I'll be right outside."

It seemed like he was saying it for the John's benefit. A warning to not try anything.

The John was wiry thin. Like a runner. Super fit. Arrogant. I could tell by how he held his nose up in the air. He also had money. Evident by the Rolex watch on his wrist. Why does a man like that have to pay for sex in a seedy motel room?

His entire demeanor changed as soon as we were alone together. He seemed angry.

"What's the meaning of this?" he asked roughly.

"I don't know what you mean," I retorted, not sure why I was feeling bad, like I'd done something wrong.

"I want my money back!" he said in a raised voice.

"I don't have anything to do with that."

"How old are you?" he asked. "Ten? I want a real woman."

"I'm more of a woman than you've ever had before!" I said with as much sass and attitude as I could muster.

"I wouldn't do you," he said angrily. "Not in a million years. You're too small. Not worth the money."

"I wouldn't do you! Cause you're too ugly!"

He became enraged. His eyes burned with anger. He took two steps toward me. I took two steps toward him. We were face to face. I could smell his cologne and fancy deodorant.

My fists were balled.

How was I going to strike him? Fists? Knee? Elbow? Round-house kick?

Jamie liked to kick Johns in the groin. She said it gave her a certain satisfaction that she didn't get from just knocking out a few teeth. She wanted him to remember her every time he had sex for months if not years to come.

My knee would do the trick.

Before I could act, the door opened, and my guard came in. His eyes widened in surprise. He'd probably heard the shouting. He took two large steps and was next to us in a flash.

The guard put his hands on the man and told him to back off.

The John didn't respond right away.

The guard pushed the John away from me.

That made the John even angrier. He swatted the guard's hand away. Then started mouthing off with the same attitude he'd shown me.

"I pay for a woman, and you guys friggin give me a kid. I don't even know if she's even a girl. Looks like a little boy to me."

He was mocking me. I didn't like it and lunged for him.

The guard put his big paw of a hand out and easily held me back. Then stepped between us so I couldn't get to the man.

"I'm going to have to ask you to leave," the guard said to the John.

He clearly was on my side. Rita had been right about the protection. I could see where the guards would be helpful to a working girl. Better than being out on the street getting into a strange car with unsavory characters.

I got the feeling my guard was street wise and tough as nails and not someone to mess with.

"I'm not leaving until I get what I pay for," the man said belligerently.

The guard took a step closer to the man. Now they were face to face. Their noses within inches of each other.

The door was still opened, so the heated exchange could probably be heard in the parking lot and in the other adjacent rooms.

"If you don't leave, I'll throw you out," the guard said.

They were about the same height. The guard had a slightly bigger build.

Suddenly, without warning, the John reared his head back and brought his head forward at a rapid pace and headbutted the gang member. Right below the bridge of his nose. The best place to strike a blow. The impact was so hard I heard the cracking sound of two heads hitting.

The guard staggered.

So did the man who hit him. He raised his hand to his head and wobbled like a drunken man.

Then fell to the floor. Unconscious.

The guard fell to one knee. He was bleeding from his nose. I knew how much a blow to the nose hurt. Then he tipped over onto the floor. His head bounced off the carpet.

They were both out.

I went to the John and searched for his wallet. I found it and put it into my pocket. Took the Rolex off his wrist and put it around mine. Then searched the guard and found his wallet. Jamie always said to use every opportunity to collect intelligence. I wanted to know who these people were. I considered taking the man's gun but thought better of it. The last thing I wanted was to get involved in a gunfight.

All I wanted to do was to get out of there as soon as possible. The door wasn't the best way of escape. More guards were outside. I could hear them coming.

I hesitated.

Decided to take the gang member's cellphone as well. He'd have contacts in it. Maybe higher ups in the organization. The few-second delay would be worth it to gather what might be a treasure trove of intelligence.

Turned out to be a mistake.

A gang member suddenly appeared in the doorway. He saw me rifling through the guard's pocket.

"What are you doing?" he shouted.

I stood to my feet and took two steps back.

He knelt down next to his friend.

"What did you steal from him?" he asked me.

This time I didn't hesitate. Nor did I answer.

I bolted for the window. I could feel him stand and follow.

I squeezed through it. Barely. He grabbed my foot as I was almost out. I gave him a kick. My shin scraped on the windowsill, and I cried out in pain, but the kick did the trick because he released my foot and I fell hard to the ground.

He wouldn't be able to squeeze through the window and follow me. That gave me a head start.

I raced down the back of the motel.

Then I saw it.

Another body. In the trees. One of the gang members.

What?

Strange.

The hesitation cost me. Before I knew it, several of the gang members were blocking my exit.

They saw the man on the ground. Looked me up and down. In disbelief.

One of them knelt beside the man. Felt for a pulse. The other two kept their eyes on me.

"He's breathing. But barely," the man said.

"Why are you beating up all our men?" another one of them asked. A smaller man. Although from the looks of him, he looked street hard. Like he would cut out your heart and toss it in the trash and not lose a second's sleep over it.

I shrugged my shoulders.

The men thought I beat up all three men. I was perfectly willing to let them think that. They might think twice before messing with me.

"I don't think that pip-squeak could beat up anyone," the third man said.

I spread my feet and took up a fighting stance. My fists out in front of me like I was ready to box them. Something Curly said not to do. Let your adversary think you're helpless for as long as possible. Always keep the element of surprise on my side.

It'd be a while before all of this was second nature to me. I could see why Jamie thought I wasn't ready. After I beat up all these men, I wondered if she'd still feel that way.

I suddenly spun. To catch them off guard.

Sent a roundhouse kick toward the stomach of the man who was mocking me.

I was too far out of range. He stepped away from it easily enough. It left me out of balance. The second guy swept my planted leg out from under me. I fell to the ground. One of them kicked me in the ribs, taking my breath away. I struggled to get it back.

One of the men jerked me to my feet. I swung wildly at his head. Without any breath behind the blow to give me energy. It glanced off his shoulders.

I saw the punch coming. Toward my jaw.

I didn't feel it though.

Everything went black.

26

If Chicago had a worse area than the one Jamie found herself in, she didn't want to see it.

She followed the gang member's car from the Central Inn to a location in the southside of Chicago. A two-story house with white siding. Noticeably, in better conditions than the other houses in the neighborhood. A driveway ran behind the houses in an alleyway, and she managed to get close enough to watch the man drag the young girl out of the car and into the house.

Jamie's heart broke as she watched it unfold. She wanted to act right then and there and free the girl and could've done so. But over the years of doing this gut-wrenching work of rescuing girls from human trafficking, Jamie had learned to focus on the big picture. She could save the one girl now or save all the girls later. Including the one in her sights.

That didn't make the decision easier, only justifiable.

Curly had ingrained in her not to go into a mission unprepared. He'd say she needed to do reconnaissance. Surveille the house. Assess the risks. Develop an extraction plan. As much as she wanted to, she couldn't go Rambo and attack the house right then and there. She had no idea how many hostiles were in the house. Where the girls were being held. If she had enough firepower and ammunition.

She had no extraction route. Jamie didn't even know if her car was big enough to hold all the girls.

The worst possible scenario would be to save the girls and find out there were so many in the house, she couldn't rescue them all. Actually, the worst-case scenario would be that she'd get gunned down as soon as she tried to enter the house. Actually, the worst case would be if she were killed sitting in her car by an assailant and a bullet she never saw.

Jamie realized that trying to surveille the house from her car put her in a precarious situation. She stood out like a clown in a church. Even though it was dark outside, she felt conspicuous. This seemed like the type of neighborhood where any unfamiliar car was treated as an intruder. It wouldn't be long before someone spotted her and came to investigate. She thought about driving around, but even cruising the neighborhood had its risk. Someone would notice her. This wasn't the kind of area where people came and went freely at night.

So, she called Alex.

"Guess what?" he said without saying hello.

"You found a hair in your ear," Jamie said.

"How did you know?"

"I know my husband well enough to know that ever since I mentioned it, you've been obsessively looking for one. All men have ear hair so I'm sure you found one."

"I did, find one."

"An epic tragedy. Like a Voltaire."

"Like who?"

"Alex! I don't have time for this. I'm kind of in a tough spot here."

"Hold on."

She heard the sound of computer keys being typed in the background.

"You are in a rough area," Alex said when he came back on the line. "What are you doing on the southside of Chicago? I hope Bae's not there."

"I've stumbled upon a sex trafficking ring," Jamie said.

"Why am I not surprised? You're like a human trafficking magnet. All you have to do is show up someplace, and you find one. You're a human bloodhound."

"Maybe it's faith. God directing my paths. Anyway."

"By the way, the house just ahead of you on your left is a known gang hangout," Alex said in a more serious tone. "The Strikers is the name of the gang that operates out of it."

Jamie was going to ask Alex to research that, but he was one step ahead of her. She started to ask him how he knew but didn't have time.

"I don't think I should stay in this alleyway," Jamie said. "It won't be long until somebody notices me."

"Yeah. Down there, they don't call the cops. They call the local gang. The gangs were doing neighborhood watches before any of us ever thought of it."

"That's why I'm calling you."

"I thought you were calling me because you love me."

"I do love you," Jamie said. "But can you find me an abandoned house nearby? Hopefully one with a view of the house. And a garage if possible."

"Do you want it to have a whirlpool and sauna?" Alex said sarcastically.

"Just a garage." She was annoyed but couldn't help but smile at the quip.

More typing on the computer keys. Alex had big hands and pounded the keys like a concert pianist playing Mozart. In their house, she could usually hear him from several rooms away.

Jamie let out a sigh. Normally, she loved bantering with Alex. Right now, she felt vulnerable. Like a deer approaching a feeding station. Knowing danger was lurking, but unable to force herself to turn around and run away as fast as possible. She needed to get to better cover, which was why she had called him. While his voice was reassuring, they were wasting valuable time. Jamie kept flinching like a bullet was going to smash through her car door window at any moment.

Curly always said the bullet that kills you will be the one you don't see coming.

The silence on the line lasted nearly a minute which gave her more time to assess her surroundings. A vacant house would be a good place to hole up in. One with a garage would give her a place to hide her car. She didn't feel comfortable leaving the car on the street or in the driveway. If the house was vacant, neighbors might get suspicious if they suddenly saw a strange car parked in front of the normally vacant house.

"Perfect," she heard Alex say.

Before she could respond, he said, "The house right behind the gang house is vacant. Can you see it? Just ahead on your right. Not directly behind but catty cornered."

"I see it. Thank you."

Jamie kept the headlights off and slowly inched back out of the alleyway.

Then came to an abrupt stop.

Headlights suddenly filled her rearview mirror. The lights were bright enough that she couldn't ascertain the make or model of the vehicle.

She started to slump down in her seat but decided not to. That'd look even more suspicious to the person in the car who was coming upon her location quickly.

She reached for her gun.

"Let me call you back," she said to Alex, then hung up before he could respond.

The car was familiar.

The Cuban lady. The one she'd seen at the inn. She passed Jamie. Their cars were so close, Jamie could've reached out and touched it if the window was down.

The lady stared straight ahead. Didn't even look Jamie's way.

The Cuban woman kept going down the alleyway and pulled in the driveway of the Striker's house.

Jamie maintained her position and watched as the Cuban lady got out of her car and walked into the house.

That sent a bolt of anger through her like an electrical current. She'd gone back and forth trying to figure out who the Cuban lady was and her connection to the Strikers. She appeared to be law enforcement, but Jamie was confused by the woman's behavior.

Undercover agents had boundaries. In the CIA, female operative couldn't act as prostitutes even if it allowed them access into the inner circle of a sex trafficking ring. Men operatives couldn't have sex with any of the victims, even if it might benefit the operation. Cuban lady appeared to be recruiting women into the Strikers' prostitution ring. Now the woman could be tied to the sex trafficking operating out of the house.

That ruled out law enforcement in Jamie's mind. Unless the woman was deep undercover. Operating under a different set of rules. She had a hard time wrapping her mind around that possibility.

She could analyze that later. Getting to that vacant house was the priority at that moment. Jamie quickly backed out of the alleyway before another car came. She drove around to the next street over and found the vacant house. It had a garage. She got out of the car, raised the garage door, and quickly pulled the car inside. Then closed the garage and said a prayer thanking God for the safe haven.

Then said a second prayer. Hoping that no one saw her enter the garage and close it. If a gang of armed men descended on the house, she might have a problem. The prudent thing to do would be to leave the garage door open for a quick getaway. But she couldn't risk someone seeing her car. If a suspicious car was seen in the garage, they wouldn't call the police. They'd call other gang members who would come to investigate.

Jamie picked the lock on the door and entered cautiously. With her gun drawn. She went from room to room to make sure the house was clear, which it was. The house was completely vacant, except for the back bedroom, which was strange. The only room in the house with anything in it. A mattress. A stool. Some trash consisting of empty soda bottles and food packaging.

The house had a perfect view of the Striker's house. It almost looked like someone had used the room for surveillance. Who?

Law enforcement?

A homeless man?

Rival gang members scoping out the competition?

Trying to figure out who'd been there was a waste of mental energy. She just hoped whoever was using it before her didn't show up that night. She liked her chances if they did. Checked her gun for reassurance.

She felt safe there and thought she'd made the right decision. It didn't take long for her to see the wisdom of her choice. Over the course of two hours, Jamie saw at least a dozen gang members come in and out of the house. Mostly, they came outside to smoke.

A few cars came and went as well. One carrying a car full of gang members. Two carrying young girls. One of the girls couldn't have been a day over sixteen. She was manhandled roughly by the gang member and basically dragged into the house.

That made at least three who were being held there.

The Cuban lady was still inside. When she came out of the house, Jamie was tempted to follow her and look for an opportunity to confront her. She rejected that idea because the opportunity might arise to rescue the girls. A plan was formulating in her mind.

During a lull in activity, she used the opportunity to do some research on her phone. The first thing she did was scope out an exit route in case she had to make a quick getaway with the girls.

She looked up everything she could find in the CIA database on a gang called The Strikers. They were the only gang in Chicago large enough to pull off this kind of operation. Jamie was impressed by the efficiency. Disgusted but impressed.

An operation that size required money. Sex trafficking was profitable, but the gang probably had other sources of income too. Drug running was Jamie's guess. Maybe arms trading, although she didn't see any evidence of that. The group might have some machine guns in the house or in the cars, but the men weren't carrying any.

Which was a relief. Jamie liked her chances against a lot of threats. Machine guns weren't one of them. Her Sig that she had on her hip had seventeen bullets in the clip. She was so proficient that seventeen bullets usually resulted in eight to ten kills. However, she didn't like her chances against Uzis—guns that could spray bullets at a rate of ten rounds per second and held up to forty rounds. Those were her worst nightmare.

Machine guns were a great neutralizer against someone with her skills, which was why the gangs loved them. The men didn't have to be good shots to gun someone down.

Jamie settled in for what she presumed would be a long night. Tested out the mattress and decided it was clean enough to use. A few hours' sleep would do her some good.

Her phone rang, breaking the eerie silence in the dark room.

Alex.

"You said you were going to call me back," he said.

"I've been a little busy."

"I have some info for you. The girl's name is Connie O'Connor."

"What girl?"

"The girl who had the cell phone Bae used to call her mom. She's a college student at DePaul. I have an address and a phone number."

Jamie had been so distracted by the turn of events she'd temporarily put Bae out of her mind for the last few hours.

"Text it to me," Jamie said.

"On its way. There's more. The license plate you sent me is unregistered. Can't find it anywhere. Are you sure you got the right numbers?"

Jamie rolled her eyes.

Alex was talking about the Cuban lady's car. She'd texted him the license plate number from the Central Inn and asked him to come up with the owner. Jamie expected him to say, the plates were stolen. Not that they were unregistered.

"If you're off one number, I can't track it," Alex added.

The comment wasn't unreasonable, although Alex knew her memorization skills were impeccable. She knew she gave him the right license plate number because she'd also taken a picture of the Cuban lady's car and had verified the number before she sent it to him.

"I'm sure," she decided to say rather than make an issue of it. "What do you make of it?"

"An undercover car, maybe?" Alex said. "FBI. DEA. ICE."

"The lady looked like law enforcement to me."

"I think you have your confirmation."

"I'll try and get a picture of her and send it to you. See if you can come up with a name."

"Will do."

"Thanks for the help."

"Always at your service. Don't be careful."

Something they always said to each other when one of them was in a dangerous situation. Curly always said that careful will get you killed. Their way of saying to each other to be careful.

Jamie's mind was spinning with conflicting thoughts and a myriad of questions. One kept rising above the others screaming for her attention.

If the lady were law enforcement, why didn't she rescue the girls from the house?

27

When I awoke, I found myself in the trunk of a car with my hands tied and my head aching. It took several seconds for the fog to wear off and for me to get my bearings enough to remember how I'd gotten into this predicament.

The first thing I did was extricate myself from the bindings which wasn't hard to do. Alex had taught me how to free myself from everything from zip ties to handcuffs. Once free, I contemplated my next move. Impossible to know, since I didn't know how many kidnappers I was dealing with, where they were taking me, or what their intentions might be.

The good thing was that I wasn't dead. Not yet anyway. Jamie said if she was breathing, then she still had the advantage. That's how I felt. My kidnappers were in for a big surprise when they opened that trunk.

That didn't mean I wasn't in grave danger. Curly said when in a predicament, I shouldn't make the false assumption that if they wanted me dead, I'd be dead already. They might be driving me to a secluded location where it'd be easier to do the deed or dispose of the body. Planning to torture me for information.

I needed to come up with a plan to keep any of those things from happening. The element of surprise was on my side. Apart from skill, Curly emphasized surprise as the biggest factor in surviving a dangerous situation.

My captors think I'm still bound by their flimsy makeshift restraints. I'd pretend I was still unconscious and fly out of the trunk like a character hiding in a haunted house. I was thankful for their incompetence. They were messing with the wrong girl, and I'd make them pay for their foolishness.

I could also let things play out and see what happens before I act. Play it by ear. Improvise. Act on the spur of the moment as the situation dictated. That might be a better plan.

This could actually be a good thing.

My luck might be turning.

They hadn't killed me for a reason. More than likely, the men who took me were lower on the totem pole, and killing me was a decision beyond their proverbial pay grades. In that case, they were probably taking me to a secure location to wait for further instructions.

Maybe they were taking me to their leader.

Even better.

It's possible that this was the best thing that could've happened to support my mission. I wanted to take down the whole organization. Jamie always talked about getting into the bowels of a sex trafficking organization.

That thought made me laugh, which eased some tension but also caused a pain to shoot through the side of my head.

"Why do you call them bowels?" I had asked her.

"Because the insides of these organizations produce the foulest, dirtiest, and stinkiest human excrement in our society," Jamie said. "They are literally the human debris of mankind. Pure evil. The lowest of the low. My job is to flush them down the toilet."

I felt emboldened by Jamie's words. It's possible these lowlifes were driving me to where they keep other girls. Maybe to their headquarters.

I'd soon know. The car began to slow. Then came to a stop.

Thank goodness. I was tired of bouncing around. It made my head hurt worse.

I reattached my bindings so that it looked like they were on but were really not restricting my movements at all. I closed my eyes and pretended to still be unconscious. If I were going to make a move, I'd be better off waiting until I were out of the trunk and standing on my two feet. If the odds were overwhelming, I would look for an opportunity to run away. If only one or two men were holding me captive, I'd look for an opportunity to knock them out. When they least expected it.

The trunk opened and I lay motionless.

A man lifted me out of the trunk and carried me toward a house. Only one man.

Easy-peasy.

From my position, I could strike him in the stomach, biceps, neck, or under the bridge of the nose. All I had to do was loosen my bindings and pretend to wake up.

Then pow!

I hesitated.

Curiosity was getting the best of me.

What was in the house? More girls? Was this the headquarters?

I decided to wait and let him take me inside.

When he got to the door, he flung me over his shoulders like I was a sack of potatoes. That made his backside vulnerable to a kidney shot or an elbow to his ribs. If I didn't act now, I'd miss the perfect opportunity.

But then I'd never know who or what was in the house.

I continued to wait.

The man used his free hand to open the door and push his way past the door and into the house. I heard two voices. I presumed they were two fellow gang members. The clang of dishes told me we were in the kitchen. I didn't dare look. As much as it was killing me not to.

"Open the basement," the man carrying me said gruffly to one of the other men.

I heard someone fiddling with a lock. I kept my eyes tightly shut.

We started descending steps.

A basement?

The bowels?

The door closed behind us.

I could feel the presence of other people in the room.

My captor dumped me onto a mattress. Then released my bindings. I continued the ruse and lay there motionless.

"Is she dead?" someone asked, in a meek voice. Sounded like a young girl.

The gang member grunted an unintelligible answer and walked back up the stairs and exited the room. I could hear the locks being reattached.

"I'm very much alive," I said as I sat up, startling the girls.

One of them let out a screech. Several let out noticeable gasps.

I stood to my feet. Felt dizzy and held my hands out to steady myself. I knew the symptoms of a concussion. If I had one, it was minor. I'd be fine.

My focus was now on the girls and my surroundings. Five young girls. In a makeshift prison cell. They looked to be fifteen or sixteen. I was clearly the oldest. Their senior. The elder in the room.

I needed to take charge and reassure them.

"My name is Bae, and I'm here to rescue you. Tell me your names and ages."

The girls were hesitant. They didn't know if they could trust me. Understandable.

"Don't worry," I said. "I can help you. We're going to get out of here. Are you being held against your will?"

A stupid question to ask. They were in the basement, with a door secured by heavy locks.

"Are they making you have sex with men?" I asked.

A look of shame came on their faces telling me everything I needed to know.

"Are you with the police?" one of them asked.

"Of course, she's not," one of the other girls answered for me. "She's not any older than we are."

"I can't tell you who I'm with," I said confidently. "But I can assure you that I'm older than all of you, and I have the skills to get us out of here."

"Your skills must not be very good, or you wouldn't be down here with us," one of the sassy girls said.

I liked the attitude, but it was annoying. I wondered if that was how Jamie felt about me sometimes.

"I let them bring me down here," I retorted. "I wanted to find where they were keeping the girls so I could rescue you."

"Another lady said she was going to help us," one of the girls said.

"What lady?" I asked. "What does she look like?"

"Her name is Rita. She has black hair. Hispanic lady."

"I've met her. You can't trust her."

Rita was the Cuban lady who had recruited me into the prostitution ring. The reason I was in that basement.

"She said she was coming for us," the girl anxiously. "That she'd rescue us."

"Don't believe her," I said emphatically. "She's the enemy. I'm your best hope of getting out of here alive."

"She's coming here today. I think. She told us not to do anything stupid. That we should wait for her."

"Don't believe her," I said. "Leave everything to me. When she comes into this basement, I have a big surprise for her. Everybody, gather around me."

The girls formed a circle.

I told them my plan to make Rita rue the day she ever met me.

***

The next morning

Rita cried all the way to work.

It broke her heart to leave the girls at the house the night before. It also pained her to recruit the girls who were working at the Central Inn. She justified it by knowing they were safer there than on the streets. That didn't make her feel better though. She'd devoted her entire career to helping girls escape the throes of sex trafficking. While operationally recruiting the girls was ingratiating her with the Strikers and giving her unprecedented access, it still felt wrong. Counterintuitive. Recruiting the girls and sitting back doing nothing while the young girls suffered was almost more than she could bear.

She wished there was another way.

While technically, the girls she recruited were there voluntarily, in a way they weren't. They were trapped. By their past. By the fact that they had no hope for a future other than selling their bodies to men. Whatever led them to that point, they weren't doing it voluntarily. Not really.

Rita wasn't sure how long she could keep doing it. The undercover work anyway. Not the part about rescuing girls. She'd never not stop helping women in trouble. Not as long as she had the strength.

But something had to give soon. The young Korean girl she rescued off the street the night before was a good example. Rita didn't know her story, but the girl couldn't have been more than seventeen even though she claimed to be twenty-one. What was so horrible in her life that she didn't think she had any other option but to sell her body to men for their carnal pleasure? Did she run away from home? Was she abused as a child?

She seemed different from the other girls. The girl had spunk. Rita had to give her that. Probably just a façade. A fake bravado. Rita knew that the girl had to be dying inside each time she had sex with a strange man.

I can't even imagine.

185

Rita's phone rang, interrupting her thoughts. Her undercover phone. The one she used to communicate with the Strikers.

She roughly brushed away her tears. Then took a deep breath and answered it, careful to make sure her voice didn't crack and give out any sign of weakness.

"Hello Reginald," she said.

They'd gotten more comfortable working together. To the point that she could speak to him in a more casual tone. Her undercover skills were good. Reginald didn't suspect a thing.

"We have a problem," he said.

Rita's heart began to race. It always elevated when she was on the phone with a Striker or in their presence. A problem wasn't what she expected that morning. She tried to tamp down her imagination which was trying to figure out what the problem was. She'd know in a few seconds.

"What's up?" she asked in a casual tone. If she didn't sound alarmed, then it'd maintain her persona as someone never rattled.

"The Korean girl you brought to the hotel last night created an incident."

Why was she not surprised? The girl did have a chip on her shoulder.

"What kind of incident?" Rita asked.

"She beat up two of our men and one of our customers."

"What? That girl doesn't weigh a hundred pounds with weights around her ankles."

"She put one of our men in the hospital."

"You're kidding! Your men must not be very good guards if they can't protect themselves from a young girl."

She'd soon know if that was the wrong thing to say.

"Shiv wants her taken care of."

A sense of dread suddenly flooded her body. To the point she could feel it all the way in her toes.

"What does that mean?"

"That means he doesn't want her around anymore."

"I agree with that. If she's beating up customers, she obviously can't be working for us. I'll fire her immediately."

"I don't think you understand. He wants her at the bottom of Lake Michigan. Where no one will ever find her."

"You're going to kill her? Because she beat up one man. It might not be her fault. He might've deserved it."

"Shiv wants you to do it," Reginald said.

"Me?"

"You got a problem with that?"

Rita wasn't sure how to answer that question and maintain her cover. It might be consistent for her to say she's not a murderer. She just recruited girls. Playing along might get her deeper in the organization.

"I don't have a problem with it per se. Seems a bit drastic, don't you think? I don't understand why we can't just cut her loose."

"That's the way Shiv is. He doesn't like it when people cross him. He wants to make an example of the girl. And he insists that you make her disappear."

"I can do that."

Rita realized the obvious. If she didn't do it, then someone else would. Agreeing to it might buy her some time and prolong the Korean girl's life. This also might be a test. To see if she really was one of them.

"In fact, I think it's my problem to deal with," Rita added. "I don't want the girl touched until I get there. I'll take care of it. I recruited her. I'll get rid of her."

"Good."

"Where is she?"

"She's in the basement at Dexter Street."

"I'll go over there this morning."

Rita hung up then pulled out her other phone and dialed Scully. He answered on the second ring.

"We've got a problem," Rita said.

28

Jamie felt like she was on a mission. It had all the rigors of a full-blown sex trafficking rescue operation. Lack of sleep. Irregular eating and drinking. Intermittent rushes of adrenaline. Fights. She'd had more confrontations with bad guys on this mission than her last three combined.

What felt unfamiliar was operating inside the United States. That and having the emotional connection to Bae, who had fallen off the face of the earth. Her only lead was the DePaul college girl who'd given Bae a ride to Chicago. Bae used the college girl's phone to call her mom. Jamie intended to pay the girl a visit that morning. She thought about calling her but wanted to have the element of surprise.

With any luck, Bae was sound asleep on the girl's couch. She'd drag Bae out of there and put her on the next flight home. If she refused to go, then at least Jamie could quit worrying about her and focus on the mission to rescue the girls which now had most of her attention.

The Strikers were bad news. No doubt about it. All gangs were, but this group of thugs was into sex trafficking. The epitome of evil. It's one thing for them to kill other gang members. Even steal property. When a group sunk to the level of depravity that involved trading in the misery of human sex slaves, then they reached the lowest of the low as far as Jamie was concerned. And they deserved to be permanently put out of business.

Something she intended to make happen, sooner rather than later.

She intended to surveille the group and gather evidence against them. Then either turn it over to authorities or take the group down herself. Either way, she intended to rescue the girls being held in the house.

First, she had to take care of the Bae situation so she could clear that out of her mind.

Jamie left south Chicago and drove toward DePaul college. On the way, she found a coffee shop called Spyhouse Coffee. The name piqued her interest for obvious reasons. She ordered a muffin, bagel, and Danish and their largest size coffee. She scarfed down the food because she was starving and enjoyed the best coffee she'd had in months.

Went back and ordered another one to go. The caffeine was so strong that within ten minutes, she felt like she'd been given a B-12 shot.

Feeling better, she drove to the address Alex had given her on the DePaul campus and found a sorority house. While it was still early in the morning, lights were on, and she could see girls already coming and going.

The door was unlocked, so Jamie walked in. The house was full of activity. Girls rushed around getting ready for class. Some were in the kitchen, others flitting in and out of the downstairs bathroom. Several greeted her. It brought back memories, having been a long time since she was in a college setting.

It also made her feel good. Maybe she didn't look as old as she felt. No one thought she was out of placc. Perhaps she still looked like a college girl.

She finally got the attention of one of the girls.

"I'm looking for Connie," she said.

Jamie didn't include the last name to make it seem more casual. Like she'd been friends with Julie all her life.

"Upstairs. Second door on the left. Connie's not here. She's in class. Her sister Julie is home though."

Jamie went up the stairs and found the room. Hesitated. Wondering if Julie was still awake. She thought about walking through all the rooms and looking for Bae herself but thought better of it. Before she could knock, the door opened and a brown-haired girl with bright eyes and a wide smile stood at the doorway.

"Are you Julie?"

" I'd better be, or my parents are in for a shock the next time they see me."

Jamie instantly liked her.

"I'm looking for Bae. I'm her aunt."

"Are you Jamie?"

An even wider smile appeared on Julie's face.

"I'd better be, or my husband's in for a shock the next time he sees me."

Even though Jamie flashed a cheerful demeanor when she said it, a flame of anger rose inside of her like someone had ignited a pilot light on a stove. She went to great lengths to protect her CIA cover. While it was probably harmless, she didn't like the fact that Bae had such loose lips. Something she'd deal with as soon as she got her hands on the girl. One of a number of things to add to the list.

"I hear ya," Julie said in a charming southern drawl. Maybe Virginia. North Carolina. Georgia.

"Is Bae here?" Jamie asked.

"Her stuff is."

Her anger for Bae turned to excitement. She was getting close.

Julie added, "She didn't come home last night. To be honest, I'm kinda worried about her."

The excitement immediately turned to concern. Concern turned to worry. Worry made the leap to dread. Jamie had an ominous feeling that Bae was going to find trouble. She hoped she wasn't one day too late.

"Do you know where she went?" Jamie asked.

"Can you walk with me?" Julie said. "I'm late for class."

"Sure."

They went down the stairs and out the door. Julie walked fast, which was good for Jamie. She hadn't had a chance to get in a good workout in several days.

"Bae told me a lot about you," Julie said.

The anger returned.

"Then you probably know I'm not her aunt."

"She didn't say exactly. Bae is very fond of you."

"I'm fond of her too. She's like a sister to me. That's why I'm here. I'm afraid Bae might be in danger."

"I hear you. She's, like, obsessed with finding bad dudes and beating them up."

"I love Bae, but she may be in over her head. Any idea where I might be able to find her?"

"She talked about a lot of things. I didn't really take any of it that seriously. Sounded kind of silly to me. She talked about going to some of the local bars and looking for bad guys there. Maybe going down on the streets and talking to some hookers. Bae kind of rambles on. It's hard for her to focus. Have you noticed that?"

Before Jamie answered, Julie suddenly stopped walking.

"Dang it!" she said. Then added, "Pardon my French."

"What's wrong?" Jamie asked, looking around but not immediately seeing a threat.

Julie turned her back, so she was facing away from the direction they were walking.

"You see that guy over there?" Julie said. "Up ahead and to the right. Behind the tree."

Jamie looked that way.

"I see him."

"He creeps me out. He's been stalking me. Since the beginning of last semester."

"Have you contacted the campus police?"

"I have. They say they can't do anything unless he breaks the law."

"That's how it works," Jamie said. "I'd just ignore him. Eventually, he'll lose interest and go away."

"I'm afraid of him."

She did look genuinely terrified. Her entire perky demeanor had changed in a flash.

"Has he ever done anything?"

"One time he came inside our house. At night. You know how it is. The door's always open. One of the girls confronted him, and he ran away."

"Wait right here."

Jamie walked toward the man with a purpose. When he saw she was headed his way, he turned and started walking away from her. Jamie quickened her pace. He started to run. Fine by her. She needed the exercise and was wearing black tights, a tee shirt, a sports bra, and sneakers. She easily matched his pace.

Jamie even let him maintain a little distance. Some buildings were up ahead, and he appeared to be headed toward them. She let him go that way so they'd be out of the view of the busy campus when she confronted him.

As expected, the man ran into an alleyway between the buildings. Then stopped running and looked back. Jamie was practically on him.

He held his ground. She stopped about three feet away from him.

"What do you want?" he said sharply.

His fists were balled, but his weight was shifted on the wrong foot.

"I want you to quit stalking my friend."

"I don't know what you're talking about."

The man was medium build. Below average in the looks department. Not at all a threat.

Jamie took two steps toward him. He unexpectedly reared back and threw a wild punch toward her head.

Everything about the punch was wrong. Wrong idea. Wrong leverage. Wrong execution.

Jamie easily stepped inside of it, grabbed the man's other wrist, and circled around so she was behind him. His momentum had carried him forward, and it took little effort for her to maintain control of his arm.

From behind, she shoved him into the wall, so his cheek was pressed against the brick That had to hurt.

He let out a sissified yelp.

Most men like this were wimps. They stalked women because they didn't have the confidence to actually engage with them normally. It was more complicated than that, and a show of force didn't always work. The man had a sick compulsion. An obsession that could turn violent. Perhaps it already had with another woman somewhere in his past. Julie might be the first. Hard to know.

"If you go anywhere near my friend again, you'll have me to answer to," Jamie said in as strong a tone as she could muster. "Next time I'll break both your arms and your legs. Do you understand?"

"You've got the wrong guy. I don't know what you're talking about."

Jamie forced his arm up higher on his back. She didn't want to break it but wanted it to be sore for a few days.

"You're hurting me," he cried out. "I'm calling the police."

"You do that! We'll tell them how you're stalking my friend. Came into her house uninvited. Tried to hit me."

"Let me go."

She released his arm. What she was doing wasn't really working and wouldn't unless she escalated the violence and actually did hurt him. Something she wasn't willing to do. She barely knew Julie, and the man hadn't actually hurt her.

Once his arm was free, the man scurried away like a frightened cat. Jamie went back to where she'd left Julie.

"I wouldn't go anywhere alone," Jamie said. "At night, especially."

"You don't think he's going to quit bothering me?"

"I don't know. But call me if he does."

Jamie gave Julie her number. "Also call me if you hear from Bae. I'm going to take her things out of the house and go look for her. Please call me. She needs to go home."

"I will."

Julie gave Jamie a hug and headed off to class. Jamie followed her the rest of the way at a distance to make sure she got there safely. Then practically sprinted back to the sorority house to get her heart pumping and a little bit of a workout in.

She found Bae's things and left.

No closer to finding Bae than she was when she got up that morning.

***

FBI field office

An argument had broken out between Rita, Scully, and the other members of the Strikers task force.

"I have to get the Korean girl out of that house," Rita argued.

"We're not saying you shouldn't," Scully said. "But do it in a way that you don't blow your cover."

The issue was that the task force wasn't prepared to act yet. They were focused on the drug angle. Rita on the sex trafficking. They were using her to get intel on the location of Shiv's drug operation. They didn't have anyone else undercover inside the organization and were counting on her to provide the intel. They were clearly concerned about the girls but not as much as they were concerned about stopping the distribution of the drugs.

Rita understood the territorial tension. This wasn't the first time she had dealt with it.

"How am I supposed to do that?" she asked after several of the members of the task force made their arguments.

"Tell Shiv you killed the girl," Scully said.

"What if he wants proof?"

"Tell him you disposed of the body."

"What about the other girls? If Shiv will kill Bae, then the other girls are in grave danger. He'll kill them too. I need to get them out while I can."

Scully leaned forward in his chair. "Find the distribution plant. Then you can do whatever you want with the girls."

Rita figured that Scully would want to take that last sentence back if he could. It didn't come out the way she was sure he meant it. That didn't mean the tone didn't make her angry.

"Why do I have to find the drugs? It's your job. You find it."

"We've been over this," Scully said. "That's why you're even in this task force. To help us get enough info to arrest Shiv. I thought you knew that."

"I do. And I'm trying to be helpful. But you've put me in a bad situation. I've got underage girls who are being trafficked by Shiv. I've got enough to arrest him on the spot."

"Then the drug operation will disappear."

"That's a good thing. We'll put Shiv out of business."

"You and I both know that Shiv will be back on the streets by nightfall."

"I'm not so sure. I've got Shiv's right hand man telling me to kill the girl."

"Do you have it on tape?"

"You know I'm not wearing a wire. Too risky."

"Exactly."

Rita started to object, but he cut her off. Technically, Scully was her boss on this task force.

"Do your job!" Scully said, raising his tone considerably. "I don't like what's happening to the girls either, but they put themselves in this position. There's a bigger picture. Shiv's drug operations are killing dozens of kids every month. It's not just about five girls in the basement. We have a chance to bring down his whole operation. Don't blow it for us."

"Fine," Rita said, then stood and walked out letting the door slam behind her.

Rita was fuming mad. While she understood their points, they clearly didn't understand hers, or if they did, they'd fallen on deaf ears. It wasn't fair that the girls had to suffer because some men in an office had bigger career goals.

As mad as she was, she'd play the part of the good soldier. At least they had a good plan for the Korean girl. She'd take her from the house and pretend to kill her. Rita needed a place to hide the girl until they could bring down the drug ring.

She drove toward south Chicago, intending to go straight to the Dexter house. On the way, she took out her phone and dialed her sister's number.

"Julia, it's Rita. I need a favor."

"Hi sis. What's up?"

"I've got a girl who's been caught up in a mess. I need you to hide her."

Her sister Rita ran a shelter for women and girls who had been abused and had no place to go.

"I can do that," Julia answered immediately, which was what Rita expected.

"You can't keep her at the shelter. This girl's in danger. The Strikers want her dead. I don't know all of her story, but we need to protect her."

"She can stay at my house."

"Perfect."

"When should I expect her?"

"Later this morning. I'll be in touch."

Rita hung up and increased her speed. Now that she had a plan, she wanted to get to the gang house as quickly as possible. She'd told Reginald not to touch the girl but didn't know if she could trust him not to. She also was worried that the girl might get in another confrontation with one of the other gang members.

When she pulled into the driveway, she felt relieved that most of the cars were gone. Only one lone car sat in the parking lot. That meant there were probably only three or four Strikers in the house.

She greeted one of them when she entered through the back-door.

"I'm here for the Korean girl," Rita said.

He nodded like he knew what she was talking about. He un-locked the door to the basement and shut it behind her.

Rita called out to the girls, so they'd know it was her. The five girls were sitting around on the mattresses playing cards. One of the supplies Rita had gotten them to help them pass the time. The guilty feeling returned. She really wanted to get these girls out of there.

"Where's the Korean girl?" Rita asked.

"She's in the closet."

"Okay."

Rita walked over to the closet and opened the door. When she did, Bae was crouched down like a linebacker in a football stance. Before Rita could react, Bae lunged at her and planted her shoulder into her stomach and drove her backward into the far wall, knock-ing the breath out of her.

She tried to shout for Bae to stop and formed the words but no sound came out of her mouth since she couldn't put any breath behind it.

Rita's head bounced off the wall, and she saw stars for a few seconds.

Bae was on top of her now.

Pummeling her.

Rita instinctively put her hands up to defend herself, but some of the blows were getting through.

She had to do something quick. The Korean girl had a fire in her eyes. Like she was going to kill her.

29

When I heard the familiar sound of the door unlocking, I got into position in the closet. I was waiting for Rita, the Cuban lady, to make an appearance. When she did, I intended to take her out, steal her gun, and rescue these girls.

My heart skipped a beat when I heard Rita's voice.

"Where's the Korean girl?" she asked.

"She's in the closet," one of the girls said.

I'd given them instructions on how to play this out.

"Okay," Rita said and then I heard footsteps.

I crouched down like a tiger about to pounce on a prey. The light to the closet was off so she wouldn't see me right away and I'd have the element of surprise on my side.

As soon as the door opened, I shot out of the closet like a bullet from a gun. I lunged my right shoulder into her midsection and kept my legs moving, driving her all the way against the wall where we crashed into it with a loud thud. I could hear and feel the air leave her lungs.

I changed positions so that I straddled her with my knees, pinned her arms to the ground and I flailed away. Not exactly like how Curly and Jamie had taught me, but I didn't want the lady to get a chance to catch her breath. The end goal was to get her gun.

I'd seen the bulge on the street when she recruited me and then at the hotel. I wasn't at the right angle to reach it, so I had to knock her out first.

Several of the blows got through her outstretched arms but were only glancing. I could tell from her eyes that she was dazed. Her head was down to try and protect herself from the blows.

I knew how to get around that.

Before I could change position, Rita raised her hips in the air and threw me forward and off balance. When she brought her hips back down, I tried to hit her with a right hook. She grabbed my wrist before the blow could strike. It took tremendous strength to stop a fist with that kind of momentum.

She held on and wouldn't let go of my right wrist, rendering it useless.

I kneed her in her left side with my right knee to try and loosen her grip. Unfortunately, I couldn't get the leverage, and the blow wasn't hard enough to do any damage but enough to let her know I could hurt her in any number of ways and that she needed to defend more than just her head.

Throwing a punch with the left hand wasn't the best option because if she took control of both of my wrists, I'd be vulnerable. A stalemate ensued for several seconds. A mistake on my part. I should've kept up the pressure with a new tactic. Rita was strong and had her own skills, and the short respite allowed her to get her wind back.

She grabbed my other wrist even though I was purposefully keeping it away from her. She had height, weight, and reach on me. That forced me to my feet so I could use my knees and feet to launch kicks at her midsection.

She countered by bringing her knees to her chest. Then pulled my arms forward.

I knew what was coming but couldn't prevent it.

A triangle.

I'd seen it several times. My mind tried to process how to combat it. The woman was too quick. Before I knew it, she'd wrapped her legs around my head, trapping my arm against it.

Instinctively, I tapped out. Then realized this was real life. Against a real opponent who wanted to harm me. Tapping out wasn't an option. The hold sent excruciating pain through my shoulder and neck area. My breathing was cut off.

I remembered enough to tighten my chin to my neck to try and prevent her from completely cutting off my air.

I had to do something quickly or I was done for.

Rita tried to scoot her body to the side so that she was perpendicular to me. A move designed to tighten the triangle.

I couldn't let her.

I brought my chest forward and my elbow down as some of my training was coming back to me. This was what Jamie meant about fighting becoming second nature. Where you knew what to do without thinking about it. The fact that I was even thinking about my training was proof that I hadn't mastered that aspect of fighting.

Thinking about it did give me an idea. I walked my shoulders and feet in the direction of Rita's ankles. Slowly at first, trying to get leverage. I could feel the triangle loosen, and I kept inching forward in the direction of her ankles to try and get them to open up.

Rita suddenly released the triangle, pulled me into her and then rolled us over, so I was on my back. Before I could react, she was on top of me in a flash.

Instinctively, I raised my hands to my face to protect it from any blows. I expected her to try and hit me, but she didn't.

A mistake on her part.

The gun.

From that angle, I could reach it.

I leaned forward and tried to reach around her, but she kept grabbing my wrists and pushing them away.

"Stop. I'm FBI!" Rita said.

I heard the girls in the room scream.

"I don't believe you," I said.

"I believe you," a man's voice from behind us said. "Get off of her!"

One of the Strikers was in the room. He was standing over us and had a gun pointed at the back of Rita's head. In all the commotion, we hadn't noticed him coming down the stairs and into the room. He'd obviously heard what Rita said.

Rita slowly got off of me. Then held her hands out in front of her and rose to her feet. Careful not to make any sudden movements.

"Take your gun and toss it on the other side of the room. That way." The man pointed toward the bathroom.

I stood to my feet and walked over to where the man was standing.

"Thank you," I said. "You saved my life."

"I wouldn't be thanking me just yet," he said in a vicious tone.

The whole picture was coming together. Rita probably was FBI. The Striker was likely going to kill her or take her captive.

Rita carefully took out her gun and tossed it several feet away from her.

"Get on your knees," the man said.

It looked like he intended to execute her.

I knew what to do.

Don't hesitate.

Without thinking, I brought my left arm up slightly in the air and then brought it down on the man's wrist. With my right hand, I grabbed the gun around the trigger and turned it sideways, then up, snapping the man's finger.

The breaking bone echoed through the enclosed space of the basement.

In one motion, I brought the sharp part of my elbow straight up, under the man's chin snapping his neck back. He collapsed to the floor in a heap. Out like a light. Maybe dead. I didn't care. My right hand still held the gun which was attached to the man by his broken finger. If he was alive, he'd never fire a gun again with that hand.

Rita leapt to her feet and started for her gun.

"Don't do that," I said, pointing the gun at her. I had to be sure. "Move another foot and I'll shoot you."

She stopped in her tracks and held her hands out in front of her.

"I'm a federal agent. You drop the gun right now."

"Not until you tell me what's going on."

"I'm working undercover. I'm trying to help you."

"If you wanted to help me, why did you recruit me to be a prostitute?"

"It's complicated. Don't shoot. I'm going to show you proof," she said. Rita reached inside the lining of her blouse and pulled out a leather wallet.

"Take this," she said. "It's all the proof you need."

I took it from her hand and opened it. It had a picture of her with the word FBI special agent written on the top. Clearly an identification card. It looked real to me.

"Drop your gun, or I'll have to arrest you," she said.

"I guess you are FBI," I said and lowered the gun. Rita took the gun from my hand and then retrieved hers.

"Who are you?" she asked me. "And where did you learn those moves?"

"It's complicated," I said. "What do we do now?"

The five girls were huddled against the wall over by the mattresses. Clutching each other. Petrified. Their eyes as wide as a full moon.

"We have to get out of here," Rita said. "Girls, get your shoes on. Don't bother taking anything with you except what you're wearing."

Rita walked over to the Striker and checked for a pulse.

"He's alive," she said.

She walked up the stairs and listened at the door. When she came back down, she handed me the Striker's gun and said, "I'm assuming you know how to use that thing?"

I released the magazine, clicked out the round in the chamber, counted the number of bullets, then reloaded it in a matter of seconds. She seemed impressed because of the smirk and widened eyes.

"I take that as a yes," she said. "Hide the gun in the back of your pants."

"I like to put it in the front of my pants. I can get to it quicker."

She shook her head no. "With that shirt you're wearing, you can see it from the front."

"What's the plan?"

"We're going to try and get out of here without having to shoot our way out. The men upstairs think I came here to take you out and kill you. I want them to keep thinking that. If we don't hurry, though, they're going to send someone down here to look for Reginald."

I assumed the man on the floor was Reginald.

"Here's what we're going to do. I'm going to walk you out of here with the gun on you."

"How do I know that you don't intend to kill me?" I asked.

Rita let out a huge sigh.

"I could've killed you when we were on the ground. I could shoot you right now."

"I'd rather take my chances alone."

"You're going to do what I say! My cover's blown because of you."

"I didn't know you were an FBI agent," I said, matching her snide attitude.

"Look. I don't have time to argue with you. I'm not mad at you. It's not your fault. It's for the best. I don't think I could've left the girls here another day as it was. You've given me an excuse to rescue all of you."

"I don't need rescuing!" I said.

"Be that as it may, the Strikers are going to be looking for you. They want you dead. After today, they're going to want me dead as well. I can handle myself, but I need to take you somewhere safe."

I started to object, but the girls were ready to go, and Rita was right. We needed to get out of there. She had a car and was my ticket out of the basement of that house. We could argue about it later.

"Bae, I want you to lead the way," Rita said. "No. I changed my mind. I'm not going to have the gun on you. I'll lead the way. Everyone needs to act like everything's normal. Hopefully, we can get out of here without anyone suspecting anything. Stay behind me. If all hell breaks loose, I want to be between you and the Strikers."

Rita started up the stairs. I followed her. Then the five girls. At the top of the stairs, I let the girls exit the basement ahead of me so I could guard their rear.

No one was in the kitchen. I'd wondered why none of the Strikers had come downstairs. That explained it. They were in a different part of the house and hadn't heard the commotion.

Rita opened the back door and motioned for the girls to hurry through. I followed them and she came out last.

"Get in that car over there," Rita said. She had a fob in her hand and the lights flickered and the car beeped, signaling it was unlocked, which also let us know which one she meant.

A four-door sedan. How were we all going to fit in there?

"What are you doing?" a gruff voice said from behind us.

I started to reach for my gun, but Rita stopped me by putting her hand on mine.

"Reginald told me to take the girls to the hotel. I guess there's a client who paid for all five girls at once."

A lustful grin came on his face.

"Lucky guy. Where's Reginald?" he asked.

"Down in the basement," Rita answered. "I guess. That's where he was the last time I saw him."

She caught my eye and we both fought back a smirk.

I liked her.

Rita motioned for me to get into the car. The five girls were already squished in the back seat.

"I'll have them back in a few hours," she told the man.

I got in the passenger seat and could see Rita's hand shaking as she pushed the button to start the car.

"That was a close one," I said.

"We're not out of the woods yet," she replied.

As if on cue, two Strikers came out of the house with their guns raised, shouting at the top of their lungs.

Rita floored it. The tires squealed as she peeled out of the driveway.

I heard gunshots.

The rear end fishtailed which was probably why the bullets missed the vehicle.

Rita drove down the alleyway at a high rate of speed, turned on to Dexter Street, and went the opposite direction of the house. She didn't slow down until we were several blocks away.

"Is everyone okay?" she asked.

I nodded. The girls in the back seat answered and said they were.

"Hand me my phone out of that glovebox," Rita said to me.

I opened it, found the phone, and handed it to her.

"Who are you?" she asked me. "FBI? CIA? You're too young to be with the bureau."

"If I told you, I'd have to kill you," I quipped.

I'd heard Jamie and Alex both say that and thought it was the coolest thing.

Rita smiled, although it didn't mask the worry on her face.

"I thought you were going to kill me there for a minute," I said.

She ignored the remark and dialed a number with her phone.

"Julia, this is Rita. I've got the girls. We're headed there now. Six of them."

Then she hung up which must've meant she got a voicemail.

"I'll send her a text." Rita began typing on her phone while trying to keep her eyes on the road.

"It's against the law to text and drive," I said.

Rita laughed out loud.

"We're kind of beyond that now, aren't we? I lost track of how many laws you broke in that basement. You assaulted a federal agent. That'll get you ten years to life."

"Are you going to arrest me?" I asked.

"Not if you cooperate," she said with a grin, making me believe the entire conversation was in jest.

"What does that mean?" I asked. "What do you want from me?"

She ignored the question and kept driving. Faster than the speed limit. Not bothering to stop at any stop signs or red lights. Breaking every traffic law in the book.

***

Striker's Headquarters

Shiv answered the phone call on the first ring. Surprised by the name on the caller ID. He didn't get a call from Carson that often.

"We have a problem," Carson said.

He was a detective with Chicago PD. He'd helped Shiv start the Striker's gang and was his inside man with the police. In return, Carson got a share of the profits which were substantial.

Shiv was used to people calling him with problems. Almost every day. Came with the territory.

"The Feds are sniffing around," Carson said, which caused immediate concern. Since Carson kept the local police at bay, the FBI was his worst fear. "Word is that they've got someone undercover in your organization."

"Do you have his name?"

"It's a she."

Shiv immediately knew who it was. The Cuban lady.

He let out a flurry of expletives.

"I have an address," Carson said. "I suggest we send some people over to her house to take care of the problem."

"I intend to."

And hung up. He didn't need to ask any questions. If Carson said the lady was FBI, then he believed him. He'd already suspected it.

Shiv's phone rang within seconds after hanging it up. This call, he expected.

"Reginald," he said as he answered.

He'd sent Reginald over to the Dexter house to make sure the Cuban lady killed the Korean girl.

"Rita ain't one of us," Reginald said.

"I know," Shiv responded. "She's FBI."

Reginald didn't say anything.

"Where is she now?" Shiv asked.

"I don't know. She took the girls. The Korean girl is FBI too. They're working together."

"What happened?"

"When I arrived at the Dexter house, I went down to the basement. I knew something was up. I pulled my gun. Korean girl ambushed me from behind. Knocked me out cold. They took my gun and Rita left with the girls."

Shiv was silent. Thinking.

"Do you want me to find the Cuban lady?" Reginald asked.

"I know where she is."

"Tell me and I'll go there now. I've got a score to settle with her."

Shiv had a score to settle with Reginald. Letting the Korean girl get the best of him and take his gun was totally unacceptable.

"I've got it covered," Shiv said, then hung up the phone and dialed another number.

"I need you to take care of something," he said.

This man had been with him for years and had never let him down. Not on purpose anyway.

"I'm going to text you an address," Shiv said. "I want you to kill the Cuban woman."

"How do you want it to happen?"

"Not at her house. Out in the open. Where everyone can see it. I want to send a message. That you don't mess with the Strikers."

"I'm on it."

"After you're done, take Reginald to an alley somewhere and put a bullet in his head."

"Will do."

That's what he liked. Total obedience. No questions.

This time tomorrow, both problems would be taken care of.

30

Jamie waited until nightfall to go back to the gang house on Dexter Street. She'd spent the day preparing. Tonight would be the night she infiltrated the house and rescued the girls. She went to a local gun range and secured more ammunition and a second gun. A Glock 19 with an extended clip and laser.

Overkill maybe. She could take out a hundred gang members with the two guns. Hers and the new one.

She'd thought long and hard about contacting the local FBI field office but decided not to. They'd want more evidence than what she had.

In reality, all she had was her opinion. She'd seen a couple underage girls taken into a seedy motel room by a couple of thugs who looked like gang members. She saw one of the girls taken into a house, seemingly against her will. That's the extent of her evidence. No judge anywhere would sign off on a warrant for a SWAT team to storm the house.

She also wanted to protect the privacy of the girls. They all had a story. More than likely, they got in this predicament on their own. Ran away from home. Started walking the streets. Put themselves in a compromising position. While Jamie didn't blame them, others might. They'd get caught up in the system. Maybe end up in a foster home. Run away again. Be right back in the same horrible situation.

Once she rescued them, Jamie would connect the girls with a Christian organization called *Save The Girls*. They'd take the girls in, provide food and shelter and counseling. Alex and Jamie's AJAX corporation funded most of *Save The Girls'* yearly budget. The organization didn't even spend all the money Alex and Jamie donated to them each year. She'd give them ten times the sum if they could use it.

She decided to put her search for Bae on hold. Julie said she'd call if Bae showed up. Since Jamie had all of Bae's stuff, she figured Bae would call her when she found out. All she could do was pray that Bae was safe. The fact that no one had heard from her for a couple of days was concerning. But what was Jamie to do? She didn't have a lead and no place to search.

And she needed to turn her attention to the girls in the house that she could save.

Jamie had spent part of the afternoon looking at the location via a CIA program that gave her an overhead view of the area. She could see everything perfectly including the house she was in and the surrounding neighborhood. A hell hole she didn't think anyone should have to live in.

Alex even managed to crudely draw up a schematic of the house based on the configuration of the windows. Based on the drawing, Alex surmised that the house had a basement. Jamie wasn't sure how he knew that, but the overhead view found evidence of one. She could tell by the location of some of the cracks in the foundation and the way in which the house settled.

With that information, Jamie was certain the girls were being held there. Underground. Where they couldn't escape.

That's where she'd look first.

This was one of those times when she wished she had one of her cohorts with her. Bond. A-Rad. The Colonel. AJAX had a team of highly skilled assassins on staff with significant experience in infiltration and extraction operations. If they weren't off on other CIA missions, she would've flown one of them in to help her.

No worries.

She'd handle it on her own.

Once she was in the vacant house, she could feel the adrenaline start to pump through her veins. It always came on her when she was anticipating a gunfight.

As soon as she looked out the back bedroom window at the gang house, the adrenaline rushed out of her like air let out of a balloon.

The house looked abandoned.

There were no cars in the driveway. No lights on.

How did that happen? Was she discovered somehow?

Jamie almost didn't believe it. She armed herself with her two guns and snuck out the back door of her house. Jumped the fence and walked cautiously up to the backdoor of the gang house. She listened for any sign of life inside.

Nothing.

She tried the door. It jammed slightly, but she was able to open it with a gentle nudge of the shoulder. The inside of the house had a feel of an empty house. Like the one she'd just come from. Except this house had signs of recent activity. Dishes in the sink. Trash bags on the floor. The musty smell of used cigarettes.

Jamie cleared each room. Certain she wouldn't find anything but wanted to be sure.

A door off the kitchen had locks on it. The locks weren't secured. No doubt the doorway that led to the basement. She decided to check it last. If someone were in the house, she didn't want them locking the door behind her.

After all the rooms were clear, that was no longer a worry. No one was there.

She reluctantly cracked open the door to the downstairs area. While she was curious what she'd find, the thought occurred to her that she might find the girls dead in the basement. For whatever reason, the Strikers had cleared out of there in a hurry. It's possible they didn't take the girls with them.

Jamie crept down the stairs into the dark room with both hands on her gun. She allowed her eyes a few seconds to adjust to the darkness. It didn't appear that anyone was there. She could feel a presence if there were. She had a sixth sense about those kinds of things. Rarely did anyone ever sneak up on her.

Jamie pulled out her phone and turned on the flashlight feature.

She didn't see any dead bodies. Nor did she smell them.

Death had a smell. An eerie presence. So did blood. They both had a distinct odor. Jamie didn't smell either. She found a light switch and turned it on. No one on the outside would be able to see it, so she felt comfortable illuminating the room.

She kept the gun in her hand just in case and walked through the room which wasn't hard to do since it consisted of a main room, a closet, and a bathroom.

It's definitely where they kept the girls. She saw plenty of evidence of that. Clothes. Shoes. Feminine things like makeup, hairdryers, shampoo, and the like. The bathroom had the smell that it hadn't been vacant for long.

Was it possible that they took the girls somewhere and they were coming back? It didn't seem like it.

Jamie turned off the light and went back upstairs. She closed up the house and went back to her safehouse. Totally confused.

Since no one knew her intentions except Alex, the Striker's weren't tipped off. For some reason, they moved the girls.

There had to be an explanation.

Jamie packed up her things, got back in her car, and drove to the Central Inn.

Her mouth flew open when she pulled into the alley across the street.

The parking lot was empty. No Striker guards were around. All the operations were completely shut down.

Why?

It made no sense. Something spooked the Strikers. It wasn't law enforcement. Police tape would be everywhere if they had raided the place.

Then she remembered.

The guy she beat up and left behind the motel. The girl who ran away. Jamie was kicking herself. Racked with guilt. That's why Curly said to focus on the big picture. She should've waited. By trying to save the one girl, the others were still trapped.

Jamie slapped herself on the hip in disgust.

Nothing she could do about it now. She had no clue where to begin to look for the girls.

She started the car and drove around Chicago for twenty minutes not sure what to do. Finally, at Alex's insistence, she found a five-star hotel in downtown Chicago and checked in. She had a big meal and a hot jacuzzi bath in an upgraded suite. Tried to relax.

But she couldn't unwind. This felt like a mission. With ups and downs. Ebbs and flows. Success and failures.

Why did this feel like a failure?

It started out as a simple search for Bae. Now it was complicated by the Strikers. She hadn't found Bae and now she'd lost the girls being held by the Strikers.

She liked her baths steaming hot. That's how she felt on the inside. A burning rage. It usually reared its head when she faced adversity and things weren't going as planned.

It served a purpose. It gave her a new resolve. Anger motivated her to action. For many, anger caused them to lose perspective and overreact. It made Jamie think more clearly.

If the Strikers thought they were out of her crosshairs, they were sorely mistaken.

31

Julie wolfed down some leftovers in the fridge and went to her room to throw on a sweatshirt and get her backpack.

She was late for class. Again.

Technically, not late yet. But she would be in the length of time it took her to walk there. She hadn't wanted to take a class at night, but it's the only time it was offered. She'd chosen Elementary Education as her major and *Education of the Gifted Child* was only offered at night with the professor she wanted to take the class under.

She also felt a certain unease.

After Jamie confronted her stalker, she hadn't seen him but had nervously looked for him behind every tree. Now she was nervous having to walk by herself to class at night.

Bae had gone with her one night, but she wasn't around, and Julie hadn't heard from her. Connie would, but she was at the library studying for a big exam. The other girls in the sorority house were busy, and she didn't want to bother them anyway. Jamie had warned her not to walk alone at night.

Nothing she could do but either skip class or walk. She could call a taxi, but that'd take awhile and would cost money she didn't have.

So, she put her shoulders back, tamped down the fear, and set off for class. Trying to look confident.

She came to a fork in the sidewalk. And a decision. If she took a shortcut and went to the right, she'd get to class faster, but it wasn't as well-lit, and she wasn't as familiar with that way. If she went left, it'd take her by the student center and library where a lot of people would congregate.

She hesitated.

Looked at her watch.

Decided to go left. Toward the student center. A safer choice.

As she started walking again, Julie saw something out of the corner of her eye.

A flash. Then recognition.

Her stalker.

He came up on her before she could scream. He had a knife.

She felt the cold steel against her back.

"Do as I say, and I won't hurt you," he said roughly.

She heard herself screaming inside but nothing was coming out of her mouth.

He was pushing her forward. Finally, she found some words.

"Let me go!"

"Shut up!"

He pushed her to the right. Onto the grass. Out of the lights that lined the walkway. Toward the area she had decided not to walk through. It didn't take long for her to realize the wisdom of her choice.

Not that it mattered now. He took her deeper into the darkness. Then veered off in a different direction.

She didn't even know his name. She wanted to use his name and talk sweetly to him. Maybe he'd let her go.

He knew hers.

"You're doing good, Julie. You might get out of this alive after all."

Soon, she didn't know where they were. He led them across a street and forced her into a house.

The thought occurred to her. If she didn't know where she was, no one else would either.

***

The next morning

Jamie woke up raring to go but with no place to go.

She had absolutely no plan for the day other than to go back to the Spyhouse for more breakfast foods and coffee.

First, she went to the fitness room and ran a brisk five miles on the treadmill. Work off some frustration. After the intense cardio, she pushed around a few weights on the machines, half-heartedly. She did it but didn't like it. Never did. After the weights, Jamie pounded out some sit-ups and pushups like a maniac then went down to her room to take a shower and got dressed.

The Spyhouse was packed. The line was out the door. Since she didn't have anywhere to be, she waited patiently. Not her strong point, but she didn't remember the last time she had coffee this good. It'd be worth the wait.

After she ordered and got her food and drink, the only seat she found was a stool along the front wall facing out toward the street. Not ideal. Jamie liked to have her back against the wall, so no threat could sneak up on her. Even though there were no threats to her life in Chicago that she knew of, the habits were so ingrained in her she felt out of place if she wasn't following the protocol of good spycraft.

She had to take the seat. Her hands were full, and she didn't know a way to navigate eating one of the three breakfast treats while holding the other two in one hand and the coffee in the other.

It didn't take long to finish them, and she considered getting back in line for a refill of the coffee. She thought about another pastry, but what was the point of the five miles on the treadmill if she were going to pack on the carbs less than an hour later.

Still, she considered it. The line wasn't out the door but would be a ten-minute wait. So, she decided to sit and stare out the window and contemplate her next move.

Twenty minutes later, she realized she had no next move.

What she really wanted was to find the Cuban lady. Find her and she'd find her answers. The Cuban lady would know what happened to the girls and the operations at the Central Inn.

Jamie was fascinated by the woman. Probably because she was totally confused by her behavior. She didn't like not knowing the truth. Was she FBI? Undercover? A rogue agent? Former agent turncoat? Low-life educated scum?

The woman drove an unregistered—likely government—car. She looked like an FBI agent or some kind of law enforcement. Walked like someone with training. Carried a gun on her hip. She also wore a gun on her inner thigh. Most people wouldn't notice, but Jamie was trained to spot that kind of thing.

But Cuban lady was also recruiting girls into prostitution for the Strikers. The FBI would never sanction that activity.

She had to be former... something. Not military. Those people had a look about them that this lady didn't have. Maybe she was an FBI wannabe who got washed out in training. That made sense. Someone with a grudge. A malcontent who turned to the dark side after being rejected by the good guys.

Jamie had seen that in the CIA. Most people didn't survive Curly's training on the Farm. They usually left embittered. Some felt like they were treated unfairly. The truth was, they couldn't hack it. Rather than accept that, they blamed everyone but themselves.

Maybe the Cuban lady had a similar story.

Satisfied she might be getting closer to the truth, Jamie stood to leave the coffee shop.

Then she saw her.

Out of the corner of her eye at first.

The Cuban lady.

Walking on the sidewalk toward the coffeeshop. She almost couldn't believe it.

Jamie sat back down. The woman was clearly walking that way and going to come inside.

Maybe she'd get answers after all.

The woman was close to the entrance. The line was back out the door and on the sidewalk.

The lady slowed her step to let someone go in front of her.

Another flash!

A black car screeched to a halt in front of the coffeeshop.

A Lexus.

Jamie had seen that car before. At the gang house.

A Striker got out of the back seat and began running toward the coffeeshop. Toward the Cuban lady. He had a gun in his hand. She wasn't looking his way. Jamie wanted to let out a scream to warn her. Instead, she bolted out of her seat toward the entrance, which was blocked by the people in line.

Jamie heard a gunshot.

Screams!

She pushed her way through the crowd of customers.

The Striker was already running back toward the car, carrying the Cuban woman's purse.

Jamie reached for her gun. Too late.

He jumped into the backseat and the car sped away.

The Cuban woman was lying on the sidewalk. Jamie rushed to her side. Knelt down and cradled her head on her lap.

She'd been shot in the chest. Once. Jamie felt for a pulse. She found a weak one. Her breathing was shallow.

The woman was conscious and looking up at Jamie. Her eyes were vacant though. Not looking for help. Resigned to her fate.

Jamie smelled the blood. And death.

"Who are you?" Jamie asked, but the woman just stared up into the sky.

She'd die soon.

Jamie leaned over the woman pretending to treat her wounds. There wasn't anything the finest surgeon in the world could do for her if he was there at that moment. The wound was right at her heart.

Jamie felt in the lady's pockets and found a phone. Pulled it out and pretended to be calling 911 with it. She stood to her feet. Drifted back into the crowd. Walked away quickly to her car.

She sat down in the driver's seat totally stunned by the turn of events.

The woman's blood was on her shirt and hands.

She turned on the woman's phone.

Scrolled through recent texts.

One from earlier that morning caught her eye.

I have the girls. Six of them. I'm bringing them to you now. The Korean girl's name is Bae.

32

Jamie had been waiting two days for Alex to get her information. When he did, the only information he had was that he had no information.

"The phone has encryption software on it," Alex said. "We can't breach it."

He was talking about the phone she'd taken off the dead Cuban woman. She was hoping to learn the woman's identity along with the name and address of where she took Bae and the other five girls.

"I thought there wasn't a firewall created you couldn't get around," Jamie said, trying not to let her frustration show. She knew if anyone in the world could penetrate the firewall, it'd be Alex and Pok.

"I've never seen this before," Alex said, not bothering to hide his own frustration.

"Why would this woman have a phone with that level of security? She was working with a gang."

"I couldn't tell you."

"Does she work for the government?" Jamie asked. "I still don't know if this woman's on our side or on the dark side."

"There's no information on the phone either way?"

A huge disappointment. The phone was her only lead. She'd wasted two days twiddling her thumbs waiting for nothing.

"Give me something, Alex."

"I wish I could. I'll keep working on it. It might take months to crack this code."

"Did Pok look at it?"

Jamie imagined the grimace on Alex's face after she said it and felt herself form one of her own. Alex and Pok had a running argument as to who was the best hacker in the world. The fact that she asked that question would make her husband think she thought Pok was better. That's not what she meant, but she was concerned he took it that way.

If Alex was hurt by the comment, he didn't say anything.

"Pok was working on it. When he ran into a dead end, I looked at it and came to the same conclusion. This encryption is sophisticated. Something new that neither of us has seen before."

"I appreciate you trying," Jamie said with an added sigh that he couldn't hear.

"I did get one bit of information from the phone that might be helpful," Alex said, momentarily raising her spirits.

"What did you find?" she asked.

"It may be nothing."

"Let me decide that."

"A few days ago, the woman got a text asking if she wanted to go to Champions Bar on Friday night. The text was from the same person who has Bae."

Today was Friday!

Jamie felt her senses heighten. They usually did when she thought she had a good development on a mission.

"Did she say yes?" Jamie asked. A couple of thoughts came through her mind. If the person on the receiving end of the text didn't know the Cuban lady was dead, he or she might show up at the bar. All she had to do was go there and find the person.

"No. The Cuban lady said she was working on a big case and couldn't."

The hope was suddenly dashed like a broken glass smashed with a hammer.

"The Cuban lady used the word *case*?" Jamie asked. Alex sometimes paraphrased things and didn't always get the details exactly right.

"That's what she said."

"Case to me, means FBI."

"I don't disagree."

"I hope so anyway. That means Bae is safe. If that's correct, then I can assume the Cuban lady rescued the girl and has them in protective custody. Whoever she was texting must be law enforcement as well."

"Sounds like a reasonable theory. What are you going to do now?"

"I'm going to Champions Bar."

"How do you know who to look for?" Alex asked.

"I don't."

She had to trust her instincts which rarely let her down. Her sixth sense might tell her when she's found the right person. Complicated because she didn't know if it was a man or a woman. But whoever it was would be looking for the Cuban lady. Watching the door. Checking his or her watch. Acting frustrated when she didn't show.

"You don't know if it's a man or woman," Alex said as if he read her mind. "You also don't know if the person is even going to show up at Champions. The lady said she wasn't going."

"Are you done?"

"Just trying to be helpful and point out some things you might not have thought of."

"I already know it's a shot in the dark. It's the only lead I have. I intend to follow up on it."

"Good luck."

"Can you check the morgue for me?" Jamie asked. "The Cuban lady had to be taken there. Maybe they have a name in the file. Will you have any problems hacking into the morgue's computer?"

"I actually called them."

Not the response she expected.

"You did?"

It caused her to smile. Alex really was going all out to try and help her.

"She's listed as a Jane Doe."

"That's strange in and of itself."

"You said the shooter took her purse. You took her cell phone. They wouldn't have any way of identifying her."

"What about a missing person's report at the police department?"

"That, I didn't look into."

"Can you?"

"You want me to hack into the Chicago PD computer? I'm going to have to double my fee."

"I'll give you a kiss when I see you."

"I said double my fee."

"I'll give you two kisses."

"Done. I'll see if anyone has filed a missing person's report. That's a good idea. I'll also find out which detective is assigned to the case. Maybe I can find his murder book on the computer if he's started one."

"Okay. I forgive you for not being able to hack into her phone."

"Aren't you magnanimous!" he said sarcastically

Ever since they started the game a couple of weeks ago, Alex had been interjecting a long word into every conversation.

"I think the word you mean is *magnaramos*," Jamie said teasingly.

She fought back a laugh. When they hung up, she was certain Alex would look it up. Knowing he was right about magnanimous. But she'd likely raised a twinge of doubt in his mind. He'd look it up, then rub it in her face the next time they talked.

"I think the word I was looking for was ignoramus. You are being ignoramus."

Alex already knew he had the right word. Not surprising since magnanimous was fairly common.

That caused Jamie to laugh out loud again. Alex joined her in the levity. No matter how difficult or serious the conversation, they somehow had a way of making each other laugh. She loved that about him.

"That's not even the proper use of the word ignoramus in the sentence," Jamie said. "If you're going to play the game, you have to get the words right."

"Like magnamerous. That's not even a word. Amorous is though. Which is what you are making me from this conversation."

"We've been apart for too long."

"Tell me about it. When are you coming home?"

Alex was still on their island anyway. If she went home, he wouldn't be there.

"Not until I find Bae. Wish me luck," Jamie said.

"I would if I thought you needed it."

"Love you."

"Don't be careful," he said.

"I won't."

33

Champions Bar

Jamie got to the bar a little after dark. Alex was right. She had nothing to go on and no idea who she was looking for, so she walked around the bar showing people a picture of Bae and asking them if they'd seen the girl.

One man looked interesting. Thirty-five years old or so. Good looking. Super fit. Carried himself like law enforcement. Did he know the Cuban woman? Did they work together? Were they friends? Had he asked her on a date and she turned him down, but he came to the bar anyway?

If so, he'd have information. Something she was desperate for.

He was on the phone, so she decided to wait to approach him until he was off. To her surprise, he hung up the phone and walked right up to her.

"My name is Cliff Ford. I'm a detective with Chicago P.D. Is there something I can help you with?"

Jamie felt the excitement rise in her. This couldn't be a coincidence.

She flashed him a smile to let him know she was friendly.

"I'm looking for this girl," Jamie said. "Have you seen her?"

She showed him a picture of Bae. A wave of disappointment came over her when she could see in his expression that he didn't recognize her.

Confirmed when he said, "Is she missing?"

"She ran away from home. I'm trying to find her."

"Is she in danger?"

"Would you want your seventeen-year-old daughter on the streets of Chicago, alone on a Friday night?" Jamie said.

"Point taken. I'll keep an eye out for her. What's her name?"

"Bae."

The detective didn't know anything. If he did, he deserved an Oscar for his ability to lie with a straight face.

Jamie continued to show the picture around the bar. Beginning to think she was wasting her time.

Then she saw a Striker sitting in the corner of the bar. She stepped behind a couple of people at the bar so he wouldn't see her. She knew he was a Striker because she'd seen him at the house on Dexter Street.

A short time later, two more Strikers entered the bar. They looked around and walked right over to the man in the corner as soon as they spotted him.

The man sitting pointed to the restroom. The two Strikers headed that way. The third man stood up and followed the other two to the back of the bar. Through the door that had *Restrooms* and *Emergency Exit* signs above the entryway.

Jamie hesitated, not sure what to do.

Her instincts told her to follow them. So, she did.

The restrooms were in a narrow hallway.

The men weren't there.

They might be in the men's restroom, but Jamie's instinct told her they'd exited the building.

Jamie peered around the corner and saw the emergency exit. The alarm hadn't sounded for whatever reason.

She opened the exit door cautiously. She heard the sound of shouting and footsteps. Then a woman's scream. She bolted out the door and into a dark alleyway. It took a second for her eyes to focus.

The Striker's had surrounded a woman at the far end of the alleyway. One of the men had his hands on her and was shaking her.

They hadn't seen Jamie. The alleyway was so dark she could be on them before they'd have time to react.

She ran toward them. She couldn't see the woman but could tell she was in danger. The woman cried out in pain.

The fight didn't go the way she envisioned it while running. Gravity and the concrete walkway did most of the damage to the men for her.

She came upon the first man. He must've heard her coming because he started to turn toward her. A bigger man, his foot was planted on the concrete and didn't move as fast as his upper body. When the heel of Jamie's foot smashed into his hyperextended knee, the force was so strong it completely dislocated the knee from the upper and lower bones, and the man fell backward to the ground, smacking his head on the concrete.

Out like a broken lamp.

The second man heard the commotion and looked at his friend lying on the ground. His back was to Jamie, and she could see his mouth twisted and his eyes squint as he was unsure what he was seeing. He no doubt heard the sound of breaking bones, but it takes time for the images in your mind to get to the brain and the brain determine the why.

He didn't have that much time. The blow to his orbital eye socket was so strong, Jamie could feel the soft tissue of the eyeball on the palm of her hand. The blow was low enough on his head that it didn't knock him out, but he fell to the ground. The man reached out to stop himself, but all his weight fell on his outstretched arm. Jamie heard more bones breaking. Probably his ulna and perhaps a dislocated wrist.

The third man was the one holding the girl. He couldn't defend himself from Jamie and keep his hold on her at the same time. So, he released his grip and reached for his gun. The woman took off running.

The Cuban lady!

That's who the man was holding.

Jamie couldn't believe her eyes.

Now Jamie was the one whose brain wasn't processing the images as fast as she was seeing them. Somehow, Jamie was able to put the questions out of her mind and focus on the threat.

Thank you Curly!

His training had saved her life more times than she could remember. *Always focus on the threat first.*

The man's hand was behind his back reaching for the gun. He was turned away from Jamie. She leapt in the air and kicked him in the back, knocking him to the ground. Before he could roll over, Jamie brought her foot down on the base of his skull and neck with such force that it drove his head into the concrete.

She heard the familiar sound of vertebrae cracking.

All three men lay motionless. No longer a threat.

She turned her attention to the woman. The lady was running toward the parking lot.

Jamie called out to her and told her she wasn't going to hurt her.

The woman stopped and turned around.

Jamie did see what she thought she saw. The spitting image of the Cuban woman!

Impossible!

The Cuban lady had died in her arms.

Jamie hadn't actually watched her die. After taking her cell phone, she got out of there as fast as possible.

Could the paramedics revive her?

No way.

Even if they did, the bullet wound was to her chest. If she did survive the shooting, she'd still be in the hospital.

Nothing made sense.

Jamie began sprinting toward the woman who was now in her car. A silver Kia SUV.

By the time Jamie got to the parking lot, the woman had already started the car and was headed for the exit. Jamie tried to cut off the angle and beat the woman to the exit, but there was nothing she could do to stop her even if she wanted to. Short of pulling out her gun and shooting out the tires.

Something she didn't even consider doing.

She did get a good look at her though. She watched as the woman drove off.

A voice called out to Jamie, interrupting her thoughts. From the direction of the alleyway.

The detective she'd encountered in the bar. Cliff Ford.

This can't be good.

While she had acted in self-defense, she didn't want to get involved in a long and drawn-out investigation. She preferred to act off the radar of the local police. He didn't know who she was.

Then she remembered that she had mentioned Bae's name, which she now regretted.

Still, he wouldn't know how to piece things together. The Strikers wouldn't talk. More than likely, none of the three would even be able to talk anytime soon. If ever.

Jamie took off running. Away from the detective. On the main street for one block then ducked behind a building and circled around. She took up a location where she could see the parking lot of the club, but no one could see her.

Her car was parked a couple blocks from the bar. The reason she hadn't parked in the parking lot. Just in case. She watched the ambulances arrive. No coroner. That was a good thing.

When she'd seen enough, Jamie went to her car and drove back to her hotel and called Alex on the way.

"Did you find who you were looking for?" he asked.

"I don't know."

"If you don't know, then who does know?"

"The Cuban lady was in the bar," Jamie said.

Silence on the other end.

"You mean somebody who looks like the Cuban lady," Alex said.

"An identical twin."

"If Cuban lady has an identical twin, how do you know the twin wasn't the one killed at the coffee shop, and the one you saw tonight isn't the one you saw at the gang house."

"I hadn't thought of that."

"I'm not just a pretty face."

"Actually, the text on her phone said she had the six girls. The dead woman has to be the one I saw at the gang house."

"I guess I am just a pretty face."

"I think Cuban woman has a twin sister. That's who she was texting. She drives a silver Kia."

"Did you get a license plate number?"

"No."

"There are probably several thousand silver KIA's in Chicago. But I'll see what I can do. If I find it, can I go back to being more than a pretty face?"

"If you keep growing grey nose and ear hairs, you won't be a pretty face for much longer."

"That's not funny."

Actually, it was.

34

After Rita and I rescued the five girls from the gang house, she drove us to meet her identical twin sister, Julia. I wouldn't have been able to tell them apart, except they were wearing different clothes. Julia ran a shelter for abused women, and we dropped off the five girls there.

Julia took me to her house. Rita said my life was in danger. The leader of the Striker gang, a dangerous man named Shiv, had ordered her to kill me. Rita explained that she was with the FBI and had infiltrated the gang as an undercover agent. Knowing Shiv, he wouldn't stop looking for me, or for her, until he found us. So, Julia insisted that I hide out at her house until the danger subsided.

For two days, Julia hadn't let me out of her sight. While I could've escaped, I needed a place to stay anyway, and this was as good as any. I also wanted to be there for Julia. Rita had said her sister's life was in danger as well. I genuinely liked Julia, and the least I could do was provide her with protection, considering how nice she'd been to me.

That didn't mean I wasn't itching to get back into the fray. Hanging around the house was getting old, and I wanted to talk to Rita and see if I could help her take down the Strikers. Unfortunately,

Julia hadn't been able to reach her. She was probably tied up in her mission.

I was jealous.

I'd gotten a taste of dangerous situations and was hooked.

It was Friday night and Julia was on a date. Sort of. She got embarrassed telling me about it. Not really a date. She met a detective at a coffee shop a couple days before. They'd hit it off. She felt a spark and invited him to meet her at *Champions Bar* tonight, but he didn't seem that interested. Said he didn't drink. She took that as him blowing her off.

I didn't think that was possible. Julia was stunningly gorgeous. What guy wouldn't want to go out with her?

I encouraged Julia to go to the bar anyway. She argued that she had no idea if he would show up or not. So, at first she wasn't going to go. She used me as an excuse. Said that she needed to stay home and watch me. I convinced her I'd be fine. I'd watch television and turn in early.

I lied.

As soon as she left, I called a cab and snuck out.

Jamie said the worst part of spycraft was all the lying. I loved it. Any fib could be justified if it helped the mission.

Mainly, I needed to get my stuff from the sorority house. My justification. That, and I was a grown woman, and it was a free country. I could go out if I wanted.

The cab took me to the college. I'd tried for two days to get in touch with Julie, but her phone kept going to voicemail. Connie's number was with my stuff, and I didn't know the number of any of the other girls in the sorority house.

As soon as I entered the house, I knew something was wrong. Normally, the house was full of life and laughter. Girls bustling around. Lots of activity. The mood was somber. Like someone had died. An eerie feeling came over me.

Some of the girls had red eyes. Several were sitting around the living room, discussing something that seemed serious, based on the tension that filled the room like a San Francisco fog.

"What's wrong?" I asked one of the girls.

"You haven't heard?" she asked.

"No. I've been tied up for a few days."

"Julie's missing. No one has heard from her for several days."

My heart skipped a beat. Maybe two.

"Where's Connie?" I asked.

"She's up in her room. We finally got her to go lie down. She's a nervous wreck as you can imagine."

"I'm going to go talk to her."

I went upstairs and stopped by my room to gather my things. My stuff was gone. I looked in the closets. Under the bed. I couldn't find them anywhere. Connie would know where they were.

The door to Connie's bedroom was slightly ajar. I pushed it open and could see that she wasn't asleep. Her eyes perked up and widened when she saw me, and she motioned me in.

She immediately stood to her feet and threw her arms around my neck. After a long hug, we sat on the edge of her bed. Her cheeks were stained with tears.

"What happened?" I asked.

"Julie didn't come home from class," Connie fought back the tears so she could get the words out. "We haven't heard anything from her. She doesn't answer her phone. I know something bad has happened to her."

"Did you go to the police?" I asked.

"We did. The campus police and the Chicago police. I filed a missing person's report. They said they couldn't do anything for forty-eight hours. It's been longer than that, and they still haven't done anything."

"Do you think her stalker did this?" I asked.

"That was my first thought," Connie said.

"Do you know his name?"

"No. I've seen him though. I'd recognize him if I saw him on campus."

Connie was gripping my hands so hard they were hurting. I didn't dare release the grip, but I did manage to move them into a more comfortable position.

"Don't worry about Julie," I said to her. "I'm going to find her. Everything's going to be okay."

"How can you be so sure?"

Truthfully, I wasn't. But it sounded like the right thing to say.

"I won't leave any stone unturned until I find her."

"I don't even know where to begin to look."

"We have to find the stalker. I bet he has something to do with it."

Connie didn't respond. She just stared into the ceiling. I was able to extricate my hands and stood up. I paced the length of the room. My thoughts were clearer when I was moving.

Then I remembered my things. I wondered if Julie being missing was related to my stuff being missing as well.

"Where are my things?" I asked. "They aren't in my room."

"I don't know," Connie said. "I mean, like, I haven't seen you for several days, I figured you took them with you. I wasn't sure we'd ever see you again."

"Who would've moved them?" I asked. "Julie?"

"I don't think so. We can ask around. Nobody has been in that room that I know of."

"Don't worry about it," I said. "I'll find them. You have enough things to concern yourself with."

I continued to pace the room. Thinking.

"What's this?" I asked. Connie had a book opened on the desk. It had the name of the University and a year on the outside cover.

"That's our school yearbook," Connie said.

I remembered that my college had one as well, but I didn't buy it. I didn't even get my picture taken for it. Jamie said I shouldn't if I ever wanted to be a spy.

I picked it up and flipped through the pages.

"Do you think the man who took Julie is a student here?" I asked.

"It's possible. I think maybe a former student. He looks a little older."

"How far back do these yearbooks go?" I asked.

"They publish one every year. I only have the last two years. I think the library would have past editions."

"Let's go look," I said.

"Why? What are you thinking?"

"Would you recognize Julie's stalker if his picture is in one of these books?" I asked.

"I know I would," Connie said with resolve. "His face is seared in my mind. I see him in my dreams."

"I think we should go to the library and look through the yearbooks. Let's start with the current year and then go back four or five years."

"Each book will have four years of students in it."

"Great. We'll look through the pictures. If he went to school here, we'll at least get a name."

Connie's face lit up. I'm glad I went there tonight. She needed hope. Jamie always said that law enforcement wasn't particularly helpful in finding missing persons. For one thing, they were overwhelmed with all kinds of cases. Murders, robberies, rapes, and other violent felonies. Add to the fact that most missing people showed up in a few days. That's why they waited forty-eight hours before they started looking. To give the person a chance to come home. Which I understood. No one wanted to waste their time looking for someone who's not missing.

Not a good thing for the one who was missing though. The lost time usually meant the kidnapper could cover his tracks. Because of that, I didn't have much confidence in law enforcement either.

I'd have to find Julie myself. The yearbook seemed like a good lead.

Connie was ready in no time, and I barely kept up with her long strides as she walked to the library as fast as humanly possible without running. She asked at the front desk, and the college kid directed us to where the yearbooks were stored.

We started with the previous year's book and Connie meticulously scanned through each page and each picture. The process was harder and slower than I'd imagined it to be. She'd stop every once in a while and stare at a picture and think maybe she recognized the person only to eliminate them after a few minutes of studying them.

"This is so hard," Connie said. "It's amazing how many people look alike."

After an hour, the pace had picked up and we'd already gone back six years.

The library would be closing soon, so we might have to come back tomorrow. For me, the whole process was as boring as my psychology class back in Richmond. I wasn't any help at all, other than being an encouragement.

A thirty-minute warning came over the intercom telling us the library was closing. I'd about given up hope when Connie suddenly let out a shriek that resounded through the entire library. Most people had already cleared out or she would've gotten in trouble for disturbing so many people.

"That's him!" Connie said in a loud voice.

She pointed to a picture on the page.

"He's definitely younger in this picture, but I'd recognize that face anywhere."

"Mitch Podowitz," I read his name out loud. Mitch had sandy blond hair. Thick lips. Creepy looking eyes. I studied the picture, searing the image in my mind. Then stood up from my chair.

"I'll be right back," I said.

"Where are you going?" Connie asked.

"I'm going to log in to a computer and search for this name. I want to see if I can find out any information on this character."

Connie closed the yearbook and followed me to the computer and looked over my shoulder.

"What are we looking for?" she asked.

Alex had taught me how to find people. Even those who didn't want to be found. First, I did a basic search. Mitch Podowitz's name came up from companies wanting to sell me a report. Alex said those companies get the information from public records. Info we can get ourselves without spending the money.

One website did give me information I didn't know. Mitch Podowitz was thirty-one-years old. He showed a Chicago address and phone number, but they were hidden. They'd be revealed if I bought the service.

"How are we going to find out where he lives?" Connie asked.

An announcement came through the intercom telling us the library was closing. I logged off the computer without answering her.

I didn't want to do it but didn't have a choice.

Once we were outside, I said, "Hand me your phone."

"Who are you calling?" Connie asked even though she pulled out her phone and handed it to me.

"Someone who can help us," I replied.

I dialed the number. He answered on the second ring.

"Alex, it's Bae. I need your help."

"Jamie's in Chicago looking for you," he said sternly.

"I know. Tell her to go home. I'm fine."

"Call her yourself and tell her that," Alex said. "And put me on the line when you do it. I'd love to hear her reaction when you tell her to go home."

I ignored the comment. I hadn't asked Jamie to come looking for me. It's her own fault if she felt like she had wasted her time. Which she had.

"I need a favor," I said. "And you can't tell Jamie I called."

Even though it wasn't my fault Jamie came all the way to Chicago looking for me, I didn't want to incur her wrath. Calling Alex was a risk. He'd almost certainly tell Jamie even if I asked him not to.

"You know that's not how it works," Alex confirmed. "Jamie and I tell each other everything."

"She didn't tell you about the good-looking guy she met in Borneo," I said.

I was glad we weren't face timing, otherwise Alex would've seen the huge grin on my face. There was no guy in Borneo. I made that up. To make a point so he wouldn't tell Jamie I called. Of course, I realized it was more likely that he'd tell her now. To confront her about the guy. I wished I could hear that phone call.

"I didn't even know she went to Borneo," Alex said roughly.

"That's what I'm saying. You guys don't tell each other everything. So don't tell her I called you. Now. Are you going to help me or not?"

"Depends. What do you need?"

"An address. In Chicago. The guy's name is Mitch Podowitz. He's thirty-one years old."

"Hang on." Alex was typing in the background.

Two minutes later he came on the line.

"45 Southwest Second Street. "

"Are you sure that's the guy?"

"Hold on."

A few seconds later, Connie's phone dinged, signifying she'd gotten a text. From Alex.

He came back on the line. "Did you get my text?"

"Yes."

"Is that the guy?" Alex asked.

"That's him," I said after looking at the picture.

"He's a little old for you," Alex said.

"Shut up! And... thanks."

"Call Jamie!" he said.

"I'm hanging up now."

While I was talking to Alex, Connie and I had stopped walking. I handed her the phone, and she looked at the picture on the text.

"That's definitely him," she said. "That's a current picture. How did you get this?"

"I have an address," I said.

"You're amazing," Connie said. "Are you some kind of spy?"

"Sort of," I said. "Where is Southwest Second Street?"

"It's a few blocks from here."

"Let's go check it out."

"Do you think Julie's there?"

"We're going to find out."

It took us less than ten minutes to walk to Southwest Second Street.

35

Alex hung up the phone with Bae and called Jamie. He could feel his hair standing on end. Jamie answered on the first ring.

"When were you going to tell me about the guy in Borneo?" he asked.

"How did you find out about him?" Jamie replied.

"I have my sources. What are you not telling me?"

"I haven't told you how big an idiot you are."

"Quit messing around," Alex said. "I want to know."

He was standing now. Walking back and forth like a caged tiger.

"I've never been to Borneo in my life."

"That's not what I heard."

"Who did you hear it from?"

"Why does that matter?"

"Because you've been given bad information. There is no guy in Borneo."

"Bae said you met a good-looking guy in Borneo."

"You talked to Bae? Why didn't you tell me?"

"Don't change the subject."

"When were you going to tell me?"

"I did tell you! Just now!"

"That little shrimp! What did she say?"

"She said you met a good-looking guy in Borneo and never told me about it."

"Not that! What did Bae say about where she is? What she's doing? Is she okay?'

"She called me for a favor."

"What kind of favor?"

"An address."

"That's strange."

"I found it and gave it to her. Some guy named Mitch Podowitz."

"Did you tell her to call me?"

"I did."

"At least she's okay. She won't be once I get my hands on her though. I got to go."

"What about the guy in Borneo?"

Jamie hung up.

36

The stalker's house was an old Victorian with two stories. A large porch spanned the entire front and looked like it could've belonged to an older couple. A porch swing with a small table beside it that had several planters with flowers in them created a homey scene.

A light was on upstairs. No lights were on downstairs except the one on the front porch. Around the back was a detached garage. I didn't see any evidence the house had a basement like the house I was held in on Dexter Street.

That caused me to pause. I couldn't see anywhere that Julie could be held as a hostage. Not in the main house anyway.

Connie and I circled the house once to check things out. I felt comfortable that if Mitch Popowitz were in the house, he couldn't see us. I didn't want a neighbor to see us though, so we went around back and hid behind some thick bushes. Confident that if we were going to see anything, it'd be from the back.

Jamie described missions for me, and this felt like one. When I stayed with Alex and Jamie at their house, she'd tell me the intricate details at night right before bed. Almost like she was telling me bedtime stories, except they were very real. I was like a sponge, soaking up everything related to spycraft that I could learn. I constantly interrupted her stories to ask questions. To the point that

I know I was annoying to her. She never let it show and patiently answered my questions. I would've continued all night if she didn't eventually make me go to bed.

One of the things I remembered vividly was that Jamie always emphasized the importance of gathering all the information you could before acting. If you think you have enough, get some more until you run out of time or you're satisfied that more planning won't be of any more use.

When you reach that point, you act unless you are facing a life-or-death situation. Then the planning was out the window, and you had to count on your training to get you out of it alive.

In this instance, I had virtually nothing to go on. I didn't know for sure this was the stalker's house. We hadn't seen him. The last thing I wanted to do was go barging into a house and scare the living daylights out of an old couple.

Even if it were the stalker's house, I didn't know that he actually had Julie. While he was a likely suspect, you're innocent until proven guilty in America. The police would never act without more clear evidence. I had a different standard, but I had to consider the laws.

Getting myself arrested wasn't a good plan.

Where I grew up in North Korea, the corrupt police didn't have such constraints. The government owned all the houses, and each person and family were assigned a place to live and a job based on their social class. The police could search a house anytime they wanted and for any reason.

That's one of the reasons I hesitated going into the house right away. I remembered how horrible living in those conditions were. I had a new appreciation for American laws even though I'd found myself breaking some of them on this mission.

Nevertheless, if the person in the house were innocent, the laws were there to protect him, and I'd consider them as well to the extent necessary to stay out of jail. On the other hand, Mitch Popowitz was far from innocent. He was a stalker. Julie had asked him to leave her alone and he wouldn't. So, if I got confirmation that this was his house, then I'd blur the line and do whatever it took. I wouldn't leave there not knowing if Julie was in that house.

All we could do was wait.

Connie understood my concern, and we maintained our cover without saying much. She was another reason I was hesitant to act. I was trained to put myself in harm's way. Connie would insist on going inside the house with me. The person inside might have a weapon. An innocent person could get hurt. I couldn't stand it if that person was Connie.

I saw activity in the house, so I knew someone was home. A shadow went past a closed curtain. It looked like the silhouette of a man, but I couldn't be sure. Certainly not enough to identify Popowitz.

A light in the downstairs suddenly came on. At the back of the house, nearest our location. It had no curtain and it looked to be a kitchen. We could see a person, a man, but not clearly enough to identify him as Popowitz.

Ten minutes later, the back porch light came on. We were well in the shadows, but we both instinctively crouched down even further. The door opened and a man appeared.

Popowitz!

"That's him," Connie said what I already knew.

I shushed her. Connie was a novice and I didn't want her giving away our position.

He was carrying something. It looked like a plate of food and a glass with a liquid in it.

That's strange.

I thought I knew what that meant but didn't voice it aloud to Connie. I didn't want to get her hopes up more than they already were.

Popowitz walked out to the garage. He balanced the food and drink with one hand and managed to open the door with the other. Before he entered, he paused and looked around. Like he was making sure he wasn't seen.

"He's acting suspicious," I said after he disappeared through the garage door.

"Should we follow him in?" Connie said.

"I don't think so. If he's holding Julie in the garage, then we can get her out when he goes back to the house. I want to avoid a confrontation if at all possible."

As soon as the words came out of my mouth, I smiled. As much as I would like to follow him in and smack the stalker upside his head, Jamie always emphasized taking the path of least resistance. Avoiding a confrontation was the prudent thing to do. If you let your emotions or desire for revenge get the better of your judgment, you're more likely to make a mistake. A lesson I was learning the wisdom of in real time.

I was growing up.

I'd gained valuable experience on this trip. I was turning into a seasoned operative. Imagine how good I'd be with years of experience like Jamie. Maybe even better than she. I had a long way to go to get to that point but not as far as I had before I started this mission.

We didn't have to wait long for Popowitz to exit the garage. The door opened, and he reappeared without the plate of food and drink. I had all the evidence I needed. Julie was in that garage. The food and drink were for her. There was no other logical explanation for the man's behavior.

I could feel the anger rise inside of me. The righteous indignation, Jamie called it. Curly called it your Kick Butt Juice. The anger fired up the adrenaline. The adrenalin produced the energy to beat up or kill the bad guys.

Again, I impressed myself with my patience. This was a good experience for me. I was learning how to control my emotions and wait. In my younger days, I might've charged into the garage like a buffalo in a China shop. Maybe the saying was a bull in a China shop. I was still learning the American idioms.

Even though the stalker was back inside the house, the porch-light was still on. If I acted now, he could see me from inside the house if he happened to look. I'd stay there all night if I had to. Eventually, he'd have to go to bed.

I was impressing myself with how patient I was being.

Getting Julie out of the garage was the most important thing, and I didn't want her to suffer any longer than necessary but waiting a few more minutes would increase the odds of success. Once I had Julie safely away from the house, we could call the police and have Popowitz arrested.

I'd considered not calling the police. But what would prevent the stalker from doing the same thing to Julie or some other unsuspecting girl? I was breaking the law even being on his property which made calling the police problematic. But trespassing was a minor offense compared to kidnapping. No policeman in his right mind would arrest me. If anything, I was well within my rights to perform a citizen's arrest.

I put those thoughts out of my mind and focused on the task at hand. We didn't have Julie yet. It'd take all of my skills to get her out. We'd worry about the rest later.

Finally, Popowitz turned out the back light, and we could move. This time I didn't hesitate.

"Wait here," I said to Connie.

"I'm coming with you," she said. "That's my sister in there."

I didn't feel like arguing, although I wished Connie would listen to me. I knew what was best for both of us. I shouldn't have to explain myself to her.

Was I this annoying to Jamie?

Probably.

Maybe I'd call Jamie when all this was over. She's the reason I was even doing this. I owe her my life. I'd found my calling thanks to her. In some ways, I was being obstinate by not calling her. She'd cared enough to take her valuable time and travel across the country looking for me.

That made me feel a twinge of guilt.

Then excitement as we came up to the garage door. The Kick Butt Juice was speeding through my body like a downhill bobsled racing through a course.

I felt invincible. Empowered. Like a real superhero. I couldn't wait to tell Jamie how I rescued Julie from the clutches of a serial kidnapper. There might even be more than one girl hidden in that garage.

The door was locked.

"Shoot," Connie whispered.

"No problem," I replied confidently. Jamie and Alex had taught me how to pick most locks. This one was easier than most.

37

It took me a couple minutes, but I got the door open. I needed to work on that skill. Jamie could've opened it in less than thirty seconds. This mission showed me how important preparation was. Opening the lock in thirty seconds instead of two minutes, meant that we weren't in the open for as long. The mission would go smoother. It didn't matter now, but it might in the future. I made a mental note to practice the skill when I was back home.

The garage was dark. As I expected.

"Turn on the flashlight on your cell phone," I said to Connie.

The garage had windows, and the light would shine through them, but it couldn't be helped. We had to be able to see. It only took Connie a few seconds to turn the flashlight on. I took in the surroundings. The garage had an old jalopy in it. It looked to be a working vehicle but had seen better days. If I imagined a car a geek like Popowitz drove, that would be it.

Tools lined the back wall along with dozens of crates and boxes that were stacked on shelves and on the floor under a workbench. The room smelled of moldy grass and I saw an old lawnmower in the corner which was the likely source of the odor.

After scoping out the garage, I was confused. Where could he be hiding Julie? Under the car? I'd seen a movie where the villain had a secret chamber under the car in the garage. I didn't think that was the case here. Popwitz didn't move the car when he went in with the food. I looked up at the ceiling but didn't see an attic or a pull-down stairway.

"There's another door," Connie said. Her voice cracked. I could feel her nerves. They were starting to get to me.

An old bookcase was up against it, which was why I hadn't seen it. The bookcase was empty and easy to move.

I tried the door.

It was locked as I expected.

Heavier than expected, like it was fortified on purpose. It looked out of place for a garage. The door was secured by two locks. It took longer to pick them.

It took all of my strength to open it.

I could feel a presence inside.

I heard whimpering.

Connie bolted through the door before I could stop her. I would've preferred to check it out first to make sure there were no threats in the room.

The room was dank and moldy, and the odor hit me as soon as I entered.

The floor was concrete. So were the walls. There were no windows.

A makeshift prison.

Connie shined the light toward the corner where we heard the whimper.

Julie!

I recognized her immediately even though her hair was matted, and she was covered in dirt and filth.

She was crouched down in the corner of the room on a mattress. The untouched food and drink sat next to her. Her ankle was chained to the wall.

Connie let out a shrill scream and ran to her right away.

Julie sat up when she recognized her sister.

"Are you hurt?" Connie asked and sat on the mattress next to Julie. With her arm around her sister.

"I'm okay. Just tired and weak," Julie said.

"What happened?" Connie said.

"I was walking to class. You know. At night. He came out of nowhere. Before I could do anything, he brought me to the house. He kept me there for a few hours and then put me in the garage. I've been chained to the wall. My stalker is the one who did this. How did you find me?"

"Let's not worry about that now," I said. "We need to get you out of here."

Connie stroked Julie's head.

"Bless your heart. You poor thing," she kept saying. "You're safe now."

"We're going to get you out of here," I said.

I looked at the chain binding her ankle. The lock was old and rusty. I wasn't sure how to pick it. It'd have to be cut off. I remembered the tools in the garage. I'd go back there and find something.

A noise!

Coming from the garage.

"What was that?" Connie asked.

"That's him," Julie said. "He's back. He always comes back for the plate."

The sound I heard was the garage door opening.

I saw a face look in the room.

Popowitz.

He had an evil grin on his face.

This was my chance to make him pay for what he did to Julie. I was perfectly within my rights to beat him to a pulp. Something I was certain I could do.

I jumped to my feet and ran toward him. My fists in a ball ready to wipe that smile off his filthy face.

Popowitz slammed the door before I could get to him. I put my shoulder against the door and tried to open it, but it was already locked.

Hmm.

I guess I should've seen that coming.

38

Jamie couldn't remember the last time she was this frustrated on a mission. For whatever reason, she hadn't been able to find Bae which was infuriating enough. Add on the fact that Alex hadn't been able to come up with the identity of the Cuban lady, and she'd spent the last two days doing the thing she hated most.

Waiting.

At least she used the time wisely. Jamie researched the Strikers. She accessed the CIA database and pulled up everything she could about the organization including the FBI file. What she found was surprising. The Strikers were the most prolific gang on Chicago's south side which was saying something. They were also one of the largest non-mafia-related criminal enterprises in the country.

They started as a high school gang. By a half dozen kids who dropped out of school and had too much time on their hands. In the early days, they were mostly into petty crime. Stealing sneakers. Bullying other vulnerable kids. Shoplifting. Over time, they turned to more violent crimes.

The group was the first in the area to use the knockout game as it's initiation ritual. To join, a prospective member had to approach an unsuspecting and defenseless senior citizen on the street and punch him or her in the face. That's where the name Strikers came from.

That was the type of senseless crime that was attention getting. When captured on videos, the sensational clips were played over and over again by the local media. The Strikers' fame grew with each knockout. Everyone in south Chicago who wanted to be in a gang wanted to be a Striker, and the group added dozens to their ranks.

Including girls.

A girl was initiated by a ritual called the dirty dozen. To become a Striker, the girl agreed to be gang raped by a dozen gang members. Literally hundreds of girls subjected themselves to the initiation, and within a few years, the Strikers had grown to nearly a thousand members.

The gang had a temporary setback in their upward trajectory when one of the girls raped was underage and one of the knockout victims died. The local authorities cracked down on them. They made several arrests, and the group disbanded for nearly a year.

They were revitalized by a man named Cade Ferry, aka Shiv. The nickname earned from his weapon of choice in dealing with rival gangs. The files didn't go into details, but Jamie easily figured it out.

Like most Strikers, Shiv never completed high school, but he was ambitious. He didn't want a gang. He wanted an enterprise. Money and power, but not fame. So, they circled the ranks. Became selective as to who they allowed as members. Shrunk their membership down to a few hundred and women were excluded.

The inner circle was even more exclusive. Shiv kept everything close to the vest. Eliminated the petty crimes. The types of things that drew attention to a gang. He focused on distributing drugs. Violence had to have a purpose to it. Revenge. Self-defense. Elimination of rivals.

Shiv had the gang prudently scale back the violence. Knockout games became a thing of the past. Over eight years, Shiv built the largest drug organization in the Midwest and brought millions into the coffers. All the while managing to avoid capture by the authorities.

In the FBI file, word was that Shiv had a mole inside the Chicago P.D. Not just a mole, but someone with significant ties to the organization. That allowed him to stay one step ahead of the authorities. Hard to believe in this day and age, but no one knew where the drugs were being manufactured and distributed.

Shiv was never seen in public. He was like a ghost. A phantom. Some wondered if he even existed. The only picture they knew existed was from his days as a fourteen-year-old, and the files of the case were sealed because he was a juvenile at the time of his arrest.

When the drug operations grew big enough, they garnered the attention of the FBI. When the Strikers ventured into sex trafficking, a second FBI task force became involved and they ramped up their efforts to bring down the organization.

Something Jamie decided to help them with.

Reading the reports had raised the ire inside of her. She hated these organizations. They were pure evil. She also wondered if Rita had been undercover. She was killed by the Strikers. The unanswered question was if she double-crossed them or they discovered she was with the Feds.

Jamie decided she'd do what she could behind the scenes. Under the radar. A skill she had considerable experience at and was highly motivated to accomplish. Shutting down sex-trafficking organizations and rescuing girls was her life's passion. Her calling. Something God had gifted her to do.

Maybe she'd already helped them even though the FBI didn't know it. She wasn't sure if she was responsible for the shutting down of the sex-trafficking operations at the Central Inn and at the gang house on Dexter Street, but they were no longer in operation, or if they weren't shut down, at least they were extremely hampered.

She must've had something to do with that. Not that she sought any credit. Just results.

The truth was that the human trafficking operations could've been moved to a new location. Since she was at a dead end in her search for Bae, she turned her focus on finding what happened to the girls. At least until a new lead emerged regarding Bae's whereabouts.

So, she went back to the gang house in search of clues. She parked her car in the garage at the vacant house and set up surveillance in the back bedroom. When she first found that house, it had occurred to her that it seemed like the room had once been used for the same purposes. She wondered if the FBI had been operating out of there at one point.

Another unanswered question.

No one was at the house, but Jamie saw signs of activity. Fresh tire tracks. Curtains that were open before were now closed. People had been at the house. That didn't surprise her. In her experience, groups might abandon a location for a period of time but usually went back there. That's why her instincts told her to check out the house again.

That, and she had nothing else to go on. She had Alex searching for Shiv's whereabouts, but he hadn't found anything yet. He was also still working on cracking the encryption on the Cuban lady's phone and hacking into the missing person cases filed at the Chicago P.D.

He'd joked with her about giving him so much work. Alex had a team of a dozen computer experts working on the island. What he couldn't do himself, he could delegate, so she didn't feel bad about it. This was the great thing about freelancing with the CIA. They could set their own missions and their own agenda. Including operating in the US. Something the CIA was forbidden by law to do based on the Constitution.

After watching the house for a couple hours, Jamie became bored and decided to take a closer look. If the Strikers were operating out of the house again, there might be actionable intelligence inside. Once she was sure the coast was clear, she hopped over the fence and raced to the back door.

She easily picked the lock and was inside within thirty seconds. Her observations were right. Someone had recently been in the house. The door leading to the basement was opened, so Jamie was certain no girls were in the house. It did appear as though preparations were being made to perhaps bring some back there again.

Bae?

Another open question in her mind. If the Cuban lady was FBI, then Bae was safe. If she was evil and one of the leaders of the sex-trafficking operations, then Bae could be anywhere.

Jamie wasn't in the house for five minutes when she heard a car drive up. She looked out the window, being careful not to be seen. A four-door vehicle pulled into the driveway.

Three men stepped out. Strikers.

They stuck their noses in the air and looked in every direction. Like secret service agents about to open the door for the President. When they did open the back door to the car, what she saw sent Jamie into a rage. She consciously made sure she was controlling it.

Two young girls were dragged out. They appeared to be fourteen or fifteen years old.

Jamie's heart began to race. She took two deep breaths to calm it.

She drew her gun.

Time to send a message to the Strikers.

She wouldn't control the punishment she was about to dole out to the three men. She wouldn't wait for them to enter the house. Their bodies needed to be littered throughout the backyard. When other Strikers found them, she wanted to send a clear message to Shiv. If he existed. If he didn't, somebody did. The organization wasn't running itself.

Jamie bolted out the door with her weapon pointed at the three men.

The two girls screamed. Crouched down on their knees in the driveway.

The men's eyes widened as they tried to process the threat.

Instinctively, they reached for their guns. A futile effort. The girls were between Jamie and the men, but it didn't matter. She still had line of sight and was a good enough shot to avoid hitting them.

Normally, when facing multiple hostiles, Jamie shot from left to right. For whatever reason, she did the opposite.

Three seconds later, the gunfight was over.

The three men lay on the ground. Red dots were on each of their foreheads, just above the bridge of their noses. The two girls had fallen to the ground. Jamie helped them to their feet.

"Are you okay?" she asked them.

They nodded their heads.

"Let's get out of here," Jamie said.

They hesitated. Looked down at the three men.

"Don't look!" Jamie said. "Run. To that fence over there. Jump over it and wait for me. I'm going to help you."

The girls sprinted to the fence and hopped over like a couple of gazelles. Jamie checked the men to make sure they were dead. Then bounded over the fence as quickly as she could so she wasn't out in the open for any longer than necessary.

She was confident no one had seen her. In a neighborhood like this, when gunshots rang out, the last thing people did was go to the windows to look. What were they going to do? Tell the cops what they saw? The Strikers would find out and pay them a visit. Most people kept their heads down and tried to stay out of the crosshairs of the gangs.

"Follow me," Jamie said to the girls.

She led them inside.

"What are your names?" Jamie asked. They appeared to still be in shock. They'd seen more in their short lives than any young girls ever should.

"I'm Shelly," one of them said. "She's Vik. Vicky."

"I'm Jackie," Jamie said. She'd just killed three men and these girls witnessed it. She didn't want them to know her real name in case they were questioned. Not likely, since no one but the three of them and the dead guys knew the girls had been there.

"We have to get out of here," Jamie said. "I'm going to take you somewhere safe."

Jamie called her local contact with *Save The Girls*. They'd been waiting for her call for several days. She'd given them the heads up that she was working on infiltrating a sex-trafficking ring in Chicago and might have some girls for them to take in.

If Shelly and Vicky didn't want to go home, they'd provide them with food and shelter and counseling. They had a good system and track record of helping girls.

After dropping off the girls, Jamie returned to the house to observe her handiwork. She was surprised to see the police activity. She figured the dead guys would be found by fellow gang members who would dispose of the bodies.

Instead, she saw a flurry of activity. Three police cruisers. A coroner. A couple of men in suits who looked like detectives. Yellow police tape surrounded the dead men and the back door.

Several beat cops were canvassing the neighborhood looking for eyewitnesses. One came to the vacant house, but Jamie didn't answer the door and stayed out of sight. When they left, she continued her surveillance from the perfect vantage point of the back bedroom.

Slowly the crowd of people left the scene. The three bodies were taken away by the coroner. The older guy, a detective, probably the boss, left the other younger detective at the scene. He became the one in charge as he barked orders to the forensic team who eventually went into the house to conduct their search.

Jamie had been careful not to leave any of her prints or DNA. Not that they could be traced. Hers were classified by the CIA and weren't in any of the databases that even the FBI could access.

Finally, everyone was gone except the detective and two cops. The detective walked out of the house and ripped down the police tape around the back door. He wadded it up and put it in his pocket. He then went out into the back yard where Jamie had shot the three men and tore down the police tape there. He then walked over to his vehicle, opened the trunk, and threw the tape inside.

A conversation with the two cops broke out. After what seemed to be an intense discussion, the two cops got in their cruisers and left the scene. The detective drove away as well.

Jamie finally allowed herself a moment to relax and wonder why the detective had taken down the police tape. A few minutes later, that respite was interrupted as the detective walked back toward the house carrying a pump action shotgun.

What?

It didn't take Jamie long to figure out what he was doing.

Not smart.

He was going against all procedures. Clearly attempting to set a trap for the Strikers. Making it look like no one was in the house. In the hopes that more of them would come, and he could arrest them and get more information.

Jamie admired the plan. It was something she'd do as well. But did he have the skills to pull it off? She almost hoped it worked and more Strikers did come back. More questions formed in her mind. How could she help him? She wouldn't mind putting a few more of them out of their miserable existence.

Something that would be harder to do with the detective there. She'd have to stay in the shadows. It was good she was there though. To have his back. Just in case.

When darkness fell, Jamie left the vacant house, hopped over the fence, and circled around to the front of the gang house to get a good sense of what was going on and what might happen if some Strikers did show up. She took up a location with a view of the front and the back driveway.

Some headlights approached. Jamie was amazed at how little traffic there actually was for a neighborhood full of houses. She crouched down further, even though it was unnecessary.

The car slowed in front of the house.

A black Lexus.

She remembered. The memory jolted her emotions and almost caused her to jump. The Cuban lady was killed by three men in a black Lexus. No question in her mind, this was the same car.

They were looking toward the gang house.

A light was on in the front living room.

She let out a noticeable gasp.

Stupid.

The detective didn't realize it, but his shadow could be seen on the wall. Jamie could see his image on the mirror above the couch. If she could see it, the men in the Lexus could as well.

The car came to a stop at the end of the block.

One of the men got out.

The other two stayed in the car and waited. The man outside the vehicle went between one of the houses and toward the back alley. A minute later, the Lexus did a U-turn and drove back to the house, pulled in front of it, and stopped.

The two men got out.

This is not good.

They were setting their own trap. More than likely, the two men in the front were going to approach the house like everything was normal. The third man would sneak in the back and ambush the detective.

He'd never see him coming.

Jamie practically sprinted down the opposite side of the street and went between the houses two doors down. She had to get to the back of the house before the other man could enter.

He was already there.

A gun in his right hand.

He'd already opened the door, and she watched him slither into the house, like a snake sneaking up on an unsuspecting mouse.

Jamie had no choice.

She followed him in.

39

"Chicago PD!" The detective said from the front living-room area. "I said to put your hands on your heads where I can see them!"

The shouting was working to Jamie's advantage. She was able to follow the Striker through the kitchen and into the hallway leading into the living room without him knowing she was there.

"On your knees, now!" the detective said.

She could envision the scene in her mind. The detective had his gun drawn on the two men. They had their guns drawn on him. A standoff. At least the detective had a fighting chance. Except that he didn't know about the third man.

The third Striker was inching toward the room. He was only three feet in front of her and clearly intended to spring from the shadows and either shoot him or jump him from behind.

Jamie wasn't going to give him the chance to get a shot off.

She came up on him and smashed the side of her hand on the base of his neck. The karate chop had enough force that he immediately fell to the floor in a heap.

Jamie came out of the shadows. The detective had his gun on two Strikers. She was relieved to see that the two men didn't have their guns drawn. Their eyes widened when they saw her. They were clearly expecting to see their buddy emerge from the darkness of the hall.

"You heard the man," Jamie shouted. "Get on your knees! Spread eagle! I'm not going to tell you twice."

If they didn't comply to Jamie's commands, she'd handle things differently than the detective. He had more constraints than she did. Not technically. This was America, and Jamie had to follow the laws as well. But the detective didn't have the White House phone number on his phone. He couldn't call the President of the United States or the Director of the CIA.

She wouldn't call them either, even though she could. One call to her CIA handler, Brad, and she'd be out of jail and on the next plane back to Washington D.C. The whole thing buried in bureaucracy.

That didn't mean Brad wouldn't chew her out. It just meant she could act with reasonable impunity. Her role with the CIA was much more important to national security than a problem she might have with local law enforcement. She'd saved many lives and would save more in the future. So, she didn't care if some local cop thought she was about to handle the situation wrong. No one in Washington would care that she killed a few drug dealers.

Jamie took several steps toward the men, spanning the gap in no time. She grabbed one of the men by the nape of his neck and unceremoniously slammed him to the ground. She planted her foot in the back of the Striker on the floor. Then pointed her gun at the other man's head.

"Three of your lowlife friends are dead," Jamie said to the two men. "Do you want to join them?"

The Striker didn't hesitate this time. He got on his knees and went spread eagle. Jamie took the guns out of the back of both men's pants and threw them across the floor toward the detective. He kicked them back behind him.

"Do you have two pairs of handcuffs?" Jamie asked the detective.

He nodded in the affirmative.

"Toss them to me," she said.

He pulled them out of his back pocket and tossed them her way. Jamie secured the men's hands behind their backs, then patted them down further. One had a pair of brass knuckles in his pocket and the other had a knife. She tossed them to the other side of the room.

"Do you have another set of handcuffs for the other guy?" Jamie asked, surprised the detective hadn't spoken a word to that point. He seemed as stunned as the two men on the ground.

"No. I only have two." His voice cracked as he said it.

"No problem," Jamie said.

She stood up and went into the hallway and dragged the body of the unconscious man into the living room.

"He's out cold," she said. "But you can never be too careful."

Jamie had a pair of zip ties in her back pocket for this purpose. She secured the man's hands behind his back and then holstered her weapon. She wiped the sweat from her brow and let out a huge sigh. Lifted her shoulders up and down to relieve the tension.

The detective still had the gun pointed in her direction. Not right at her, but toward her. His finger was on the trigger, and that made her nervous.

"You can put your gun away," Jamie said.

"Who are you?" he asked.

Jamie pointed toward the kitchen. "Let's go in there where we can talk."

She was also still nervous even though she tried not to let it show in her demeanor. More Strikers could show up at any time.

Finally, the detective put away his weapon.

Once they were in the kitchen, Jamie asked him, "What's your name?"

"Cliff Ford, Chicago PD. Homicide."

For whatever reason, the name made her grin. Could be nothing more than the release of tension from the confrontation. Then she remembered that she'd seen him at Champions Bar. The night she

263

beat up three other Strikers. Couldn't be a coincidence. Especially since she didn't believe in them.

"May I call you Clifford," she asked kiddingly.

Surprisingly, he nodded.

Jamie reached out her hand, and he shook it.

"Your plan was a good one," she said as she leaned back against the kitchen counter. "Take down the police tape and wait for them to show up. If you hadn't done that, I intended to."

Not exactly. She didn't know if she would've thought of it, but it was a good idea.

His mouth twisted to the side like he was confused. Probably that she had seen him do all of that. His mind was probably wondering where she had watched it all.

"How did you know the Strikers would show up?" he asked.

"The same way you did. Intuition. It seemed logical. Three of their men are dead. They'd be curious. They'd also be livid. They'd want to know who took their guys. Several of them already drove by during the day. They slowed down when they saw the cruisers and the coroner hauling off the bodies."

"Did you kill the three men?" Cliff asked.

A question Jamie wasn't prepared to answer. She'd answer his question with one of her own.

"Like I said, your plan was a good one, but it had a fatal flaw. Do you want to know what it was?"

"What's that?" he asked.

Jamie was thankful he hadn't pushed the point and asked again who shot the men. She suspected he already knew.

"Your shadow," Jamie said. "They could see it through the window. I saw them drop off one man down the street. Then they drove slowly back to the house, so he had time to sneak in through the backdoor. I had intended on seeing how it all played out, but I figured you needed help. He was coming from your blind side."

"You probably saved my life," he said. "I owe you big time. Thank you."

"You're welcome."

He asked Jamie more questions. He wanted to know if she was CIA, FBI, or some other kind of law enforcement. She deflected again.

"I'm someone who can help you," Jamie said. "I've been following these three thugs for a while. These are the guys who killed the girl in front of the coffee shop."

Cliff's eyes widened, and his mouth gaped open. Jamie had hit a nerve. Something that was personal to him.

"What do you know about the girl in the coffeeshop?" he asked.

Jamie told him everything she knew. About how she was there. Saw the black Lexus. How the woman died in her arms.

She did learn some things from the conversation. Cliff wasn't the detective investigating the case but had a lot of information. Another detective was investigating the murder. Something that clearly bothered him. They didn't know the woman's identity or if she was law enforcement.

Cliff changed the subject and asked about the events of Friday night at Champions Bar. This was getting uncomfortable. He was the one who had chased her out of the parking lot.

Her turn to change the subject.

"Do you know where they took the girls who were in this house?" Jamie asked.

His turn for deflection. We were engaged in a ping pong conversation.

"I saw you at Champions Bar. Friday night. You beat up three gang members in the alley. I need to take you in for questioning."

That concerned her.

Jamie didn't want to resist an officer but would if necessary. There's no way she'd go to the station voluntarily, and a quick look at him left her convinced that he couldn't make her.

She uncrossed her arm and stood straight up so he'd know she considered that comment a threat.

"Good luck with that," Jamie said.

"You're obstructing an investigation!"

"From my vantage point, I just solved your investigation. Run ballistics on the gun. You'll see. That's the murder weapon. You wouldn't know that if it weren't for me. You'd also be dead right now if I hadn't come along. So, drop the obstruction nonsense."

He seemed convinced by her argument.

"Look," Jamie continued. "We need to work together on this. I'm looking for a girl. The gang kidnapped her and were holding her in this house."

Jamie didn't know that for sure but was convinced that was the case.

"I can confirm that," Cliff said. "Your girl wrote her name on the wall downstairs. Bae."

She couldn't believe what she heard.

40

"That's right," Cliff said, gaining some confidence. "We found a list of names written on the wall. Behind the dresser. Presumably the names of girls held in this house. Bae was one of them."

"Do you know where they took them?" Jamie asked.

"No."

"Well... those scumbags in the other room know. Let's go question them."

Jamie started to walk that way, but Cliff held out his hand and touched her arm to stop her.

Don't touch me, she wanted to say but held her tongue. Her anger for the Strikers was right on the surface, and she could easily take it out on Cliff.

"I need to read them their rights," he said.

"Let me do it. Follow my lead. You play good cop."

Jamie knew his limitations. She could get more out of the guys than he could. The men were face down on the floor and buried their heads when they saw her walk in. She grabbed one of them by the scruff of his neck then flipped him over.

"Where did they take the girls who were being kept in this house?" she asked roughly.

The man glared at Jamie then turned his head to the side in defiance.

Jamie pulled the gun out of her holster. She put it against the man's forehead. While she wouldn't kill him in front of the detective, the low life on the ground didn't know that.

He tried to squirm away, but Jamie had him pinned down.

"You have the right to remain silent," Jamie said to him. "If you choose to remain silent, I have the right to put a bullet in the back of your brain!"

She pushed the gun harder against his forehead. He'd have an indentation on it when she eventually pulled it off.

"You can't do this," Cliff said.

Exactly what she wanted him to say and what she meant about playing good cop.

Jamie took her intensity up a notch. "You have a right to a coroner." Jamie was almost shouting now. "If you can't afford a coroner, one will be provided for you at no charge. Do you understand your rights?"

He didn't answer.

"Do you understand your rights?" Jamie shouted.

"Yes," he said weakly.

"I'm going to ask one more time. Where did you take the girls?"

The man's eyes flitted back and forth. He didn't know exactly what to say. Gang members had a code. The man was probably thinking he was dead either way. Dead if he talked. Dead if he didn't.

"I'm done with you," Jamie said. "After I blow your brains out, I bet your friends will talk."

She made a gesture like she was about to pull the trigger. At least she wanted him to believe she was about to.

"No!" Cliff shouted. "Don't kill him!"

While he was playing the role of good cop, he was also serious. He didn't want Jamie to kill the guy. She didn't want to either. She wanted information. When she was done with them, Cliff would arrest them. Once they were taken down to the station, they'd clam up. Get a lawyer. The police would never get information from them. Jamie didn't know how much they knew, but they knew more than they were letting on.

"I'm going to count to three," Jamie said. "You'd better answer me, or you're as dead as your three friends who were hauled away by the coroner earlier today."

She probably just confessed to killing the three men.

"One!" Jamie shouted.

"Two!" she said even louder than before.

"I'll talk!" The man caved. "Don't shoot me. I know where the girls are!"

Jamie could tell the man was lying. He'd say anything to save himself. She let up and removed the gun from his forehead though.

"Where?" she asked.

"Shiv has them."

The man had just confirmed something important. Shiv existed. The man might not know where the girls were taken, but he would know where Shiv was.

"Address?"

Jamie pressed the gun back down on his forehead.

"He's in a warehouse on the south side. Down by the docks. That's where he's at. I don't know where they took the girls, but he'll know."

"Which warehouse?"

He muttered out an address. She could tell from his expression that he was telling the truth.

Jamie stood to her feet, and the man let out a noticeable sigh of relief.

"Alright. Detective, you need to put the police tape back on the front and back doors. Seal off the house. Then call for backup. Take these three in on suspicion of murder."

Cliff read the men their rights. Jamie went into the kitchen, walked out the back door, and went back to the vacant house.

She got in the car and dialed a number while she was driving away.

Alex answered. "Do you know that I haven't had sex in three weeks?"

Jamie couldn't help but grin widely. She'd just been in a life and death situation, and a few minutes later Alex was cracking her up.

"I'm glad," Jamie answered. "Considering that I haven't seen you in three weeks."

"I don't think I can go much longer," he said.

"Me either. If I don't see you soon, I'll have to call the man in Borneo."

"I thought there wasn't a man in Borneo!"

"There isn't. I was only kidding."

She immediately regretted the comment. She'd broken a cardinal rule in their relationship. They never joked about cheating on each other. She couldn't help herself though. Alex deserved it for even questioning her about such nonsense.

"Why are you calling me?" Alex asked coldly.

"I have an address. I need everything you have on it."

"Everything? Or anything?"

Jamie knew what he meant.

"I want the works. I think I found Strikers' headquarters. I want schematics. Ingress and egress. Satellite photos. Anything you got."

"What do you intend to do?" Alex asked. "I'm almost afraid to ask."

"I'm going to pay Shiv a visit."

41

The drug manufacturing and distribution center was a series of interconnected warehouses at the Chicago shipping docks. They looked like dozens of other warehouses in the area, which was probably why the authorities never found the operations.

Alex came through and provided Jamie with great intel. He sent her architectural layouts of the entire facility with an educated guess as to where the main offices would be located. She didn't have real time overhead satellite pictures but was able to observe the warehouse over two days and had a good idea as to the number of armed hostiles she might encounter.

Alex provided her with an infiltration plan, but Jamie decided to walk into the place like she belonged there and got deep into the warehouse before anyone noticed her.

"I'm here to meet with Shiv," she told the armed Striker who finally asked her what she was doing. After she'd pretty much cased two thirds of the facility.

"And who are you?" he asked.

"Who are you?" she fired back.

"I work for Shiv," he said. "And I don't know you."

"I work for Shiv too, and I don't know you," Jamie retorted.

Curly taught her that trick. If you were somewhere you weren't supposed to be and were questioned about it, keep repeating the person's questions back to them with an attitude and watch their confusion. The tactic made it sound like you belonged there as much as that person did.

At some point she would have to explain herself, so she did. "I'm the one who replaced Rita. I recruit the girls now."

Jamie saw the recognition in the man's face when she mentioned Rita. A confirmation that her intel was correct. Even though she'd thrown out Rita's name, he still seemed skeptical. He was likely high up in the organization which was why he had the authority to stop and question her anyway.

"No one told me," he said.

"I guess you aren't as important as you think you are."

He scowled at her. She scowled back.

Then he continued to ask questions, so she pulled out her gun and shot him in the head and hid his body in a nearby closet. No one else saw the shot, but several Strikers heard it and scurried around with their guns drawn, looking for the source.

Since things were getting hotter than she liked, Jamie decided to get out of there. She'd seen enough and knew exactly what to do.

Something law enforcement could never do.

The manufacturing part of the facility was a sophisticated, fifty-thousand-square-foot lab on the north end of the building. It'd qualify as a superlab by most standards. Drug distribution wasn't Jamie's area, but she knew enough to know what was in the large liquid storage bins. Ammonia. Acetone/ethyl alcohol. Red phosphorus. Highly flammable liquids that would explode with an igniter.

Something like a bullet shot into the center of a tank.

Jamie got in position. She covered her nose from the strong smell of the chemicals. One bullet in one tank did the trick.

Actually, more than the trick. The tank exploded and ignited the others.

She hightailed it out of there. Almost not quick enough. The explosion was so loud, it reverberated in her ears, and she could feel the ground shake like an earthquake had just hit Chicago's south side.

When she looked back it was like a war zone after a bombing raid. The warehouse was no longer there. Nothing more than a rubble of twisted building material with large dark smoke reaching hundreds of feet in the sky.

A bullet bounced off the ground next to her. The war wasn't over. Six hostiles were running toward her with guns drawn. Jamie put bullets in each of their heads and chest. Left to right, this time. Because of necessity. The other way wouldn't have made logistical sense.

Not before the men got more shots off. Fortunately, the bullets whizzed by her or bounced harmlessly off the concrete near her feet. She knew from experience that most bad guys weren't good shots. That didn't mean they couldn't get lucky, so Jamie didn't stick around to see if anymore came after her.

She sprinted to the cover of other businesses which were far enough away from the blast radius that they weren't damaged. Alex had pre planned her escape route, and she'd memorized it and followed it almost perfectly. Almost, because she had her own plan.

The explosion at the docks leveled an entire block. Blowing up the Strikers headquarters hadn't been Jamie's plan. That was a bonus.

She ran toward a building two blocks over. Climbed the fire escape in the back to the top of the building where she had a good vantage point to observe her handiwork.

Not Alex's plan. He said she should get out of there. Jamie wanted to see who showed up at the scene. It might give her information she didn't have.

Over the next fifteen minutes, the expected arrived. Fire trucks. Ambulances. Chicago PD. DEA. FBI.

Then the unexpected.

Cliff Ford.

The homicide detective she met at the gang house.

She had information he might be interested in. Alex found Cliff's personal cell phone number, and Jamie had it on her phone. She dialed it.

From her vantage point, she could see him answer it.

"Clifford. How are you?" Jamie asked.

"How did you get my number?" he said in a confused tone. He recognized her voice but was clearly shocked that she'd called him.

"I see you are down at the docks," Jamie said nonchalantly.

She laughed inside as she could see him looking around for her.

"I'm sorry the FBI took your case from you," Jamie added. "You deserve the credit for solving it."

"How did you know... "

Another way in which Alex had come through. He found the name of the Cuban woman in a missing person's report by hacking into the Chicago PD server and looking for anything filed in the last few days.

He also found the Jane Doe online case file and learned that the FBI had taken jurisdiction over it.

"Why did they take the case from us?" Cliff asked.

More information Alex had gathered for her. Once he had a name of a person, he could find out the last time they trimmed their fingernails. Not really. But it seemed like it.

The information was still raw inside of her and had hit her like a semi-truck carrying a ton of bricks.

"The woman who was shot at the coffeeshop was an undercover agent with the FBI," Jamie said.

Grief rose up inside her a second time. She thought taking down the Strikers would ease the pain of it, but it hadn't. Knowing Rita was in the business of rescuing girls was downright excruciating. Like one of her own had been killed. In essence, she had. The circle of people who put their lives in danger to rescue girls was small. Losing even one was devastating to the cause.

"You were right," Cliff said. "The guy at the house was the shooter. Ballistics were a match."

"I told you they would be," Jamie said. "The Strikers killed her. More of an execution, really."

Even saying the words brought a tear to Jamie's eyes. She estimated that more than a hundred Strikers died in the explosion. One thousand wouldn't be enough to compensate for the death of someone with the courage of Rita. A woman willing to go undercover in the seedy underworld of a male-dominated gang and risk her life for six girls. Including Bae. Jamie regretted she hadn't known all the facts sooner and perhaps could've protected her.

"Why would the Strikers want to take her out?" Cliff asked. "Had she infiltrated their gang?"

"Not exactly," Jamie said. "She worked in the sex trafficking division of the FBI. Her job was to rescue girls. The Strikers were taking girls off the street and holding them as sex slaves. The woman wasn't undercover in the sense that she was part of the gang, but she was working surreptitiously to get girls out. Her work was robbing them of their most valuable commodity. Young, beautiful girls. Saving the girls was her passion. My kind of girl. I'm sad we lost her."

"Me too," Cliff said. "And the Strikers have one of the girls you're looking for. Bae."

"Had," Jamie said.

"As in, they don't have her anymore?" he asked with surprise in his voice. "Was she still alive? Was she in the warehouse?"

Jamie hesitated. She'd already given him a lot of information. A good judge of character, she felt like Cliff was someone she could trust. It wouldn't be hard for him to deduce that she was behind the explosion at the docks, along with the death of the men outside the warehouse, so she didn't figure she had that much to lose.

"I take it you still haven't found her?" Cliff asked Jamie.

"No."

"Is that why you blew up the warehouse?"

"That was an accident. So to speak. The Strikers had a meth lab in that warehouse. A stray bullet set off the explosion." This was a way to cover her backside.

"The explosion brought the whole place down," Jamie added. "But to answer your question, they weren't keeping any girls there."

Jamie confirmed that before she set off the explosion.

"Why are you telling me all this?" he asked.

"The dead woman has a sister. Her name's Anna."

More of Alex's information he had gathered.

"How do you know Anna?" Cliff asked.

Jamie could hear the excitement rise in his voice.

"The dead woman's name is Rita Navarez. Her sister filed a missing person's report on her earlier today. The FBI hasn't notified the next of kin yet. My guess is that the family didn't know what she really did for a living. Look up the missing person's report. They need to know what happened to their family member."

"How can I get in touch with you if I have more questions?"

"I'll text you a number. You can call me at that number. Don't bother trying to trace it, though. It's a burner. Untraceable."

Jamie hung up.

Convinced she'd done the right thing by sharing that information with Cliff. She thought back to the conversation with Alex to see if she'd left anything out.

"There are two people reported missing," Alex had said. "There are more, but these are the only two who fit the description of your girl. Although, one of them is probably too young to be your girl."

"What are the names?" Jamie asked.

"Julie O'Connor and Rita Navarez."

Jamie had been positive Rita was the name of her girl. O'Connor was Irish. Navarez was Cuban or Hispanic, so putting it together wasn't hard. The O'Connor name sounded familiar, but Jamie couldn't figure out why, so she moved on. She was thrilled that she finally had the name of the dead woman.

The police were starting to cordon off the area, so Jamie thought it best to get out of there.

Alex was working on finding Anna's address. When he did, she was going to her house to find Bae.

42

"Why can't I find the little monster?" Jamie asked Alex with as much exasperation as she could put in her tone.

She'd gone to Anna's house and found nothing. No one was home, and it didn't look like they'd been in a day or two. Certainly, no evidence that Bae was ever there.

"You're the one who taught Bae how to stay off the grid," Alex said.

"Don't remind me."

"It might be because you're emotionally invested. You know how it is. When we let our emotions get the best of us, we lose perspective."

"Are you saying I've let my emotions get the best of me?" Jamie asked angrily.

"What I'm saying... " He said the words slower than before. Obviously trying not to tick her off any more than he already had.

"What I'm saying is that Bae is like a sister to you or a daughter. That makes it harder to see the forest for the trees, as the saying goes."

"You aren't emotionally invested in Bae?" Jamie asked.

"It's different for men."

"This I gotta hear."

"Let me explain," he said.

"Feel free."

She was more than willing to let him keep digging himself into a bigger hole.

"Bae is annoying," Alex said.

The comment and the way he said it caused Jamie to laugh, easing the tension some.

"That she is," Jamie agreed.

"I focus on that," Alex said. "When I'm working on Bae's stuff. I think about how annoying she is. That overcomes my emotional attachment to her."

"That's an interesting hypothesis you presented there, young man."

"More of a theory than a hypothesis."

"You may be on to something. If you ever go missing, I think I'll try that. Focus on how annoying you are."

"Back at you."

Jamie hung up the phone. Alex had a point.

Bae was as annoying as it got. She'd focus on that. See if it helped.

***

Jamie actually considered going home. Alex left the island and was flying back to DC. and she desperately wanted to see him. It was one thing to be apart for long periods of time when she was being productive. Quite another when she faced one dead end after another.

Actually, taking down the Strikers had been a huge success and the only reason she wasn't despondent. Bae was the problem. It shouldn't be this hard to find a ninety-pound North Korean girl on her own in Chicago for the first time.

She had a lead, Rita's sister, but it wasn't going anywhere.

Jamie staked out Anna's house for hours, and the woman never showed up. That gave her a lot of time to research Anna. The woman was a high school guidance counselor. Jamie called the school. Anna wasn't in and hadn't been for a couple of days.

Was she missing as well? Did the Strikers learn that Rita took the girls to Anna? Were the Strikers still after Bae? She had a lot of unanswered questions.

Jamie felt like she was no closer to finding Bae than the day she arrived in Chicago. For all she knew, Bae could've left Chicago and was in Timbuktu, as her mom used to say when she didn't know where someone was.

Jamie pounded her fists on the steering wheel of the rental car, then shook it out of frustration. She'd done everything she knew to do.

"This is ridiculous. I'm going home," she said aloud even though no one was around to hear it.

As she started the car, her cell phone rang, startling her and interrupting what had been hours of silence. Not *her* cellphone, but the burner phone. She'd only given that number out to one person.

"Hello Clifford," she said.

"I know where Bae is," Cliff blurted out.

Out of all the things she expected him to say, that wasn't one of them.

"Where?" Jamie said excitedly.

He gave her an address. Then explained.

"Rita has a sister. Bae is staying at her house."

Jamie's heart sank. She already knew about Anna. She was sitting in front of her house.

"I know about Anna," Jamie retorted with a hint of anger. "I'm the one who told you about her. Bae is not at her house."

"Rita has two sisters," Cliff said. "Anna and Julia. Julia is the name of the third sister. They are identical triplets. What are the odds?"

The rush of adrenaline returned. Even stronger the second time. This would explain why she hadn't found Bae at Anna's house.

"Astronomical," Jamie said. She couldn't even fathom the odds. "I've never heard of it before."

"One in two hundred million is what I heard. Anyway, it doesn't matter. I think the sister's lives are in danger. Shiv is alive."

Jamie would've fallen off her seat if she wasn't sitting in the confined area of her car. She didn't believe for a minute that Shiv could've survived the explosion.

Cliff continued. "We never recovered his body at the explosion site. So, he's still on the loose. Probably looking for you as well. Keep your radar up."

"I'll be gone before he can find me," Jamie said. "As soon as I get Bae, we're out of here."

"That's a good idea."

Jamie needed to know something she wasn't particularly worried about it, but it might complicate things.

"Have you told your boss about me?" Jamie asked.

"Your secret is safe with me," Cliff answered.

She let out a sigh he wouldn't be able to hear over the phone. A sense of relief washed through her.

They talked for several more minutes.

As the conversation wound down, Jamie said, "Thanks for the intel on the girl." She sincerely meant it. She was growing to like Cliff Ford.

"The Strikers will still be looking for you," Cliff said a second time.

Jamie wasn't sure they even knew who she was. Certainly not how to find her. She had half a mind to go looking for Shiv but thought better of it. She needed to find Bae and get out of town as soon as possible. Shiv was Chicago's problem. She had crippled his organization to the point that it no longer existed. If Chicago PD let him resurrect it, then shame on them.

"Hopefully, Bae will go with me," Jamie said with some resignation. "She's very stubborn."

"I think she thinks she's a female Reeder Rich," Cliff said, which surprised Jamie. He obviously knew more about Bae than she'd realized.

"Like I said, the girl is a little crazy," Jamie added. "She means well, but she got in over her head with the Strikers. Hopefully, she's learned her lesson. I'm glad to hear she's alive. If I don't talk to you again, thanks for everything."

"You're welcome. Good luck," was the last thing he said.

Jamie hung up and looked up the address Cliff had given her. She was only a few blocks away from it. She couldn't believe the unexpected turn of events. That's how missions were. They had ebbs and flows. Leads often showed up out of the blue. Rarely as unusual as this one.

She drove to the house. A silver SUV, Kia model, sat in the driveway. The same vehicle Jamie had seen driving out of *Champions* bar on Friday night. A third sister. Identical triplets. Who'd have thought that was possible? Julia was obviously the person at the bar that night. Jamie had possibly saved the woman's life.

She'd lead with that. The woman might deny Bae was staying with her if Jamie just showed up out of the blue asking questions. If she mentioned the bar and the Strikers, that might get her to open up.

A woman answered the door. The spitting image of Rita and the girl at *Champions* bar.

"I know you," the woman said. "You're the lady at *Champions*. You saved my life."

Jamie was glad she remembered. That'd make things easier and bullying the woman unnecessary.

"May I come in?" Jamie asked.

"Of course."

Julia was pleasant and had a welcoming smile. She led them into the living room. Julia sat on the couch and Jamie on a chair next to her.

"First of all, let me express my condolences to you for the loss of your sister," Jamie said as she noticed the woman's eyes were bloodshot. Obviously from crying. "I'm sorry about Rita. I really am."

Tears welled up in Julia's eyes and the cheerful demeanor was replaced with grief. "Thank you," Julia said. "How did you know Rita? Did you work with her?"

Jamie decided not to answer. Leaving that vague would work to her advantage.

"Your sister was a hero," Jamie said. "I was there when she died. A gang called the Strikers killed her."

"I know. A detective with the Chicago police department came by and told me everything."

Jamie didn't know if she was talking about Cliff, but it seemed like a safe assumption.

"What's your name?" Julia asked.

"My name is Jamie," she said. She couldn't think of a reason to lie. "I'm looking for a girl. I understand she's staying with you."

"Bae?"

Jamie felt like she'd just had a B-12 shot.

"Yes! Is she here?"

"No."

Not the answer she expected to hear. Her demeanor changed in the same way Julia's had.

"I was told she was staying here," Jamie said, still trying to keep a friendly tone. "That Rita brought her to you."

"She was here. But she left. I haven't seen her in a couple of days."

Jamie's anger returned. Not at Julia, but at Bae. The girl was like a squiggly worm Jamie remembered trying to get on a hook when she went fishing as a little girl.

"Do you know where she went?" Jamie asked.

"I have no idea. Maybe the college. Bae talked about some girls she met on DePaul campus. At a sorority house. Connie and Julie, I think. She left her stuff there. I assumed she went to get it. If you can find them, they might know."

When Julia mentioned Connie and Julie, something triggered in Jamie's mind. Something Alex had said.

There were two missing person's reports. Rita Navarez and Julie O'Connor.

Jamie met Julie. At the sorority house. She had a stalker. Was Julie's last name O'Connor? Maybe? It seemed like it might be.

Oh no!

She put some pieces together. While she didn't know if they were right, she had a strong feeling they were.

"I've got to go," Jamie said, abruptly standing to her feet.

"I'm sorry I wasn't more help," Julia said.

"You've been a big help. Once again, I'm terribly sorry about your sister. I think she was an amazing woman."

"Yes. She was. We're going to miss her."

"Take care. I'm sorry I can't stay longer," Jamie said and left.

After she was on the road, she called Alex.

"I think Bae's gotten herself in the middle of another mess," Jamie said.

"What is it this time?"

"Who filed the missing person's report on Julie O'Connor?"

"Funny you should ask," Alex answered. Not the response she was expecting.

"A girl named Connie O'Connor filed the report. She's listed as a sister."

That confirmed in her mind that Julie was the one missing.

"Okay. I know about Connie," Jamie said.

"A missing person's report was also filed on Connie," Alex said.

What?

"How do you know?" Jamie asked, not believing it. What were the odds of both girls going missing? About the same as three identical triplets.

"I set an alert on the Chicago PD website," Alex explained. "When a missing person's report is filed, it notifies me."

"You never cease to amaze me."

"I thought I never ceased to annoy you."

"That too."

Jamie remembered something. "When Bae called you, she asked for an address. Do you still have it?"

"You bet," he said.

The phone was silent for a good thirty seconds or more. A text suddenly appeared on her phone along with a picture.

Of the stalker!

Jamie couldn't help but think the worst. Bae went to confront the stalker. It obviously didn't go well because Connie was missing now.

When Alex came back on the phone, Jamie said, "I've got to go. I need to clear my head."

"My head's always clear."

She thought of a funny comeback but didn't have the time.

43

The stalker's house was only a couple of blocks from campus and easy to find. It didn't appear like anyone was home.

Jamie wasn't going to wait around to find out. Normally, she'd do surveillance. Stake it out for a few hours. For some reason, she didn't think waiting was a prudent thing to do. In a missing person's case, time was of the essence.

She might be wrong, but it made sense that the stalker grabbed Julie. Bae went looking for her. Connie probably went with her. The stalker nabbed them as well. If that were the case then Bae was in grave danger. Maybe dead for all she knew.

No wonder Bae was so hard to find. She was probably being held in that house or some other location. She needed to confront the stalker and get answers. All her powers of persuasion would make him talk. That, and her Sig revolver which she realized she couldn't use as anything other than a threat. If she killed the kidnapper, she might not ever find the location of the missing girls.

Other methods would be more persuasive. Jamie had ways to invoke pain in a subject without leaving a mark. He might resist for a while, but the man she confronted once before was a wimp. She wasn't much worried about his ability to fight back. Jamie had been underwhelmed by his physical attributes and toughness, or lack thereof.

In fact, she was surprised that he got the best of Bae. Even Bae had the skills to beat that guy up in a fight.

Jamie picked the lock to the back door and searched the house. There wasn't any place inside where he could hold three girls against their will. She was about to go search the backyard and garage when she saw headlights.

The car turned into the driveway. Then pulled up to the garage. A man got out, opened the garage door, and pulled the car in. After he closed it, he walked toward the house.

Jamie went into the living room and sat down on a lounge chair.

The door opened, and the man entered. She was out of his line of sight. She could hear the sound of keys clinking on what she presumed was the kitchen counter. The man opened the refrigerator door. Silence for a few seconds. Then footsteps. Coming toward her.

The living room was dark except for the light from the street casting an eerie shadow into the room.

He entered the room and turned on the light with a drink in his hand.

"We meet again," Jamie said.

He jumped, but quickly composed himself. He acted surprisingly calm. Took a sip of his drink and stood there like he was the one in control. Jamie didn't buy it. The man was about to pee his pants.

"Where did you take the girls?" Jamie said with intensity behind the words.

From his face, Jamie could see the recognition. More than three of his body and facial expressions told her he knew exactly what she was talking about.

"I'm calling the police," he said. "You can't just break into my house."

Jamie stood to her feet. He took two steps back and set his drink on an end table.

"That's a good idea," Jamie said roughly. She pulled her phone out of her pocket with one hand and her gun with the other. "Let's call the police. Missing person's reports have been filed on two girls. I think the police will want to question you about their disappearances."

"What do you want?" he asked roughly.

"I want to know where the girls are!"

She took two more quick steps toward him with the gun raised.

He was no longer acting cool and collected. The concern showed deep in his face as his eyebrows were raised and he cowered back against the wall.

She stayed a couple steps back from him. So she could control the situation better. Until she knew what she was going to do. Too many unknowns. Were the girls in the garage? Did he take them to a different location? A cabin on the lake. A hole in the ground somewhere. Like in the movies.

Were the three girls dead? Jamie didn't allow her thoughts to go there. She'd play the cat and mouse game with the guy a little longer until she had a plan. The garage would be a place to start.

"Why don't we take a look in the garage," Jamie said, making an animated gesture with the gun so he'd be reminded of the threat.

She could see his mind trying to come up with his own plan. His eyes were flitting back and forth. Like he was trying to figure out how he could get out of this predicament.

The cocky demeanor suddenly returned.

"Fine," he said. "After you." He held out his hand like he wanted her to go first.

Jamie thought she knew what his plan was. Maybe the same one he'd used to trick Bae. She wanted him to think she'd fallen for it, so she walked ahead of him. If he tried something, a quick backward kick would make him regret it.

When they got to the garage, he unlocked the side door that led into it.

He turned on the light and they stood there looking at each other for a minute.

"As you can see, there are no girls here," he said. "I don't know what you're talking about, but since you have a gun, I guess you call the shots."

He grinned, then let out a geeky laugh. "Shots. Did you get the pun?"

Jamie noticed a door on the far wall. "What about the back room? What's in there?"

"That's just storage."

"Let's take a look."

He grew considerably more nervous and started to fidget with the keys. That's where the girls were. The stalker was trying to hide it, but Jamie could tell he didn't want to open the door.

She waved the gun at him.

"Open it."

"There's nothing in there."

Jamie gave him a shove.

"Hey!"

"Open the door! I'm not going to tell you twice. I'll shoot you and open it myself."

"Okay," he said. "You don't have to get pushy. But you're making a big mistake."

"Won't be my first one," she said.

He unlocked the door, pulled it open, then said, "After you." He held out his hand for her to go first. She expected it. Jamie was right about his plan. She had one of her own.

She walked through the door ahead of him. As soon as she crossed the threshold, she whirled and grabbed his collar with her hand and flung him into the room with one motion like he was a ragdoll.

She heard a yell, "Jamie!"

Bae!

The room was dark except for one small lamp plugged in on the back wall. Bae, Connie, and Julie were chained to the wall.

Jamie turned her attention back to the man. She holstered her weapon and picked him up again with two hands and slammed him against the far wall. He fell to the ground in a heap and laid there writhing in pain. She searched his pockets for a key to unlock the chains.

He had several keys on the keyring.

"Which key opens the locks?" Jamie said to the man roughly. She got on one knee and in his face. Now that she had the girls, she didn't care what he did. If he resisted and she roughed him up or killed him, then it was his own fault.

"Which key?" Jamie shouted.

She handed them to him. He fumbled with them, then selected one.

"Unlock them," Jamie said as she kept the weapon pointed at him.

That gave her a chance to look at the girls. They seemed okay, considering what they'd been through. The room was dank and smelled of mold. They all sat on one mattress. The room stank.

The man's hands shook, but he managed to unlock the chains.

When all three of them were free, Bae reared her leg back and kicked the man in the shin. Like Jamie had taught her.

"Take that!" Bae said.

He fell to the floor again and grabbed his leg. Jamie knew how much kicks to the shin hurt. Bae kicked him in the side of the ribs for good measure. She didn't blame her.

"Let's go," Jamie said, pointing to the exit.

"What are we going to do with him?" Julie asked.

"Give him a taste of his own medicine," Jamie said. "Let's see how he feels locked in this room for several days."

44

Boy was I glad to see Jamie.

I had a plan to escape out of the garage, but Jamie coming along made it easier. We chained the stalker to the wall and locked him in the garage.

Jamie intended to leave him there overnight then call the police to come and arrest him. Julie was adamant that we should call the police right away. I didn't care either way.

"I feel so bad for him," Julie said. "No one will know he's there. What if he dies?"

"After all he put you through?" Jamie asked in a cold, exacting tone.

Julie was practically pleading with Jamie. "I know. He's a bad person. I want him off the streets. But I don't want him to suffer."

Jamie let out a huge, noticeable sigh then took out her phone and called somebody. A homicide detective she knew named Cliff Ford. He came to the house and interviewed Connie and Julie. Then arrested the man. Jamie made me hide in the car, and Connie and Julie agreed not to mention I was even there.

Fine by me. Saved me from having to come back and testify against him.

When Jamie finally got in the car, she said Connie and Julie were going down to the station for questioning and then to the hospital for a medical examination.

We went and checked into a hotel.

Later that night, Jamie got an unexpected call. I didn't know who she was talking to, but they had a long conversation. I heard Jamie say, "Why are you telling me this?"

A few seconds later, she said. "Sorry. But I'm getting out of Chicago. I've helped you all I can."

The conversation got more heated.

"And I appreciate it," Jamie said. "I got the girl in the middle of the night. She's with me now. We're going home soon."

Was she talking about me? Better not be. I'm not a girl. I'm a woman now. If they were talking about me, shouldn't I be included in the conversation?

"How do you know my name?" Jamie said.

Uh oh.

Jamie paused to let him answer.

Then Jamie said in a strong tone, "You got my name from Bae! That little weasel. I thought I taught her better than that."

Jamie glared at me.

Who did I tell about Jamie? Then it dawned on me. I told several people her name. Something she'd drilled in me that I should never do.

How was I to know she'd ever find out about it?

Jamie hung up the phone. I braced for her to chew me out. Instead, she said, "The leader of the Striker gang is on the loose. His name is Shiv. The detective who met me over at the stalker house wants my help finding him. I owe him a favor. I guess we can't go home yet."

The plan was to leave Chicago first thing in the morning.

I started bouncing up and down on the bed. "I want to help."

"No! Shiv is a dangerous man. First I have to find him." Jamie paced the room.

"I'll tell you where he is, if you let me help."

That stopped Jamie in her tracks.

"This isn't a game, Bae. If you know something, spill it!"

I didn't know where he was, but I had an idea. I'd heard some of the Strikers talking about Shiv's hideout. On Seger Street. I crossed my arms and laid down on the bed in a reclining position.

"You're not going to tell me?" Jamie asked in a serious tone.

"Not until you promise to let me help."

Jamie jumped on top of me, and we started wrestling. It didn't take long for her to get the upper hand. I wasn't really trying to resist.

Before long, we were laughing.

We hadn't done that in years. Then she started tickling me, which always got me. I begged her to stop.

"I miss these times," Jamie said when she rolled off of me.

Both of us were out of breath.

"Me too."

Then her tone turned serious again. "Now tell me where Shiv is or I'll take you into the bathroom and waterboard it out of you," she said.

"I'd like to see you try."

Jamie rolled back on top of me. This time for real. I could see by the look on her face that she meant it.

I put my hands up and said, "Okay! Okay! I'll tell you. His hide-out is on Seger Street."

"How do you know?"

"I heard some of his minions talking. That's what they said."

Minions was a term I'd heard Jamie use a thousand times to describe bad guys.

"Do you have a street number?" she asked.

She was still straddling me, sitting on her knees. Holding me down.

"I don't, but it shouldn't be hard to find. It'll be the nicest house on the block."

Jamie got off my bed and called Alex. She gave him the street and asked him to confirm my intelligence. It ticked me off that she didn't believe me.

A few hours later, we got confirmation from Alex that the house belonged to the Strikers and was in one of Shiv's shell companies. That's about all he knew. I wanted to say, *I told you so*, but thought better of it.

"We'll go check it out," Jamie said to Alex.

A jolt of excitement went through me. She said *we*.

"Get dressed," she said to me.

While I was getting ready, Cliff Ford called back. Jamie let me hear his side of the conversation this time.

"Anna is missing," he said. "I think Shiv has her. Tell me you're still in town."

"I am. Was just going to call you in fact. Your ears must've been burning."

"Why were you going to call me?" he said.

"I've been working on finding Shiv," Jamie replied.

What?

I told her where to find Shiv. The least she could do was give me the credit for breaking the case. If not for me, she'd still be looking for him.

"Do you know where he is?" Cliff asked.

"No luck so far," Jamie answered.

She was lying!

Then she added, "He's clearly gone into hiding. That gives me an idea. Do you know Anna's cell phone number?"

"I do."

He gave it to her.

"Let me call you back," Jamie said.

After she hung up, I asked Jamie, "Why did you lie? You already know where Shiv is."

"We don't know for sure. He might be there, or he might not be. Either way, it's going to be dangerous. It's personal for the detective. Shiv had his wife killed. I'm doing it for his safety."

That made sense. It also made me wonder how many times she had lied to me about things to protect me. I decided to ignore those thoughts. Lying came with the territory. I'd have to get used to it since I was going to be a spy like her. Rather than judging, I needed to pay attention. I might learn something.

Jamie called the detective back. "I found Anna's cell phone."

Another lie. The woman was good.

"How did you do that?" Cliff asked.

"She's in South Chicago."

"What's the address?"

"No. Not so fast. It's not the part of town you want to go charging into."

"Tell me the number! If she's in a bad part of town, then I was right. Shiv kidnapped her."

This was what Jamie meant about the detective being too emotionally invested. Jamie had warned me about that. I was watching it play out firsthand.

"Ask yourself this question? Why would Shiv leave her cellphone on?"

"So we would know where she is."

"Exactly. He wants you to come there. It's a setup. Shiv doesn't want Anna. She's the bait. He wants you."

Jamie was creating a huge elaborate story. I was impressed. I'd never actually seen her in action in a real-life mission situation.

"Then I'll oblige him," Cliff said.

"It's too dangerous."

"I can handle myself."

He sounded like me.

"I'll get back with you," Jamie said. "Go back to your office and wait for my call. Don't tell anyone about this. Not yet."

"Jamie! Give me the address."

He sounded desperate. I knew Jamie. Once her mind was made up, she wouldn't relent. This was for the best. We didn't need the detective getting in our way.

Jamie hung up on him.

45

Taking down Shiv had been the most fun I'd had in my short life. We found his house. Jamie used me as a decoy. She even let me have a gun.

A loaded gun!

I went around the front of the house, and she went around back. We communicated by cellphone. On her cue, I fired several shots in the air.

Shiv and another man came running out. I hid in the bushes. They looked around but didn't see anything. When they went back inside, Jamie was waiting for them. When it was safe, she called for me and told me to come into the house.

The two men lay face down on the floor with their hands and feet tied.

Then she taught me how to hogtie them!

That was hilarious!

After I was done, Jamie checked it to make sure it was tight enough.

"You did good, Bae," she said to me. That warmed my heart.

"Watch them," Jamie said. "I'm going to go see if Anna is here."

Another thing that made me feel good inside. Jamie was beginning to see me as her equal.

I put my gun on them, although they weren't going anywhere.

A few minutes later, Jamie returned with a woman who looked identical to Julia and Rita. If they were standing side by side, I wouldn't be able to tell them apart.

Jamie pulled out her phone and typed in a text message.

"What are you doing?" I asked.

"I sent the detective the address. Let's get out of here."

"You don't want to wait for him?" I asked.

"If I wanted to wait for him, that's what we'd be doing!"

Okay. Smarty pants. She didn't have to cop an attitude. I was just asking a question.

We took Anna to our car, dropped her off the police station, and headed out of town. East.

"I want to get out of here as fast as we can," Jamie said. "Before we get drawn into something else."

She called Alex to let him know we were on our way home. Alex also had more information. He found dozens of banking transactions between one of Shiv's accounts and a cop with the Chicago P. D. Jamie told Alex to send the information to the local field office of the FBI. They'd know what to do with it.

"Do you want me to send A-Rad with the plane?" Alex asked.

"We're going to drive," Jamie said.

So, we settled in for what I knew had to be at least a twenty-hour drive. Looking back, I think Jamie wanted to drive so she could lecture me the whole time.

"What you did was stupid!"

"You could've gotten yourself killed."

"Your mom is worried sick."

"You're not ready for this. You need more training."

"You need to finish your degree."

Blah. Blah. Blah. Blah. Blah.

The harangue was nonstop. Then it turned more personal. Around the time we crossed the Kentucky border.

"I risked my life to save you," Jamie said. "Do you know why?"

"Why?" I asked.

"Because I love you. I don't want to see anything happen to you."

Tears welled up in both of our eyes.

"I know that," I said. "I love you too. And I appreciate what you did for me. But what do you want me to do? This is my calling. This is what I want to do. And I'm good at it."

I told her about the man's life I saved in Ohio. About saving Rita's life in the basement when the Striker had a gun on her.

"I found who took Julie," I argued passionately. "She'd still be in that garage if not for me."

"I get it," Jamie said. "I know what it's like. It's why I get up in the morning. It's why I risk my life for others. People I don't even know."

Tears still filled my eyes. One escaped and I could feel it on my cheek.

I was ready with a comeback. "When I was at The Farm, Curly said something to me. If you can do anything else, do it. If you can't, then do what you have to do. If deep down in your soul, you have a driving passion to risk your life for other people and you're willing to die for someone you don't even know, then do it. Become a spy. That's who I want to get in a foxhole with."

I think the argument resonated with Jamie.

"Promise me one thing," Jamie said. "Wait until you get your degree and more training. Curly would tell you the same thing. I spent six months on the Farm before I went on my first mission. I went back dozens of times after that for more training. In this business, you're always learning."

She made me promise. Several times.

I promised her I wouldn't do anything this stupid again. She actually made me say it that way. I was already convinced of that. I needed more training. It also made sense to finish my degree. My mom and dad spent all that money, and I couldn't waste it by not finishing. Jamie reminded me that she had a degree and that you can't be a CIA officer without one.

I wasn't sure I wanted to join the CIA. Too restricting. I liked freelancing as the female Reeder Rich. Still, I wanted to leave my options open.

I didn't need a lecture from Jamie to know what I did was stupid.

And impulsive.

Even though I did some good things on the mission, I made some mistakes. I didn't tell Jamie about them or she would've reamed me out some more. As it was, the lectures continued, off and on for the rest of the drive.

Honestly, when we pulled into the parking lot of my college campus in Richmond, I was relieved. Twenty hours alone with Jamie was long enough.

I love her, but she can be so annoying.

The last thing she said to me before she drove off was, "Remember what I said. Promise me your Reeder Rich days are over for a while. Not permanently. But for a while."

"I promise," I said.

She made me promise several more times.

Geez! I get the point.

We hugged and she left, and I went upstairs to my dorm room. My roommate wasn't in, so I unpacked my bags, took a shower, then laid down on the bed to take a nap.

I'd go back to my classes tomorrow.

I was just starting to nod off when my roommate, Ruby Blake, burst into the room. She slammed the door behind her. She was out of breath. Practically in tears. She walked over to the window and looked out.

"What's wrong?" I asked.

"I have a stalker!"

I bolted out of bed and went over to the window.

"See that guy over there?" Ruby asked.

She pointed at a guy who was standing next to a tree in a knoll across from our dorm.

"I see him."

"He's a creep. He's been following me. For a week! I'm scared of him."

I went to my closet and got my sneakers and put them on.

"What are you doing?" Ruby asked.

"I'm going to go take care of it."

"No. You can't do that. He might be dangerous."

"Don't worry about it," I said. "I have experience dealing with stalkers."

"Wait here," I said to her as I left the room and went down the stairs.

I had the man in my sights.

Adrenaline was pumping through my veins like water through a firehose.

"I'm back, baby!" I said aloud.

The female Reeder Rich is back.

Not The End

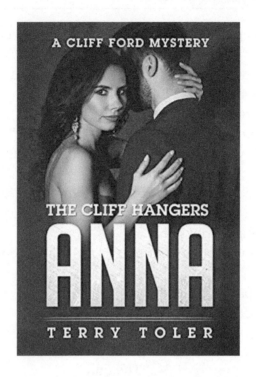

FROM THE AUTHOR

Anna's storyline overlaps with Save Me Twice. It's from Cliff Ford, Rita, and Anna's perspective. I took the opportunity to introduce Cliff Ford as a new character in Anna. I hope you read it. It'll fill in more of the story. In the future, they'll be more of Cliff and more of Bae in their own spin off series.

Thank you for purchasing this novel from best-selling author, Terry Toler. As an additional thank you, Terry wants to give you a free gift.

Sign up for:

Updates
New Releases
Announcements

At terrytoler.com

We'll send you the first three chapters of *The Launch*, a Jamie Austen novella, free of charge. The one that started the Spy Stories and Eden Stories Franchises.

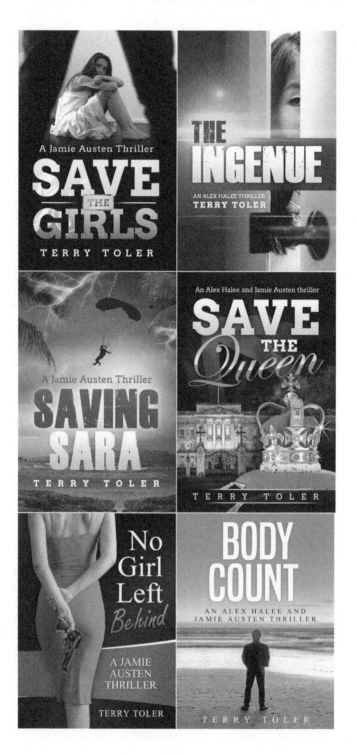

Coming soon in 2022
More Jamie Austen Thrillers

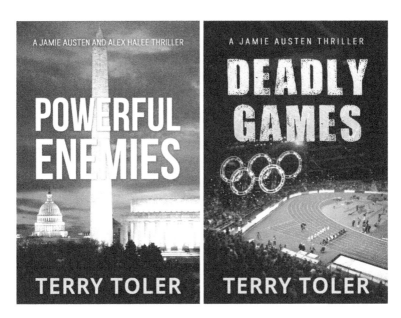

Made in the USA
Middletown, DE
07 September 2024

60387279R00188